Watch for other titles from

Deep Indigo Books and
Calvin Davis

indigoseapress.com

The Phantom Lady of Paris

By

Calvin Davis

Deep Indigo Books
Published by Indigo Sea Press, LLC.
Winston-Salem

Deep Indigo Books
Indigo Sea Press, LLC
302 Ricks Drive
Winston-Salem, NC 27103

Copyright © 2011 by Calvin Davis

First Deep Indigo Books edition published December, 2015
Deep Indigo Books, Moon Sailor, and all production designs are trademarks of Indigo Sea Press, used under license.

For information regarding bulk purchases of this book, digital purchase and special discounts, please contact the publisher at indigoseapress.com

Cover design by Stacy Castanedo

Manufactured in the United States of America

ISBN 978-1-63066-200-4

Chapter 1

The Phantom Lady of Paris? I knew her well. On the other hand—as I later discovered—I didn't know her at all. The woman did everything wrong. She did *nothing* wrong. She was a Jezebel, deceptive in every way. I've never known a more honest and straightforward person. During our relationship, she kept me constantly jittery and perturbed. The happiest days of my life were those I shared with the Phantom Lady of Paris. They were the golden days, the good times, good, that is, until...

Don't let her name mislead. She was not an apparition, nor a creation of some writer's fantasy, a fiend-like character in, say, an Edgar Allen Poe tale or one by Stephen King or Franz Kafka. No, she was real all right and, above all, she was human, more human than anyone I'd known and, I'm sure, will ever know again. And in spite of my blundering ways, she taught me what it really means to be a human being.

The Phantom Lady was a down-to-earth mortal possessing a unique dream, one fabricated from her passion for living, some of which passion she shared with me and with others fortunate enough to have known her.

As her name suggests, she lived in Paris, lived there during the most turbulent times the city has known since the bloodletting and mayhem of the French Revolution. She resided in The City of Light during the Vietnam War and peace protests in the United States and Europe, Sorbonne student riots on the Left Bank and worldwide clashes between "The Establishment" and "The Flower Generation." It was an era of cataclysmic social eruption and revolutionary clashes of ideas and age groups.

I was a grown man when I met the Phantom Lady. All was going well with me. My life was in balance, and I knew how to live it. In spite of that, the moment the Phantom Lady and I met marked the real beginning of my life. Everything preceding that instant was meaningless prologue. During our initial chat, which lasted about three hours—though it seemed a fleeting moment, I learned for the first time what life is all about and how I should live mine.

On the morning we met, she taught me many things about myself that were, until then, mysteries. And what did I learn about her? Very little. Basically, I learned that she was more question marks than periods, and that something mysterious lurked behind each question mark. I wasn't prepared for what the hidden thing turned out to be. But looking back at what happened the morning I met her and everything that ensued, I wonder, what human being could have possibly prepared for the *startling* revelation that developed and how it would change not only my life, but hers…and change both forever?

Who could have been prepared?

No one.

Chapter 2

Skies over northern Virginia were as dazzling as Tiffany diamonds the August afternoon in 1968 when I stepped aboard an Air France jetliner at Dulles International Airport. Destination? Paris, France. On a year's sabbatical from my job as an English teacher in Baltimore, Maryland, I was en route to The City of Light to learn more about French culture, to practice speaking the language, and to write. What better place to do all three than on the Left Bank in the jewel beside the Seine?

Within hours of arriving in the French capital, I checked into a small Latin Quarter hotel on Boulevard Saint Michel, just above where it crosses Boulevard Saint Germain. Then, as it is now, this famed intersection of two main boulevards in the Left Bank was a beehive of Sorbonne students, common laborers, expatriates, artists, would-be artists, writers, and tourists from every continent on earth. Cafés at this celebrated crossroad were always packed, remaining that way each day until early morning.

After being in Paris a couple of days, I began searching for a permanent residence, ideally a studio (one room) apartment. Finding one wasn't as difficult as I thought it would be. I soon discovered that in The City of Light anyone who wished to buy, sell, trade, or lease practically anything, considered it his God-given right to post flyers on walls, doors, and light poles or anywhere else he deemed suitable and space was available. The result? Placards, flyers, and frayed scraps of paper were stuck everywhere.

Strolling down Boulevard Saint Michel one afternoon *("Bul' Mich'"* Parisians called it), I happened upon a flyer tacked to a tree. The advertisement announced that several nearby studios were available for immediate occupancy. Within the hour, I signed a lease for one, and the following day I moved into a furnished studio at Twenty-One Rue Galande, just off Boulevard Saint Germain, in the heart of the Left Bank. Not very spacious by American standards, this two room apartment would be my home for the next eleven months.

I soon settled into a daily routine that seldom varied. Each morning at six-thirty I arose, showered, and dressed. At around seven-twenty I dashed down stairs, en route to the bakery and dairy across the street to buy a few items for breakfast: usually a croissant, a baguette, a cup of yogurt, and sometimes a liter of milk (in France, bread and milk were government subsidized, thus inexpensive). After making these purchases, I stopped at the mailbox in the foyer of Twenty-One Rue Galande.

Unlike apartment mailboxes in America, the one in my building wasn't compartmentalized: that is, one box for each apartment. Nor was it locked. The postman dumped all correspondence addressed to residents of the building into a single wall-mounted, rectangular wooden structure. Each tenant had to sort through the pile to find his mail.

In many cities, such a mail distribution system probably wouldn't work for long. Checks and credit cards would levitate from the receptacle as if inflated with helium. However, during my stay in Paris no one stole a single letter of mine. Other things belonging to me they pilfered from the mailbox, yes—as I'll explain—but never a letter.

The postman delivered mail twice daily, punctually and reliably, at seven in the morning and two in the afternoon. My mother wrote me once a week and my sisters occasionally, but beyond their letters, I didn't get correspondence on a regular basis. I did, however, receive a subscription copy of the *Herald Tribune* every morning. The *Herald Tribune* was an English language newspaper published in Europe. Reading a newspaper in English was akin to having an invisible link to my country while I lived abroad.

After breakfast each day I'd tuck my copy of the *Herald* and a composition book under my arm and exit the building. With a pencil or two in hand, I'd head for my favorite "writing cafe," Cafe Le Balkan, which was just around the corner on Boulevard Saint Germain. There I'd sit in the glass-enclosed terrace, basking in morning sunlight. I'd sip an espresso or a cappuccino while mulling over the newspaper. Then I'd write for several hours. This routine was the prologue of my day, easing me into the reassuring sameness of a well-trod schedule.

On this particular morning with a liter of milk, a croissant, and a cup of yogurt in hand, I hurried into the foyer of Twenty-One Rue Galande. I flipped open the mailbox, and, to my dismay, my *Herald Tribune* was missing. Had the mail carrier made his rounds? He always did, religiously and on time, regardless of the weather. Besides, mail for other tenants was in the box. So why wasn't mine?

I rummaged through the huge mound of letters, finally fishing from it an address band with the *Herald's* logo on it, beneath which was my name, address, and that day's date. I didn't need to be a forensic scientist to realize that some midget-minded SOB had stolen my newspaper, and, to add insult to injury, brazenly left the address band in the mailbox. Of all the rotten, dirty…

With the discarded mailing band in hand, I glanced at the bulletin board that was just above the mailbox. On it was a note addressed to me, scrawled on a piece of torn notebook paper. A hastily scribbled peace sign adorned the top.

> *Dear Mr. Paul Lasser,*
> *I borrowed your newspaper. I would say, Thank you, but as nice as I know you are, I don't have to thank you. Do I? Of course not, darling. So, why bother?*
> *And oh yes, do have a good day! I'm sure I'll have one. Reading the morning paper always makes my day—as I'm sure it makes yours. For your information: the weatherman predicts mild temperatures, sunny, cloudless skies. Should be a gasser. So, enjoy. Peace and love.*
> *Signed, your neighbor and fellow-newspaper-lover,*
> *The Phantom Lady of Paris.*

I crumpled the note in my hands. The hussy! The wench! What nerve! Of all the unmitigated gall! Just who did this misbegotten person think he or she was? I include "he" because in spite of The Phantom Lady label, the culprit could have been, and probably was, a male lurking behind a female alias. Face it, I was dealing with a first-class reprobate, and I didn't expect such a lowlife to tell the truth about anything, including gender.

But of whatever sex the slime ball was—male, female, or something in between—I was determined she/he would pay and pay dearly. Reading that paper, written in my native tongue, was a vital part of my day. Feeling bereft of my daily link to home, I stood there fuming; how could I communicate my rage to the thief?

I hurriedly devised a plan. If the robber, I reasoned, could post a note on the bulletin board, why couldn't the victim do the same? I rushed to my studio on the third floor, plopped down at the table and removed the cover of my Remington 502 and typed.

> *Dear Phantom Lady,*
> *You stole my Herald. Borrowed is the phony word you used. I repeat, you stole my paper, and I don't like being ripped off. I've known scores of scumbags, in fact, the*

scummiest of the scums, but you, Miss Phantom, have added a new term to the lexicon of scummism: the ultra-scummiest of the scum. Ad infinitum.

Is a person of your character—or lack of the same—able to understand that what belongs to others does not belong to you? Or is this concept too intellectually challenging? I'd say one needs an IQ of at least eighteen to comprehend it, a sum that probably leaves you about twenty-one points short.

I look forward to meeting the lowlife who pinched my paper.

I remain yours, with all due respect—none,
Paul Lasser

Feeling somewhat vindicated, I placed my response on the bulletin board. The next morning the memo wasn't there. In its place, the perpetrator left a note penned on pink stationery; roses adorned the side of the paper. Countless flourishes and curlicues written in red ink embellished each line. Obviously, the writer wished to impress me. I *wasn't* impressed—*damnit.*

Dearest Pen Pal and Newspaper Buddy Paul,

I hope you don't mind if I call you Paul. I do so because of our note exchange, which makes me feel close to you, as close as a family member.

I'm disappointed that you got so hyper over, of all things, a mere newspaper. Be cool, pen pal. If you aren't, you're certain to blow an artery, and we wouldn't want that now, would we? Keep this in mind: I didn't use your journal as a dog pooper scooper. Nothing so gross. I merely read the damn thing. Isn't that why they're printed?

You say my IQ is minus three. Not so. It's a documented plus three. I don't want to sound immodest, but I'm proud of that. Anyway, it's not one's IQ that's important, it's one's integrity. But you say I'm deficient in that, too. Seems I can't win, can I, Paul?

Incidentally, don't bother looking for your newspaper today, I have it. OK, stole it, purloined it, borrowed it. Whichever word turns you on.

Before you call me dirty names again, let me explain. Today's Herald carries a continuation of Tom Effertton's column, and I hate starting a series and not finishing it. I'll bet you're the same way. Aren't you? Tell the truth, Paul. 'Fess up.

Paper pal, what do you say we get together? I'd be delighted to meet you. Until I do, I remain, as always yours, The Phantom Lady of Paris: that's W--O--M--A--N, the Glorification of Adam's Ribs, Man's Better Half, or, as you'd probably phrase it, "DAMN BITCH."

So, the slime was finally ready to crawl from under her rock and show herself. Would I, she brazenly asked, like to meet her? What an asinine question! *Of course* I would. I couldn't wait to lay eyes—if not hands and a foot—on the wench. With that in mind, it didn't take long to dash upstairs and type a reply to Her Royal Slimeness, then post it on the bulletin board. I was beginning to enjoy the zaniness of our bulletin board correspondence, a battle of wits, if you will.

Dear P.L.,

I hope you enjoyed Effertton's column. I too like his work, but due to circumstances beyond my control, I couldn't read his piece today. Sadly, a non-subscriber has my subscribed-to-and-paid-for-by-me copy. One of the main reasons I get the Herald is that it carries Effertton's insightful comments. I see you had a similar motive for subscribing to my paper. We do have something in common, don't we? You LIKE the Herald. I BUY it.

You asked if I'd like to meet you. Name the time and place.

Signed, Paul, a.k.a.. The Aggrieved Party.

The next morning my newspaper was where it should have been: in the mailbox. There was no memo from Miss Mystery Person. Obviously, Her Slimeship had second thoughts about rendezvousing with me. I glanced at the empty bulletin board and shrugged. A feeling of disappointment swept over me. I had enjoyed our note exchange, chuckling to myself at the audacity of this mysterious person.

An inner voice whispered that the matter of the purloined *Herald* was now relegated to my cold case file, and there it would probably languish and be forgotten. Time proved me wrong, for when I entered Twenty-One Rue Galande two days later, I saw a communiqué on the bulletin board from PL.

Hi, Paul,
Will you be free tomorrow evening? Say, sevenish?
Looking forward to meeting you. Where? In the foyer? Does
that sound OK? Be there. I'm in a rush, so, until our
rendezvous, au revoir.
Signed, the Phantom Lady of Paris

Wishing to be punctual for my date with The Journal Jerker, I ate supper early the following day. At six fifty-nine, I headed downstairs. Seven o'clock found me waiting in the foyer, leaning against the mailbox. So did seven ten. The same for seven fifteen. At seven thirty, what was my batting tally? Same as before. Zero. No Phantom Lady. No note. Nothing. Had she chickened out? Was her invitation a ruse, another of her dirty little tricks? I was anything but pleased.

At seven forty, nothing had changed. My batting average remained zilch. Seven forty-eight—the same. Eight fifteen? A carbon copy of the seven thirty-nine report. A goose egg.

So, the Phantom Lady stood me up...big time. But, why? The note she posted the following day answered that question...in part.

Dear Paul,
Sorry I couldn't meet you as promised. Unavoidable. I
hope I can get a rain check. One day I'll explain why I was a
no-show. One day. But I'm not certain you'll understand
even after I explain, for I realize that there are some parts of
the explanation that are difficult to grasp—even for me. But
if you don't understand immediately, maybe you will in time.
I hope so. Until then, straight ahead, chin up, and keep the
faith. Meanwhile, I'll be in touch.
Your Newspaper Partner, the Phantom Lady of Paris

Chapter 3

Two days later when I walked into the foyer of Twenty-One Rue Galande, I glanced at the bulletin board. Empty. Not a word from the Phantom Lady. Good, I told myself, although a part of me missed our lighthearted, screwball messages. At around nine that night, after undressing, showering, and snacking, I got into bed and within minutes was sound asleep.

"Bam! Bam! Bam!" I jerked awake. Someone was knocking, no, *pounding* on my studio door. The pounding continued. Who could it be? And at this *ungodly* hour? More pounding. My door shook from the force of it.

Pulling the chain on the lamp beside my bed, I peered at the clock on the table. I blinked a few times to focus my sleep-heavy eyes on the dial. The time: four a.m. I'll be damned. Probably some drunk who'd forgotten his way home. The pounding started again. "Yeah," I growled, "what-cha want?"

"How about opening the door?" said a female.

Great! A female drunk. "Who...who is it?" I sat up in the bed, rubbing the sleep from my eyes.

"Me! So open up."

"Who?"

"*Me, Bonnie Silver.*"

"You must have the wrong studio. I don't know anybody named Bonnie...Bonnie..." I yawned. "Ah, what'd you say your last name is?"

"Silver. Bonnie Silver."

"Like I said, I don't know anyone by that name!" I turned out the light, flopped back on my pillow, and pulled the sheet up to my chin.

"Wrong. You do."

I groaned. Please, can't a fella get some sleep around here? "Look, I should know who I *know* and who I *don't!*"

"Well, you know me," the voice insisted.

"Again, I say, I *don't!*"

"And again, I say, you *do.*"

I reached over and yanked on the lamp chain again. Why I felt I needed a light on to argue with a complete stranger was beyond my sleep-hazed thought process at that point. "Are we gonna have to ride that merry-go-round again? Like I told you, I *don't* know a Bonnie Silver."

"OK, lemme put it to you this way: I'm P. L."

"P.L.? I draw a blank on that name too." I yawned and rubbed my eyes, turned, and looked longingly at my pillow.

"P. L., *damnit!* Paul, did you have a brain meltdown during the night?"

"Of course not!" I was getting really ticked off by this point.

"You'd think so. Either that or you've got a short in your cerebral circuitry. P. L.!" she shouted. "Get it? As in, the *Phantom Lady.* Now open up! It's chilly out here!"

"Oh-h-h-h," I swooned. "So, it's *you at last,* The Phan-n-ntom Lady." After scooping up a pair of Levis lying on the floor and pulling them on, I hurried to the door and jerked it open.

"About time," the visitor frowned, leaning against the doorframe. In her early twenties, she was slender, almost wispy. Her ebony hair, parted down the crown of her head, flowed over her shoulders. Like that on a Grecian bust, her nose angled to a point. Atop its bridge perched a pair of silver wire-rimmed "granny glasses." These highlighted her jewel-like, aqua-blue eyes, which scanned and rescanned me from head to toe. The Grand Inquisitress' examination finally completed, she entered the room, whisking past like a spring breeze.

"So, why don't you come in?" I said sarcastically, after eyeing the blur that had just streaked into my apartment.

"Don't mind if I do," my uninvited guest shrugged, plopping down on the stuffed chair in the corner. "Boy, I'm tired."

"And while you're at it, why don't you make yourself at home and have a seat?"

"I think I will," she sighed, toeing off her sneakers and wiggling her toes. She wore bell-bottomed jeans and a tie-dyed t-shirt of yellow, orange and navy.

Perhaps a heavier dose of sarcasm was required with this early-morning intruder, I thought. "And don't be bashful: take off your shoes and relax your feet."

"Don't mind if I do." Now seemingly comfortable, she scrutinized my studio. "Not a bad looking joint you got here."

"You think so?" I crossed my arms over my chest and leaned against the door.

"Uh-huh. My place is on the fourth floor." After further perusal, she continued, "For some odd reason though, my studio looks smaller than yours." She shrugged her shoulders. "Probably just an illusion. Anyway, let me compliment you. You did a good job decorating this place."

"Thanks."

"Except," she frowned, "for that print hanging near the window. I can't give you any points for that. What was the artist trying to say in it?"

"The print is a Claude Vanderbilt. He's the latest thing in a new school of modern art called Psycho-terra Exposition."

"Hum. So, two wiggly blue lines intersecting at a right angle on a red background, you say is an example of...ah...what'd you call it, Psycho-terra Exposition?"

"Right."

"But what's the work's message? What's the artist attempting to say?"

I cleared my throat. "It's untitled."

"Untitled? Does that mean the painter doesn't know the point of his own work—assuming it has a point—and he won't admit his ignorance, so he calls it...'untitled'?"

"Of course not! Don't be ridiculous!" I could feel myself tensing.

"OK, but I ask again, what's the print trying to say?"

"That's simple. It conveys different meanings to different viewers." I hated the defensiveness in my voice; it sounded like I was allowing her remarks to get under my skin. Who cared what the Phantom Lady thought?

"I can go along with that. So, what's it communicating to you?"

"Well," clearing my throat, I was determined to sound casual, more enlightened. "The artist delineates the peaks and valleys of humanity's inner landscape." I stepped toward the painting, waving my hand as I spoke. "He addresses mankind's universal longings, the forlornness of the human spirit and its quest for identity and fulfillment."

"All of which means," she tittered, "that you're like me."

"How so?"

"Like me, you don't have the faintest notion what that damn print is trying to say. The only difference is...I admit my ignorance."

"Look," I sizzled, "I hope you don't make it a habit of barging into a guy's studio at four in the morning and lecturing him on modern art!"

"Lecturing? Who's lecturing? Not me. You were the one doing that."

I shook a finger at her. "Hold on. Just one minute! We're getting off the subject."

"Are we? I thought we were talking about Psycho-terra Exposition Art and Claude Vanderbilt's depiction of—what'd you call it?—'the forlornness of the human spirit.' Whatever the hell that means," she giggled.

"But Psycho-terra Exposition Art is *not* the subject!"

"Oh? What is?" Her eyes blinked behind the granny glasses.

"My newspaper!"

"Oh, the paper?" she shrugged. It was obviously a topic she didn't care to discuss.

"Right, the paper. You stole it. Or have you forgotten?"

She idly ran a finger over the arm of my chair. "I don't like the word...stole." Then she focused those aqua blue eyes on me.

"Look," I groaned, "are we going to play silly word games?"

"No, we don't have to."

"You can call it what you want, but the bottom line is you ended up with a newspaper mailed to me, one I subscribed to, *paid* for, and therefore...rightfully owned. You can label that act anything you care to—'borrowed,' 'requisitioned'—*anything*, but whatever you call it, taking what doesn't belong to you is wrong." I felt like I was lecturing one of my students.

When I'd finally finished my Paul Lasser Lecture Series, she twinkled a smile, highlighting the dimples now illuminating her cheeks. Following this, she bubbled a sniggle. "Paul, anybody ever tell you that when you're peeved there's a twitch in your cheek?"

I straightened. "No."

"Well, there is."

"Are you sure?" I could feel my eyebrows wrinkle in question.

"Why would I lie?"

"In which cheek?" I fought the urge to charge into my tiny bathroom and check my image in the mirror.

"Both."

"A moment ago, you said 'cheek,' not 'cheeks.'"

"I meant cheeks." The corners of her mouth twitched as if she were trying not to smile.

"Either way, you *are* putting me on, aren't you?"

"No." Her hair undulated in waves when she shook her head.

"Is the twitch that noticeable?"

"Quite. Trust me."

I groaned inwardly as my mind traveled back to the students in my classes the previous school year. Had they noticed the twitch? Talked about it with fellow students? Laughed about it? I swallowed. "I mean is it...*really* noticeable?"

"Take my word for it."

"No one has ever brought it to my attention before."

"There!" she squealed, palming back a giggle. "You're twitching again." Unable to suppress it any longer, she ignited a string of sniggers. Though I tried to restrain myself, I couldn't, and a second later, I laughed, uncontrollably, even louder than she giggled.

"Wait a minute...just...one...minute. Why the hell am I laughing? I should be furious."

She wrinkled her forehead as if studying me. "Mind answering a question for me?"

"What?"

"Why are you so damn uptight? Why take yourself and life so seriously, huh? Smile. You've got to learn to snap your fingers in life's face." She snapped her fingers, displaying a go-to-hell expression. "If you don't, life'll make about as much sense as that Vanderbilt print you tried to explain—and couldn't. Because it *and* life are filled with contradictions and inconsistencies and just plain nonsense, most of which is tragic or laughable...or both.

She pushed her long dark hair back from her face. "Face it, either you laugh at life or you'll find yourself doing a lot of crying. Look, life is something to savor, to *enjoy*, not analyze as you would a math problem. Isn't it enough that we accept that life simply is, that it exists? So, learn to laugh and find pleasure in it...while you can." She paused, then smiled. "All of which brings me back to your..."

"Back to my...what?"

"That *sanctified* newspaper." She exhaled a long, loud sigh.

"Finally."

"Look, I've got a bulletin for you. That paper of yours was not a tablet chiseled in the clouds by God's angelic scribes. It was merely a newspaper. Nothing more, nothing less. At any rate, I'll tell you what I'll do."

I crossed my arms over my chest. "I'm listening."

"I'll make you a proposition."

"Go on."

"I'll pay for the paper on two conditions."

"Paper? No, you mean...papers."

"OK, OK, *papers*, if that'll make you happy."

"It will," I conceded. "Anyway, what are the conditions?"

"One, you must convince me that the mortician's expression on your face isn't permanently chiseled there."

Though I struggled not to, I smiled. "I...I..."

"See, you can smile." She winked. "And twice in one day, too.

Hurray! Let's dance in celebration! Peace and love, the man can smile!" With abandon, she waved her arms and danced sprite-like about the room. "Come on-n-n, join me!" she bubbled, beckoning.

I don't know why I did, but I joined her in her choreography of lunacy, and for the next several minutes we giggled and cavorted as energetically as school kids at recess. She hummed the Beetles "Yellow Submarine" as the beat for our pre-dawn milieu. Finally exhausted, we plunked onto the sleep sofa, "Whe-e-e-e!" she ventilated, "wasn't that fun?"

Grudgingly, I concurred. After panting for a couple of seconds, I said, "Bonnie?"

"Yeah?"

"You told me I'd have to meet two conditions before you'd pay me for my papers. What's the second?"

"That you go with me to a café—it's not far from here—so we can sample some of their onion soup everybody raves about."

"Onion soup? At *this* hour?"

"Ah-h-h," she groaned, slapping a thin hand over her eyes.

"What's wrong?"

"You don't know?" Her voice rose in question.

"No."

"The problem is I think you're relapsing."

I crossed my arms over my chest. "Meaning?"

"Meaning you're getting that undertaker-expression on your face again."

"Hold on for a second, will you, while I pull on a shirt and shoes."

"Sure." When I reached for a necktie draped over a hanger in my closet, her eyebrows shot up. "You really are an uptight, establishment kind of guy, aren't you?"

Minutes later as we stepped outside, dawn winked over the eastern horizon, prising shafts of violet and gold that painted the spires and buttresses of Notre-Dame Cathedral like a gigantic impressionist's brush. I had witnessed the beauty of Left Bank dawns many times. Often, restless and unable to sleep, I arose at five or six in the morning and strolled Boulevard Saint Germain when it was all but empty, the thunder of silence pounding like kettledrums.

"In which direction are we going?" I asked.

"This way," she said, heading down a narrow street toward Notre-Dame Cathedral. When we reached the cathedral, we turned left. Later, nearing the bridge, *Pont Neuf,* she stopped.

"What's wrong?" I asked. Why'd you stop?"

14

"I want to show you something," she said, pointing to a group of about twenty or thirty seemingly homeless people, mostly men, under the bridge's arch. "What you're looking at is something tourists seldom see: the City of Light's underbelly."

Many of those beneath the bridge were in sleeping bags or partially hidden under makeshift tents. A few sat with their backs propped against concrete buttresses of the *pont*; others lay on the ground with only the bridge's arch as protection from the morning's chill.

"So many," I mumbled, both shocked and disturbed at what I was witnessing.

"Every night they assemble there. Usually about the same number, though in winter, there are more."

"I wonder if French tourist books list Paris bridges as a four or five star accommodation."

She chuckled. "Neither! There is one thing and one thing only that compels them to seek shelter under that bridge: the will to *live, to survive.* Later this morning, they'll roll up their sleeping bags and then turn the Seine into a giant washbasin and toilet. After that, they'll once more face the problem *du jour.*"

"Which is?"

"The same one they faced yesterday and the day before that: how to go on breathing. And, ironically, their struggle for survival takes place in, of all places, Paris, the theme park of self-indulgence and pleasure seeking. Beneath that arch, they plead their case for continued existence. For them, the span is a court of appeal, in some cases, the final court of appeal."

"No doubt. And look, there're so many of them. I wonder...I wonder where they all come from?"

She looked up at me with those aqua blue eyes. "The answer is simple. Pick a country. *Any* country, for Paris attracts people like flames attract moths. I once heard someone say if you stand on the Champs Elysees long enough, everyone you've ever known will eventually walk past."

"There's probably some truth to that. By the way, I thought you said we're going to a café for onion soup?"

"We are."

"So why are we standing here talking?"

"Because from time to time, I need to *remind* myself how unforgiving life can be. And looking at, what I call, 'the bridge people,' jolts me with a lightning bolt of reality and brings me back to earth."

"Back to earth? Do you ever leave earth?" I smiled down at my free-spirited friend, for that was how I was regarding her, as both a free-spirit and as a new friend.

"Of course. In my thoughts, I often become extraterrestrial. You see, I have this uncontrollable urge to invalidate the laws of gravity, to slice through space like an eagle, and like an eagle, to taste freedom. You ever get the feeling you'd like to fly like an eagle? Mountain high. Beyond earth's gravity. Unfettered. And...free."

"Not really. Although, being an American, if I was going to fly like a bird, I'd pick an eagle. By the way, when you fly, where do you go?"

"To faraway, uncharted lands. But the destination isn't the important thing."

"Oh? What is?"

"The ecstasy of flight and the feeling of liberation it brings."

"What brings it on?"

"Brings what on?" She aimed those incredibly blue eyes on me as if I were dense for asking.

"This need you have to feel free."

"I'm not sure. It might be some abnormality in my genes," she shrugged.

"Or...or perhaps those who don't share your urge to fly, to be free, those who are fettered to the earth, mentally and physically, maybe those are the ones who have a genetic abnormality. Not you."

With a flicker of her hand and a glittering smile, she brushed aside a wayward strand of dark hair that draped her cheek, and then said, "That may be. That just may be. Anyway, let's get started? We still have six blocks to go."

"Six? You said the café was nearby!"

"Oh-h-h, you poor darling," she teased. "Come on, momma's baby, I'm sure you can survive. If you don't, I'll see that you get a good Christian burial. I'll have the eulogist mention how you died pursuing the excellence of French cuisine, how you walked yourself to death for a noble cause: a bowl of onion soup. Oh, the French will love you for that grand gesture. I'm sure they'll pin a medal on your tombstone engraved with the words '*Grande Fleur de la Soupe,*' and the prime minister will declare a national day of mourning, order black buntings draped around the Arc de Triomphe, and—"

"Bonnie."

"What?'

"Cut the bull!"

"Bull? I was only trying to be helpful."

"You wanna help?"

"Yeah. How?" She linked her arm in mine.

"Don't help."

"I'm shocked you feel that way," she shrugged, eyes twinkling a smile.

"Miss Shocked, will you *please* come the hell on?"

"Coming, master. Coming."

Six blocks, Bonnie said, was the distance to the café. Nine was the actual count, but because of the energetic pace of our conversation, it seemed only a block or so. Like the cadence of her speech, her steps were lively and bubbly. I often lagged a half pace or so behind and from there I watched her hair, ebonized silk, fluff as she fluttered along like a human butterfly.

When she spoke, she fingered the air, seemingly feeling for not only the right word, but also the correct exuberance when uttering it. Conversing with Bonnie was like watching sprinkles of stardust streak the western horizon.

We covered an array of topics; among them, how Frenchmen spent hours lounging at sidewalk cafés, sipping wine, and conversing. Americans, if they did the same, would feel guilty, convinced they had "wasted valuable time." We were in perfect agreement that it would be a sad day when fast food outlets replaced Parisian sidewalk cafés. When people no longer valued the healing therapy of conversation over a cup of espresso or a crystal of champagne, a large part of the charm of Paris would be lost.

We walked through a labyrinth of side streets—some I had never seen—to a neighborhood near *Pont Neuf* and there we stopped at a little café almost obscured by buildings flanking it. Bonnie and I sat on the terrace and looked down a narrow side street toward the Seine, where tethered boats bobbed.

A middle-aged waiter approached our table. *"Monsieur et Madame, vous desirez?"* In almost flawless "Parisian French," which is spoken with machine-gun rapidity, Bonnie exchanged a few pleasantries with him and then ordered a couple bowls of onion soup and two espressos.

As the waiter reentered the café, I leaned back in my chair. "Bonnie, I'm impressed. Your French is remarkable. Where'd you learn to speak the language so well?"

"In a little town in the Blue Ridge Mountains of Virginia: Goode, population, roughly two thousand, that is," she grinned, "if you include coon dogs, hogs, and workhorses. Tell me something? Have you ever heard of Goode, Virginia?"

"No. Although I'm from Virginia myself: Hampton. But I've never heard of Goode."

"Well, what'll ya know, a fellow Virginian. No wonder we clicked. As for your not hearing about Goode, I'm not surprised. Most people know absolutely nothing about the place. In fact, only a few maps even bother to include it."

"That small, huh?"

"Right. A couple of stoplights and a go-slow sign, that's Goode. Want to hear what its chief industry is?"

"What?"

"Attempting to do the impossible: grow fruits and vegetables on rocks and in nutrient-starved red clay."

"So, you learned Parisian French in Goode, Virginia, huh? You'd think in a town like the one you just described, the only language spoken would be Grand Ole Opry-ese, not Parisian French. Yet, you say you learned the language there. The facts don't compute."

"OK, I was only toying with you. True, I learned to speak French in Goode, and yes, the locals there communicate in Smokey Mountain, their favorite expression being 'Y'all have a good day.' Still, they are great, caring people. The best."

With a movement of her wrist, she flicked her hair back over her shoulder. "What I didn't mention was that my mother—God rest her soul—was a French native, born and raised right here in Paris. After she married my father, a well-off American business executive, they eventually moved to Goode. Both fell in love with the region's quaintness and the majesty of its surrounding hills. So, contrary to what I teasingly led you to believe, I learned French from a Parisian, my mother, and, believe me, she was the best teacher and mother a gal could have."

"Well, that explanation makes *some* things a little clearer. But it still leaves one or two things murky."

"Like what?"

"Like why a person from the Blue Ridge Mountains of Virginia ends up an ocean away in, of all places, Paris, France?"

"Well, there're a couple of reasons. The first is the *important* one. The second is..." She shrugged, aborting the sentence, as if, though incomplete, it communicated all she wished to say on the subject—or all that she felt I needed to know. Glancing at the sparse traffic breaching the stillness of the early morning, Bonnie gave an audible sigh and continued, "Reason one made itself known when I finally realized I *had* a problem. When the revelation came, I'd been a student at the University of Virginia for nearly two years."

"What was your major?"

"I didn't have one."

"Are you telling me that after two long years in college, you still hadn't decided what to study?" I'd known many students like that. As for me, I'd always known I wanted to major in English. I'd had a love affair with words since Mrs. Reynolds, my ninth grade English teacher, introduced me to William Shakespeare.

"Right."

"Why? Didn't anything spark your interest?"

"That's right. I couldn't decide on a major. Like my attention span wasn't long enough to stick with one thing." The waiter brought our soups and espressos.

I lifted my soup spoon and looked at her. "Why? Didn't anything hold your interest?"

"Not for long, I'm afraid. The reason turned out to be my problem, though, as I said, I didn't know I had a problem. Anyway, I woke up one morning and, like a flash, it dawned on me that the coordinates of my life were as scrambled and disoriented as I felt inside. Where was I heading? What was the destination, the end goal of my life? To these questions, I had no answers.

"My North Star had been blasted from the heavens. My college transcript was a hodgepodge of disconnected bits and pieces, courses chosen on either impulse or mood, in some cases on both, and in all cases, leading to the same destination." She shook her head once. "The Lost Land of Dead End Streets. Finally one thing became clear."

"And what was that?" I lifted a spoonful of steaming soup and blew on it, my eyes still focused on her.

"That the compass of my life was busted and that I needed to find myself. I thought maybe I could do that in Paris. Do you understand what I'm fumbling to say?"

"Thoroughly."

"Do you *really*?" She folded her arms on the tiny café table and leaned toward me, an earnest expression in her eyes.

I took a sip of my espresso. "Why do you doubt me?"

"It's just that—" She looked away for a beat as if struggling with something.

"Look, what you went through, I suspect more people than you have done the same. So, yes, I understand. It's a journey through loneliness, confusion and pain."

"Mine was worse."

I leaned back in my chair, enjoying conversing to an American in my native tongue. I hadn't realized how much I missed it, hearing French spoken all day, everywhere I went. "Why do you say that?"

"Paul, I felt like someone crawling through a field of land mines, all primed with tenpenny nails. But look," she said, face suddenly lighting a smile, "my disorientation and lack of purpose may have slowed me. It did, but it didn't *stop* me. Hell," she winked, snapping her fingers, "I vowed long ago that nothing will ever stop me...*nothing*... death included."

The waiter returned, asking if we wanted anything else. Bonnie told him we didn't, but that if we changed our minds, she'd beckon him. Wiping his hands on his apron, he reentered the café.

"So, Paul, you say you've never tasted French onion soup?"

"Right, never. Until now." A refuse truck rumbled to a stop and men in green uniforms scurried to empty trash containers set along the street.

"It's great, isn't it? Better than first-time sex."

I choked on the hot soup. "Better than first-time sex? You're putting me on. First-time sex and onion soup? What a comparison: like comparing the Grand Wizard of the KKK to Mother Theresa."

"I think it's a *good* comparison," she stated, lifting her spoon.

"I don't."

"Ah, to hell with it," she laughed, snapping her fingers. "Bad analogy, good analogy. Who gives a damn? Enough. Let's eat. I'm famished."

Bonnie was right, about the soup, I mean. It was like none I'd tasted, putting canned, water-rich concoctions sold in supermarkets to shame. A wedge of melted cheese topped each bowl, surrounded by heaping servings of sautéed onions, ripe and juicy. I don't know that I'd have compared it to first-time sex, but I was fast learning that Bonnie's viewpoints were as unique as Bonnie, herself.

Before I knew it, we were halfway through our second order of soup. "You told me there were two reasons you're in Paris. One you explained. What's the other?"

"The other?" Bonnie stared into her soup as if it held the answers to the universe.

"Yeah...the other." I waited while she fingered the handle of her spoon. Then she lookayed intently into my eyes, smiled, but gave no response. I waited some more. "So, are you going to tell me about the second reason?"

"The second? Ah, what do you know?" she chirped, glancing at her watch. "I had no idea it was so late. I'd better get back to my pad and cop some shuteye. I certainly could use some. What about you?"

"Same here." I pulled out my wallet to pay our bill. "I think this place will become one of my favorite eateries in Paris."

On the way back to Twenty-One Rue Galande, we neared the bridge, *Pont Michel.* "Paul?" she said. "Are you game?"

"Game? For what?" I glanced around, trying to figure out what in the world she was talking about.

"Come on, let's *do* it."

"Do? Do what?" This woman could be the most mysterious person at times.

"Cross the bridge."

"Why should we do that? Didn't you say you're sleepy and needed rest? So why do you want us to cross the bridge? Doing that won't take us toward Rue Galande, but in the opposite direction. We live in The Latin Quarter, the left side of the Seine, not the right, in case you've forgotten."

"Ah-h-h," she twinkled, tugging my hand, "don't be a killjoy. Come on-n-n." To my amazement, she climbed onto the bridge's baluster and, with arms outstretched like a circus high wire acrobat, she inched toward the Right Bank.

"Idiot!" I blurted, "I thought you meant cross the bridge the *sensible* way, by walking on the sidewalk, like *normal* people do, not walking the railing."

"Whee-e-e!" Daredevil Lady squealed, almost toppling into the Seine. "Whee-e-e!"

"Bonnie Silver, what's gotten into you?"

"Whe-e-e! Ladies and gentlemen, *Mesdames et messieurs*," she announced, mimicking a ringmaster and waving her arm for emphasis, "feast your eyes on the world-famed daredevil of Goode, Virginia. Observe as she performs the ultimate of death-defying challenges, an act never viewed by mortal eyes! Whee-e-e!"

"Are you completely nuts?" My heart was tripping like a jackhammer. I frantically peered around, searching for the French police.

"Whee-e-e!"

"What are you trying to do? Get your name in the Goode obituary?"

A police patrol car cruised toward us. Its driver, head angled out the window, eyed Bonnie just as *Mademoiselle* Audacious Aerialist ignited another squeal. "Whee-e-e!"

Hearing the other-worldly sound, the cop raised his shoulders in an eloquent Oh-My-God-Not-Another-One-Of-These-Kooks-On-My-Shift shrugs, shook his head, slammed the cruiser into first gear and screeched off, leaving about a streak of rubber on the pavement. So much for legal intervention.

Meanwhile, the high wire exhibition kicked into high gear. "Come on, Paul," Bonnie exclaimed, urging me to join her. "You'll love it. I kid you not. Come on!"

Contrary to rational thinking, I climbed onto the railing and inched toward the Right Bank, and for some strange reason—one I still can't explain, even today—I had the sensation of disengaging from my body, as if transformed into some gaseous element thinner than air.

Later, as we walked back across the bridge—the sensible way this time, on the sidewalk—she leaned toward me, breezed a kiss on my cheek, and said, "Welcome, my friend."

"Welcome to what?" I gave her a smile.

"To the most exhilarating of human joys, the thrill of flight and the wonder of feeling free. Remember I told you how I love flying because it brings a sense of liberation? Well, in walking the railing, I'm sure you felt a little of what I'm talking about, felt what an eagle must feel when flying mountain high. How'd-cha like it?"

"Fantastic...fantastic." My earlier actions were so out of character for me. I was so conservative, rarely taking any chances. Having done so, I had to admit that it did bring a sense of liberation.

Later, as we stepped into the foyer of Twenty-One Rue Galande, I glanced at the bulletin board over the mailbox. Seeing it reminded me of the note the Phantom Lady posted on it, promising to meet me, then standing me up. "Bonnie."

"Yeah?"

"Let me ask you something."

"Sure."

"Why didn't you show up that night you said you would?"

"Well, I really don't expect you to believe what I'm about to tell you, but the truth is, I didn't intend to stand you up."

"So why did you?"

"I had no choice. You see, I got the times confused. I had an engagement—ah, an appointment—at the same hour I'd promised to meet you. I'd forgotten it, or maybe I didn't want to remember it, if you get my meaning. You know how these things go. Over time, all of us accumulate an assortment of clutter in the storehouse of our minds. We tell ourselves that one day we'll sort through it and discard some of the unpleasant things in the inventory, in a kind of garage sale of bitter memorabilia." She walked up one step, stopped, and ran a hand over the banister of the ancient, wooden stairway. Something caused her expression to change—worry, perhaps, or sadness. "But we postpone the sale because we know that going through the stored items will only bring…pain."

"You couldn't break it?"

"Break what? The door to memory's storehouse?"

"No, break the engagement, or the appointment, or whatever you call it."

"If I could have broken it," she said slowly, as if in deep reflection, "believe me, I would have done so in a New York minute, because it was the kind of meeting I didn't want to attend. But life often boxes us in, and we do what we don't want to, but…must. And when that happens, you search for exits and discover there are none. You find yourself trapped."

"You're right about that. Life does play tricks on us all. Then one must add the fact that things and people seldom turn out the way we expect."

"That's for sure. Anyway," she yawned loudly. "Thanks for a delightful evening. Did I say 'evening'? I meant morning. But either way, it was great. Anyway, I gotta catch some sleep."

"Sure. When will I see you again?"

"Who can say?" She suddenly sounded very weary.

"What do you mean, 'who can say'? You, Bonnie Silver, you can say. Who else, but you?"

"Look, I really don't know when I'll see you again. The truth is, I can't even say…if we'll meet again. And the meaning of that last statement, I'm sure you don't understand."

"Right, I don't. Do you?" Why the mystery?

"The 'what' part I understand. I understand well. But the 'why' part I don't understand, and I may never understand. But at any rate," she said, a smile brightening her lips like the blush of dawn, "I had a marvelous time." She started up the stairs once more.

"Same here. Oh, by the way."

She stopped and looked back over her shoulder. "Yeah?"

"Thanks for mentoring me through my first solo flight across *Pont Michel*. It was a real blast."

She blew me a kiss. "See-ya 'round, tiger."

"Sure. But when?" No answer. "Did you hear me? When?"

"I heard."

"So?" I knew I was stalling; I hated for our time together to end. For some reason I needed to know we'd get together again. Soon.

She continued up the stairs. "Goodbye, Paul."

"Never say goodbye. Say *au revoir*." I followed her up the steps.

"*Au revoir*." Her voice fading as she rounded the corner to the next flight of steps toward her apartment.

"*Au revoir*, Phantom Lady…*au revoir*."

Chapter 4

Bonnie and I saw each other briefly every day for a week. We'd bump into one another, catch up on our respective activities, and afterward retreat either to his or her own studio, or one of us would head out to enjoy the beauty that is Paris. Then, for the next two weeks, I didn't see Bonnie Silver/the Phantom Lady. I wondered why, for it was not unusual to pass her in the morning or evening as she bubbled up or down the stairs. But for fourteen days, nothing. It was as if an alien spaceship plucked her from the Latin Quarter and sped her to another universe.

Thinking perhaps she'd changed her daily routine and was leaving the building earlier, at say, five A.M. or there about, I got up at four thirty one morning and waited in the foyer, hoping I'd see her going to wherever it was she went each day. The vigil was futile. I must have seen just about every tenant of Twenty-One Rue Galande exit that morning—everyone, that is, except The Phantom Lady.

Two days later, I decided I'd use a more direct tactic: I'd go to Bonnie's studio to find out if she were home. Halfway up the stairs, I had second thoughts. Maybe, I reasoned, one of her relatives unexpectedly flew in from the States, and she was busy showing him or her a few must-see tourist attractions: the Louvre, the Arc de Triomphe, etc. Or perhaps she might be staying with a sick friend, or maybe… The possibilities were endless. I soon scrapped the idea of knocking on her studio door. After all, what right did I have to violate her privacy by barging in unannounced…and uninvited? None.

Because I'd finished my quota of writing for that day (twelve pages), in fact, for the following day also, I decided I'd take a break and go somewhere to lounge away the afternoon. What better place to do that than at the most entertaining show spot in Paris? The Moulin Rouge? Folies Bergere? The Lido? None of these. They were all tourist traps where the cost of a bottle of champagne was astronomical and admission prices, obscene. Besides, gaining admittance to any one of them often meant standing in an endless line. For me, buying a ticket to one of these "spectaculars" would annihilate my budget, which wasn't much to begin with.

The only show I could afford was one with no cover or

minimum. There was such a presentation whose entertainment was consistently the best in Paris—and the cheapest. Price of admission? Zero. However, those wishing to make a donation were free to do so, in fact, were encouraged to. But whether spectators gave or not, the show went on as scheduled.

The site of the presentation was on the sidewalks fronting The Cluny Museum. Housing a collection of medieval artifacts (including a Roman bath dating to 200 A.D.), the museum was in the remains of a Middle Ages building at the intersection of boulevards Saint Germain and Saint Michel. Sidewalks there were exceptionally wide, an ideal stage for street performers.

Filling it most of the day, often into early morning, was a smorgasbord of itinerant entertainers. Usually among them were several artists who, using chalk, sketched on the pavement. A few of them were quite talented, others mediocre at best, while some should have considered other professions (house painting, for example).

In addition to graphic artists, there were usually one or more acrobats, jugglers, fire-eaters, mimes, jazz musicians playing conventional instruments: trumpets, trombones, clarinets, etc. Others played unconventional ones: goblets, bottles, jugs, or anything capable of producing sound, thus snaring the attention and money of passersby.

Drawing crowds was an essential part of the sidewalk entertainment business, and performers went to great lengths to lure spectators, embellishing their acts with all kinds of bizarre attention-grabbers. Any gimmick was acceptable, and forgivable, as long as it produced an audience, preferably a generous one.

When I arrived that morning, the show was already underway, with the usual performers holding center stage. The most remarkable of the group was Eddie Thomas, a balladeer from Durham, North Carolina. Strumming his Sears and Roebuck guitar and singing, or what he *called* singing, he circulated through the crowd as he usually did. "Working it," he called the practice. Eddie could only play three chords, all in the key of "E," but, sadly, he sang in the key of "C"— and not too well at that.

"John Henry" was the tune he rendered when I arrived. As always, he belted the lyrics with great zeal. "Cap'n said to Joh-n-n-n Henry, gonna bring me a steel drill down!" To Eddie, gusto and earsplitting volume were acceptable substitutes for talent.

In spite of his musical limitations, audiences loved Eddie. Convinced that no one could naturally sing so poorly, listeners were convinced his seemingly lack of musical refinement was affected to create an earthy *persona,* and that when he sang off key he did so to flavor his performance with the stuff of "true folk artistry." If his admirers had only known the truth.

Encouraged by his listeners' response, Eddie for years continued strumming his three chords, singing his limited repertoire, collecting the few francs tossed into his "kitty," a hat, and remaining true to his "artistic integrity." Secretly—to me he admitted this only once—he dreamed a recording agent would discover him. All he had to do, he felt, was to continue singing on the sidewalk in front of an obscure museum in Paris, and that one day his dream would come true. When? "Soon," he assured me. "Soon."

Sadly, years later, Eddie would still be entertaining on the same street corner, hoping a recording executive would happen by, hear him, and realize what a gifted artist he was. Recently, a friend who lived in Paris told me that Eddie, a much older man, continued to stand at the intersection of boulevards Saint Germain and Saint Michel, still strumming, singing, waiting…and dreaming.

On this particular morning, having passed Eddie, I strolled to a cluster of about twenty people further up the street. Bodies pressed together like packed sardines, they formed a semicircle around a male street performer. Those at the rear tiptoed and, necks craning, strained for a better view over the wall of onlookers. I hopped onto the ledge of the fence, and from there I saw what everyone stared at.

Wearing a grimy white shirt and tattered jeans, a balding, diminutive man in his late fifties, sat on the sidewalk, his back angled against the fence. A topless shoebox containing five white mice rested in his lap. Unhurried, the performer placed his hand into the container, cornered one of the animals, scooped it up and lowered the rodent to his forearm. Apparently trained, the mouse sniffed a path up the showman's arm, making its way toward his shoulder. Once there, the mouse inched toward the man's neck and when the animal reached it, the performer's head tilted back until it rested against the fence. When it did, his mouth opened and the animal darted into the cavity, which immediately snapped shut, leaving only the mammal's vacillating tail visible.

"My God!" a female behind me gasped. "Will you look at *that.* Sickening! Disgusting! How can anyone do such a thing? Jesus!" The voice sounded familiar. I turned and, to my astonishment, the Phantom Lady, Bonnie Silver, stood within inches of me. "Paul," she twinkled, "what're you doing here?"

"Same as you, my friend, studying Sidewalk Zoology one-oh-one."

She chuckled. "Isn't this guy sickening? Makes you wanna puke."

"Does at that. He's certainly not recommended watching on a full stomach."

"For sure. Oh!" Bonnie chirped, snapping her finger, "I nearly forgot: I'd like you to meet a friend of mine, Roger Anderson."

A black man in his early twenties stood beside Bonnie. Over six feet, he dwarfed her. His hair, styled in a bush, ballooned high above his head, accentuating his height. The dashiki he wore, longer than most, ended below his knees. "Nice meeting you, Roger."

"Same here." He hesitated, ignoring my outstretched hand, his eyes wary. After a few seconds, I withdrew my hand. "Ah, what'd you say your name is?" A scowl distorted his face.

"I didn't, but it's Paul, Paul Lasser." I smiled and offered my hand again, my good manners ingrained, thanks to my Mother's training. Tentatively he extended his. His grasp was spongy. Mine tightened. A second later, his did also.

Something in his eyes seemed to change, as if my persistence in getting a handshake from him elevated me in his estimation. "Pleasure meetin' ya, Paul."

"Same here. So, you're a friend of Bonnie?"

"Right. She's my ace running buddy, the kind-a broad you can't help but dig. In fact, a man would have to practice in order *not* to like Bonnie Silver. Know what I mean?" He shot Bonnie an affectionate glance and smiled.

"Yes, I think I do. In fact, I'm in agreement with you on that," I replied.

"Look," Bonnie said, "I can't speak for you guys, but standing here watching this clown convert his mouth into a Holiday Inn for rats is turning my stomach upside down. Why don't we go to a café and talk?"

Minutes later, we sat on the terrace of a nearby café. One of the most popular in the Latin Quarter, it was usually packed, as it was that day. We were lucky to find seats, let alone three on the terrace, where most customers preferred to sit. From there patrons had the best vantage point for seeing and being seen while watching a never-ending flow of pedestrians.

No university—Princeton and Harvard included—provided a better education in the study of "people-ology" than the one you could obtain with an alert eye and a terrace seat at a sidewalk café in Paris, in what I called, the University of Human Studies.

For a modest tuition fee, the price of a cup of coffee, there was no end to the knowledge you could acquire observing the walking volumes that promenaded before you. You were able to sit all day if you cared to, confident that your tuition wouldn't be terminated by some zealous waiter asking you to move on, reminding you that a single cup of Java didn't entitle you to endless schooling. Pay for the coffee and you've met the school's financial requirements, placing you in good standing and entitling you to all the rights and privileges of the Left Bank Sidewalk Café Scholars' Society.

Bonnie and Roger ordered white wine, I, an espresso. For a while, we chatted about sundry things, all trivial matters. Then Roger put his elbows on the table and focused his wary eyes on me. "So tell me, what's a guy like you doing in The City of Light?" I explained that I was on a sabbatical and planned to do some writing.

"That's cool." He nodded, his eyes scanning the crowd.

I peered at Roger, sensing misery under his feigned relaxed facade. "And you, what's your story?"

"Well, I'm here for two reasons. One, to do my part for The Civil Rights Movement in the States. And two, like you, I'm on a sabbatical…of sorts."

"I'm confused. I don't understand how you can help The Civil Rights Movement in America by being *here* in Paris."

"Well, I got my reasons for not walking picket lines in America. Some people can do that sort of thing and do it well. But me? Like I said, I got my reasons." He glanced at Bonnie, who immediately looked away. Again, he turned to me. "You see, by *not* being in America, I'm actually helping The Movement. You know what I mean?"

I didn't have the *faintest* idea what he was talking about, but it was obvious he didn't want to pursue the matter. Uneasiness in his voice convinced me it was time to change the subject. "So, you're on a sabbatical?" I inquired.

"In a way of speaking, yes."

"A way of… What do you mean?"

"Frankly, I don't think you wanna hear about it. It's a complicated story, and it'd take far too long to explain." He sipped his wine as if that closed that topic of conversation.

"I can't speak for Bonnie here, but as for me, I have nothing *but* time." My curiosity gene was kicking in; there was nothing I loved more than digging around in someone's psyche. More than one person had called me nosey in my lifetime but, the truth be told, I was the way I was—damned inquisitive—or so my sisters had told me countless of times.

"Well, she's heard the story before…often." He glanced at Bonnie, who mirrored his smile but remained silent, fingering a strand of love beads at her neck. "The fact is, she's my chief confidant and listener. Ain't that right?"

She covered his hand with hers. "That's right, my friend."

"Without her, my life would be a sewer. So, yes, she's heard my story. When I've needed somebody who'd listen, and that has been often, she has always offered me her ears."

"So, that leaves only me who *hasn't* heard the story. Right?"

"Right. Like I said though, I don't think you want to hear it." Roger paused. "But," he continued, "now that I think about it, maybe I can give you a condensed version. The short version goes like this. I was born and raised in Flatwater, Mississippi, in the heart of the Delta. Then, thank God, one day I left the damn place...for good. End of story."

"Is that it?" I asked, reaching for my espresso.

Roger shrugged. "What more is there to say?"

"I don't know, but I'm sure there must be *volumes* sandwiched between 'I was born in Flatwater, Mississippi,' and 'I left.'" What was the big secret, I wondered.

"You're right, there is, in fact, there is another whole Library of Congress sandwiched between the beginning and the end."

"And I suspect that the part which is between 'I was born' and 'I left' is the crux of the matter." My writer's active imagination was starting to kick in, imagining all kinds of scenarios. I sensed a despondency about him which drew me in, yet turned me off at the same time. It was a compelling combination.

"You're right, it is. Let me tell you a few things about my hometown. In Flatwater, they have ways of dealing with people like me. They silence them...forever. And this they planned to do to me, and would have, but thank God they couldn't get their hands on me, so they switched to their Plan B."

Concern suddenly clouded Bonnie's eyes as she turned to Roger. "Are you sure you wanna go into all of that? You know how it upsets you."

"I know, but it'll be OK. Trust me. It'll be fine." He faced me, his dark eyes boring into mine with an intensity that I found unsettling. "Let me ask you something. Do you have any idea what it's like to have someone *mentally* castrate you, then douse the wound with the turpentine of terror?"

I stared right back. "No." How was one supposed to answer a question like that?

"I do," he confessed before taking a gulp of his wine.

In the far distance, the wail of an emergency vehicle's siren splintered the morning air. Gradually the volume intensified, nearly blotting out cafe noises. The siren came closer, so close it seemed to emanate from the café's interior or perhaps the adjoining building. "W-E-E-E-E . . . W-A-A-A-A . . . W-E-E-E-E . . . W-A-A-A-A."

Jetting to the front of a line of cars waiting for the red light at the intersection of boulevards Saint Germain and Saint Michel, an ambulance streaked into view. Tires screaming, it darted to the opposite side of the thoroughfare, then slammed to a halt within feet of the Cluny Museum. Almost instantly, the vehicle's cabin doors swung open and two paramedics, one carrying a black satchel, hopped from the ambulance and bolted toward the sidewalk where street entertainers performed.

Bonnie stood, trying to get a better view of what was happening. "Wonder what's going on."

"Beats me," Roger said, draining his glass. "Wanna go over and check it out?"

"Why not? You coming, Paul?"

"Sure." I gulped the rest of my espresso and stood.

As the three of us crossed the street, the two paramedics wedged a path through the wall of onlookers. Nudging and elbowing, they finally cleared an opening leading to a man sitting on the sidewalk, his back propped against the fence. Almost as soon as the breach opened, it closed. To get a better view, Roger and I pressed forward, hoping to leverage spectators aside. We couldn't.

"*Revenez!* " the taller paramedic shouted. "*Revenez!* Back up!" With the viscosity of chilled molasses, the mass of voyeurs finally relented, parting near its center.

"*Pierre!*" yelled the other attendant who now knelt beside the prone patient.

"*Oui?* "

"*Il n'y a aucun besoin d'expedier...pas maintenant.* " (There's no need in rushing...not now.)

"*Tu veux dire--.* " (You mean—")

"*Oui.* "

Pierre shook his head and groaned. "*J'esperais que nous pourrions epargner le pauvre gars.* " (I was hoping we could save the poor guy.)

He removed a stretcher from the ambulance and walked toward the dead man. All spectators were now eerily silent—a dark and brooding silence, the type heard exclusively at burials, wakes, and memorial battlefields. Holding it by its tail, the paramedic kneeling next to the corpse dangled a bloodstained mouse.

"What happened?" a woman asked.

"Beats me," someone replied.

"*Madame*, did you see what happened?" the woman asked someone else.

"No. I just got here."

"That guy is sure a goner all right," one bystander observed. "Look at those eyes, will you? Like frozen marbles."

An elderly woman approached the paramedic who held the mouse. "Young man, I do wish you'd get rid of that nasty thing. It's *disgusting*."

"Certainly." The emergency worker, the one named Pierre, reached into his black leather bag, removed a roll of gauze, snipped off about a foot of it, circled the bandage around the mouse, then dropped the corpse into a sewer opening."

"Satisfied, *Madame*?"

"Quite. *Merci, monsier*."

Ever the polite Frenchman, he gave a slight bow. "My pleasure." Pierre turned to his partner. "Well, I guess we'd better put that stiff on the stretcher and haul him out of here. It's close to our break time." Seconds later, the ambulance, tires screeching, lights flashing, sped up Boulevard Saint Michel.

"Pardon," Bonnie said, speaking to the woman who complained about the dead mouse, "do you know what happened?"

"I can't say for sure, but I'm told that as a part of his act, the dead man placed a mouse in his mouth, and for some strange reason, the animal went berserk, clawing and nibbling its way down the victim's throat. Seemingly, it got stuck and ended up choking the poor wretch. Anyway, when I walked up, I saw the paramedic tugging to pull the animal free, but it fought to go in the opposite direction. Finally, he yanked it loose. The rodent was drenched in blood. A most sickening sight!" She shook her head in sadness. "What a grisly way to die."

The wail of the siren echoed as the ambulance streaked toward the crest of Boulevard Saint Michel, leaving an air of misery and loss.

"So sad," I murmured.

Bonnie rested her head against my arm. "Death is always sad, isn't it? Let's go somewhere away from here. This is too depressing."

Roger extended his hand. "Look, you two, I'm gonna split. Nice meeting ya, Paul."

I clasped his and noticed his handshake was much warmer than when we'd met earlier. "Same here."

"What do you say we get together again? Soon, real soon?"
I smiled. "Sounds great. I'd like that."
"I'll dig you guys later, be cool." He placed a hand on Bonnie's shoulder.
"Sure thing." Bonnie rose on her tiptoes to give him a hug. "Take care, my friend."
"Peace, Bon." Roger kissed her gently on the forehead and strolled away, leaving an atmosphere of melancholy in his wake.
Bonnie and I headed for Twenty-One Rue Galande. En route, we chatted about *Easy Rider*, a film playing at a little Left Bank theater. We also discussed the new movie by the Beatles, *The Yellow Submarine*. As we stopped at a corner, waiting for a break in traffic, I said, "You know, this has turned out to be one heck of an afternoon, hasn't it? In less than an hour we've seen death twice."
"Twice?" She peered up at me through her granny glasses, a questioning look on her face.
"Yes." I couldn't seem to shake the despondency in Roger's eyes, the hopelessness in what he said.
"I don't follow you. OK, the first time we saw it was when we saw the old man choked by the mouse, but what's the second time?"
"When we met Roger."
"Roger dead? That's ridiculous. What's wrong with you? He's alive, as alive as you and I are."
I peered down at her for a minute. "Is he?"
"Of course, we just left him, remember? Are you operating on all eight cylinders here?"
"I think you're overlooking something." Traffic slowed and I took her arm as we crossed the street.
"What?" she asked, hurrying her steps to keep up with my long stride. "What am I overlooking?"
"Not all dead men are in coffins. Some walk among us. Every day."
We reached the sidewalk and stopped while a street cleaner, dressed in the city's green-as-grass utility uniform, swept away debris. Bonnie fisted her hands on her slender hips. "And exactly what does that mean?"
The realization hit me that I was talking about one of her close friends, and that evidently Bonnie was very loyal to her friends. Once more I'd philosophized at the wrong time. I sighed audibly, running a hand through my hair. "Sorry. That was just a flippant remark. I meant nothing by it. Nothing at all."
We dropped the subject and, both silent, walked on. I was

surprised that Bonnie didn't understand what I meant when I, speaking of Roger, said that not all dead men are in coffins. Usually we were in tune about such things. Later, she would perhaps, but for now she was too emotionally involved to see her friend's emotional dilemma.

Chapter Five

The apartment building in which I lived was a few blocks up from Notre-Dame Cathedral, just off Boulevard Saint Germain. If you walked from Twenty-One Rue Galande to where it intersected Boulevard Saint Germain, you passed an assortment of small businesses—a dairy, a pharmacy, a grocery, a furniture store, a ladies' boutique, cafés, etc. The only business not represented was a funeral home. So varied were the businesses that a resident, if he cared to, could spend his entire life within a two square block area—except for his burial.

During most of the day, Rue Galande was a beehive of pedestrians: shoppers, laborers, bohemians, and always, scores of Sorbonne students scurrying to or from classes, while others sat in cafés and poured over books.

After living on Rue Galande a couple of weeks and becoming familiar with some of the neighborhood regulars, I began to sense the "personality" of the street and to observe many of the daily occurrences. Case in point, at around seven each morning four unkempt men and a couple of women—even more unkempt—pushed a vendor's cart piled with used clothes up Rue Galande and parked it at the entrance of a narrow street across from my studio. For several hours, they buttonholed pedestrians in their effort to hawk their merchandise, turning the sidewalk into a bustling open market.

Usually at around noon, the vendors shut down their business for the day and, after rushing across the street to a grocery store, returned with a couple of bottles of cheap red wine, and by two o'clock—sometimes three when business was slow—they curled up on their cart or on the sidewalk or, more often than not, in the gutter, and there they snoozed. The fact that they were irretrievably drunk seemed of no concern to the neighborhood cops who, chatting and twirling their batons, strolled past as if the intoxicated men and their discarded wine bottles were natural components of the scenery, like trees in a forest or grazing cows on a farm.

During my eleven months in Paris, I never saw a policeman arrest a single drunk on Rue Galande, though countless lushes afforded them many opportunities to do so. In some cases, the drunks lay boldly, no, defiantly, on the sidewalk in the direct path of the patrolling officers, and the cops walked around or over them,

35

continuing to converse nonchalantly while twirling their nightsticks.

Rue Galande was a remarkable street, populated with an assortment of remarkable regulars. One of the regulars, "The Gypsy Lady,"—a name I gave her—was even more remarkable than the street. At around seven each morning she, cradling a baby, stood on the sidewalk fronting the cafe across the way and panhandled for an hour or so. If an approaching pedestrian looked prosperous or tried to sidestep her, she pounced on him like a used car salesman on a Mongolian idiot. She could also be solicitous, as she was the morning she stopped me.

"*Monsieur*, my child is starving, hasn't had a morsel in days. I pray that the generous gentleman will be so kind as to help this poor, impoverished mother save her beloved child."

"How old is the child?" I asked.

"Six months," she said, cuddling a well-nourished offspring of at least twelve months.

"Six months, you say. I see. Your husband, does he provide for the baby?"

"I have no husband," she swooned, slipping her gold-banded wedding ring finger under the blanket that circled the child. "The father abandoned us. Sad, *monsieur*," she sobbed, though, her eyes were tearless. "Very sad."

"Sad indeed." I handed her a couple of francs, not out of pity for her plight or that of the child, but as a tribute to her acting skills. The woman was talented, capable of delivering Oscar-winning performances on cue, one of which she had just given—minus the tears.

"You are too kind, *Monsieur*," she said, taking the money with a sweeping and blurred movement of her hand.

"You're right; too kind. Good day, *Mademoiselle*...or *Madame*...as the case may be."

By eleven each morning the "destitute mother," still cuddling "her starving child," sat at her usual table on the terrace of the little café near the corner, and, as was her custom, she ordered a bottle of Moet Chandon, an expensive wine. Promptly at eleven thirty, a man joined her, the same one each day, and later they, amid much chatter and laughter, ended the rendezvous with an elaborate meal, paid for by the *impoverished* mother. The next day the *starving* child would again be in the mother's arms as she stood on the corner in about the same spot. Often she held a different baby, by my count, ten different ones in an eighteen day period, which was mystifying because the mother was young, no more than nineteen at the most, too young to

36

have produced such a litter.

The Gypsy Lady was indeed a mystery. But after living on Rue Galande for a while, I discovered that there were others on the street just as mysterious.

One was *Madame* L'Enfant. I'll always associate her with the dairy across the street from my apartment building. Entering it at around eight each morning, as I often did, was quite an educational experience. By then, the shop bulged with prattling housewives. Each carried a netted shopping bag, for few stores in Paris provided them. The only exceptions were the large department stores like *Au Printemps* and *Galeries Lafayette*.

Immediately upon entering the dairy, shoppers rushed to the cheese case as if it were a trough and they, famished animals. Each elbowed and shouldered for advantage over her competitor who, like everyone there, was eager to lay hands on a packet of Camembert cheese, then the most popular cheese in Paris, probably still is. Much bickering accompanied the stampede, for it was every shopper for herself. There were no rules of protocol. No timeouts. No holds barred.

Like the cheese case, the checkout counter was the site of many confrontations. There a housewife might insist that she be served first since the shopper at the head of the line hadn't waited "her proper turn," or someone else might demand that the last container of raspberry yogurt, her "favorite," not be sold to the woman who'd bullied others aside and claimed the prize for herself.

There were ceaseless allegations of price gouging. Some housewives were walking computers, capable of naming any item in the store whose cost increased a single centime during the month. The store's owner was the target of their wrath. Shoppers often "double-" or "triple-teamed" him; the poor guy couldn't squeeze in a word. Or sometimes they employed a tag team tactic. Regardless of the strategy, the proprietor could never win. He was outgunned or out maneuvered, or both.

At around a quarter after eight each morning, amid a flood of chattering and bickering, a frail old woman hobbled into the dairy and, as she always did, brightened and warmed the place with her presence. After greeting everyone, calling each by name—how she could remember so many names I didn't know—she always purchased a liter of milk, slipped it into her frayed net bag, wished all a pleasant day, and, beaming a smile, headed for the door.

Whenever the aged shopper entered the store, squabbles over Camembert cheese, line cutting, price gouging, etc. ceased, resuming only after she exited and, tapping the sidewalk with her cane, made her way up Rue Galande.

"The old woman," I said to the storeowner one day, "who is she?"

The storeowner smiled with obvious affection. "Ah, that, *monsieur*, is *Madame* L'Enfant."

"She's like a sedative to your customers, isn't she?"

He nodded as he handed a customer her purchase. "Always."

The next time I mentioned *Madame* L'Enfant to the proprietor, he nudged me to the end of the counter. "*Monsieur*, you are new in the neighborhood, are you not?"

"Yes."

"So naturally you don't know."

"Know what?"

"That, though *Madame* L'Enfant's smile is a vivid one, and she wears it always, the old woman is dying of an incurable disease. Those who have lived in the neighborhood for a while are aware of this. Sadly, her doctor says her time draws near, *very near*."

"So, her doctor thinks she'll die soon?'

"As surely as we speak."

"I say if her doctor believes she'll die, the man is an idiot."

"An idiot?" He straightened himself to his full 5'4" height.

"Yes."

"It's obvious you don't understand. You see, her doctor, Doctor Degur, is not your ordinary physician. Why, he is a recognized expert in his field."

"I'm sure what you say is true, and as her doctor predicts, the old woman will soon be in her coffin. But her doctor does not recognize that people like *Madame* L'Enfant never die."

His eyes flashed question marks. Obviously he hadn't understood what I tried to say. He handed me my change, wished me a pleasant day, and I left.

That was the last conversation I had with the shop owner about the old woman. We didn't talk about her any more because there was nothing else for a couple of males to say about a frail and dying old woman who made our masculinity seem puny, and squabbles over a few ounces of Camembert cheese, the most trivial of matters.

Though I returned to the dairy many times after speaking to the manager about *Madame* L'Enfant, I never saw her again. Someone told me she died and morticians buried her or, to be precise, doctors declared her dead and morticians lowered a corpse into a grave. But *Madame* L'Enfant didn't die. Many claim the old woman, shopping bag in hand and a smile lighting her face like dawn, still walked Rue Galande, and those who knew her best say they were willing, under oath, to swear that they saw the old woman every day.

Chapter 6

Exiting Twenty-One Rue Galande one morning, I noticed a man loitering on the sidewalk near the entrance. Neighborhood regulars I recognized, having seen them day after day, but I'd never seen the loiterer before. Nonetheless, I paid him little mind, thinking he was just another idler. The Left Bank had scores of them. Perhaps, I thought, he might be waiting for a friend or, having nothing better to do, enjoying a few minutes of girl watching, a popular Parisian pastime, almost as popular as walking dogs.

On the other hand, he might have been…well, the possibilities were endless in my vivid imagination. The following morning I saw the same man in almost the identical spot. Again, I gave him little thought. But when I saw him the third morning, keeping in check both my writer's imagination and my natural trepidation for anything mysterious became impossible.

Who was this guy? What was he up to? Was he meeting a friend? If so, who? Or did he have other things in mind? Mischievous things? Sinister or felonious things? Perhaps he was casing the building, plotting to burglarize some or all of the apartments, noting the hours that occupants departed and returned. But whoever he was and whatever he was up to, he was beginning to make me nervous, very nervous.

He was wearing the same gray business suit, a conservative tie with slanting bars of black and amber, and an equally conservative fedora. The hat he cocked with almost geometric precision several degrees to the right. His suit was always immaculately pressed, shirt starched, and shoes buffed.

"Morning," I greeted the man on the fourth day I saw him dallying in front of the building.

"Morning." He nodded his head slightly.

"I trust your day will be as pleasant as forecasters say the weather will be," I stated, glancing up at the azure blue sky.

"You're most kind," he murmured.

"My pleasure." Sensing that our cryptic conversation was over, I walked on. Sparing him a glance over my shoulder, I decided that this man required watching. Two could play this game.

I ducked around the corner into the side street between my building and the *boulangerie,* or bakery that I normally visited each morning. By American standards, the side street was an alley. I flattened myself against the side of my large white brick building and very slowly peeked around the corner. There he stood, in the same spot, lighting a cigarette with his hand cupped over the flame and looking up at the windows. Who was he waiting for? What was he after? I stood there for several long minutes watching him watch the building. It was like watching milk curdle—and about as exciting.

My empty stomach grumbled a protest, reminding me that fresh-baked croissants were waiting for me in the bakery. I waited some more; so did he. I sighed, running a hand through my hair still damp from my morning shower. What a waste of time, I thought. Still, I couldn't bring myself to leave my vantage point just yet.

The concierge of the building stepped out onto Rue Galande, net shopping bag in hand, nodded at the stranger in the hat, and preceded across the street to the dairy. The stranger pulled a small notepad from his hip pocket and wrote something down, checking his wristwatch as if noting the time. Interesting.

My stomach growled louder, any louder and the stranger would be able to hear it, I thought. Time to bring my spying mission to a close. James Bond, I wasn't. Hungry, I was. Leaving my vantage point, I hurried to the bakery with my growling stomach leading the way.

The next morning I was in the foyer opening a letter from my mother when the stranger entered. Up close, within the confines of the small foyer, he seemed shorter than he did in the openness of the street. By my guess he was about 5'6"; I stood 6'2".

"*Bonjour,*" I greeted, surprised at the man's audacity, entering the building after observing it for several days. Just what was he up to? I intended to find out.

"*Bonjour.*" The man acted as though he had every right to be there. He made me uneasy.

Trying to appear nonchalant, I said, "It seems we might have a few showers later on."

"Yes, it does. You're Paul Lasser, aren't you?"

"That's right." Wait. *Wait!* How did this total stranger, know my name—first and last, no less? Was he psychic? Absurd. Maybe, I reasoned, he saw my name scrawled in my mother's slanted penmanship on the envelope I'd just removed from the box. Glancing down, I noted that the address side of the envelope was face down. So, it was impossible for him to have seen my name. So, the question remained: how did he know who I was?

He looked up at me and smiled. "You don't mind if I call you Paul, do you?"

"Not at all." The level of my unease ratcheted up a notch or two. He wasn't getting ready to make a pass at me, was he? I'd hate to have to pound his Frenchy fedora down to his collarbone.

"Paul, I wonder if you'll share with me a minute or so of your time?"

"Certainly." I was determined to find out what this man was about.

"I appreciate that."

"Ah, perhaps you're searching for someone, and I can be of assistance."

"Well, the subject," he said, enunciating slowly, "she—"

"Wait! Did you say '*subject*'?"

"Correct. *Monsieur*, allow me to get to the point. And the point is, during the past several weeks you made the acquaintance of an American who lives in this building, a *Mademoiselle* Bonnie Silver. Is that not correct?"

Chills started crawling up my backbone. "Yes." First, the guy knew my name. Then, he knew that Bonnie Silver was my friend. Exactly what was going on?

"Perhaps you can tell me if you've had a recent conversation with the subject, ah, I mean, the person mentioned, *Mademoiselle* Silver, on the matter of—"

"Wait." I held up my hand in a stop gesture.

"What's the problem, *Monsieur*?"

"The problem is that this conversation is moving too fast for my tastes, and I'm not comfortable with it. Let me see if I've got this right. You—to me a total stranger—walk in here and expect me to answer questions of a personal nature about private conversations I've had with a close friend? Is that what you expect?"

"*Monsieur*, I—"

"How do I know who you are or how you'll use this information? Maybe you have blackmail in mind, character assassination or…worse?"

"My apologies," he smiled briefly, like an oil slick lapping against the pier. He whipped a little leather folder from his inside coat pocket and flipped it open, revealing an identification card and badge. The card read *Inspector Charles DeMure, Agent of the National Investigative Force.* "Forgive me. I blundered. I should have identified myself," he tilted his head to the side as if in apology.

"Well," I sighed as I examined his ID, comparing the attached photograph to the irritating man standing in front of me, "from all indications, you are official."

"Quite." From his hip pocket, he removed a notepad. In it, he jotted my responses to a catalog of questions. Where did I meet Bonnie? Under what circumstances? Who introduced us? During the introduction, did someone accompany her? Did Bonnie mention where she spent her days? Upon leaving the building, did she sometimes carry a handbag? A purse? A briefcase? "Perhaps," he said, voice oozing insinuation, "a small parcel of an unusual shape and size."

He was especially interested in two of Bonnie's friends, an Algerian, Abdul Bushaeve, and an American, Roger Anderson. He showed me snapshots of both. I told him I'd met Roger. As for Abdul Bushaeve, I said I'd often seen Bonnie with a man who resembled the one in the photograph. Hearing this, he smirked as if he'd just discovered a crucial clue.

About Roger, he had a long list of questions. Did I know his means of support? Had I seen him flash large wads of cash? Had he purchased a "big-ticket item" recently—a luxury sedan, diamonds, a condominium, etc., and if so, was the sale in cash? Did he carry a weapon? Had I seen him accompanied by someone who spoke with an Italian accent? And finally, did he tend to glance at the nearest entrance when talking to me?"

"Look," I said, "would you mind telling me what the hell this is all about?"

"And, *Monsieur*," he continued, seemingly ignoring my question, "during the past week did you at any time see *Mademoiselle* Silver either enter or leave the premises?"

I crossed my arms over my chest. "Neither."

"Do you know of her whereabouts during the period in question?"

"Again, the answer is no." This man was really beginning to irritate me.

He lowered his notepad and probed my eyes. A second later, he redirected his attention to the notepad, seemingly convinced I had told him the truth. "I see."

"Inspector DeMure, what kind of trouble is Bonnie in?"

"You've been most helpful," he smiled, snapping the notepad shut. "Most helpful. It's a pity all those I interview are not as cooperative as you. Sadly, some aren't. So, for your assistance, I'm grateful."

"You're welcome, but, again, what I'd like to know is, has

Bonnie done anything wrong and if so, *what*?"

He clasped my hand and, smiling, pumped it. "Once more, thank you." He walked to the door, eased it open, and peered outside before speaking. "People from all corners of the world gather here in The City of Light. In fact, I'm sure if you randomly selected, say, fifty or so, from any street on the Left Bank, you could start your own little United Nations."

"I don't think you'd need fifty. Fifteen would do."

"No doubt, and, of that number, some would be good and honorable people, others, well, less so. Sadly, my job brings me in contact with the less honorable, the scum, the lowest of humans, liars, schemers, opportunists, and yes…even murderers. But Paris, of course, must be protected. Needless to say, in my line of work one becomes cynical of humans and their motives. Even so, I have made it my life's work to rid Paris of scum."

What was he getting at talking about liars, schemers, and murderers? Scum, he mentioned. I felt my ire rise; scum and Bonnie Silver did not belong in the same sentence. Obviously he had no clue what kind of person she really was. Perhaps I should be more concerned about *what* kind of person Inspector DeMure was, I thought. Bonnie, I knew; him, I didn't. Why wouldn't he answer my question about Bonnie? It was a simple question, after all.

"But enough about the negative," the inspector continued. "One should always be positive, always. And speaking of positive things, I see the sun is peeking through. In spite of today's earlier bleak forecast, it's a rather pleasant day, isn't it?"

"It was."

"*Was,* you say?" He turned to look at me.

"Yes, was until you showed up and bombarded me with questions about my friend, Bonnie Silver."

"Nothing personal, you understand. Asking questions is what I do for a living, distasteful though it sometimes is. But one has to do what one has to do."

"Indeed. Yet you've refused to answer my question regarding what it is you think Bonnie has done, for I assure you she could never do anything wrong."

Once more he spoke as if deaf to anything I had to say in Bonnie's defense. "At any rate, it has been a pleasure chatting with you. And I do hope you'll have a good day, Paul." He stepped over the threshold, stopped, and faced me. Obviously, he was waiting for me to wish him a good day, as he had wished me.

I didn't.

What reaction would you anticipate from an American in Paris when told French law officials were investigating him? Chances are his reaction(s) would include a selection from the following menu. Option A: discontinue doing what authorities suspected he was doing, which was probably something illegal or the French government wouldn't have one of its top agencies probing him. Option B: hire a good lawyer, one with influence in high places. Option C: contact a travel agency and book a flight on the next plane bound for anywhere...outside of France.

Regardless of the option or options chosen, the American when told he was the target of a criminal probe would, at a minimum, show concern, if not apprehension.

That evening when I stopped Bonnie in the hall as she passed my apartment and told her of my conversation with Inspector DeMure, what was her reaction? Option one? Two? Three? Or some combination there of? Answer, none of the above. Instead, she laughed.

"Bonnie, I don't think you understand the *seriousness* of the situation."

"Wrong." She shifted her net bag of vegetables, wine, and a baguette from one hand to the other.

"Then maybe you didn't hear everything I said."

"Heard every word."

"And you *still* think it's funny?" Sometimes the woman could be damned irritating with her Pollyanna outlook on life.

"Yes, I think it's funny. Don't you?"

"Of course not! And I'll lay you odds French law officials aren't rolling on the floor with laughter either."

"They should be because, I ask you, why would anyone in his damn right mind want to waste French taxpayers' money investigating me, Bonnie Silver? It'd make more sense if French officials used public funds to do something practical, like requiring dog owners to use pooper-scoopers so pedestrians can walk a straight line on sidewalks, instead of having to hopscotch. Or maybe fix the telephones, because half the time most of them don't work."

"About both you're right, but the fact is the French government isn't using tax money for the purposes you suggest, as wise as those suggestions may be. Instead, they're investigating *you*. Face it: someone thinks you're doing something wrong."

"There you go, overreacting again." She clucked her tongue a couple of times in a tisking manner as she slowly shook her head.

She reminded me of my mother after I'd done something that disappointed her. "And you're wearing that undertaker-glum-expression again," Bonnie said on a sigh.

"It's my teacher look," I ground out through clenched teeth. I was *not* overreacting, damn-it!

She rolled her eyes. "Look, whoever thinks I'm doing something wrong is the one who's wrong, not me. Anyway, if they want to find out about me, why don't they come and ask *me*, instead of slithering behind my back like a sidewinder?"

"Ask you? But that's not the way police conduct an investigation, at least not during the initial phases. Need I remind you that we're in a foreign country where the rules are different than in America, where one is presumed innocent until proven guilty?"

She shifted her bag again, flicked her long hair over her shoulder and glared at me. "I've done nothing wrong. Beyond that, I don't know what the hell to tell you. "

"Listen, if what you say is true, that is, you haven't done anything wrong, maybe it's not you, but your friends, Roger and Abdul, they're after."

"Abdul and Roger crooks?" she guffawed. "That's crap, grade A, homogenized crap! OK, I admit that by conventional standards, both those guys are a little kooky. But in one way or another, about one thing or another, aren't we all a little kooky? In this cockeyed world, where good is bad and right is wrong, where dishonorable men are lauded, and honorable ones hanged, jailed, or crucified, being kooky may be the only *sane* reaction to an upside down and insane world. So, kooks both Roger and Abdul may be, but crooks they ain't."

"For your sake, I hope you're right. Anyway, that brings us back to…"

"To why they're investigating me? Well, maybe," she grinned. "Maybe because they think I'm so sexy I'm a threat to French womanhood."

"Bonnie, do you take anything seriously?"

She batted her aqua blue eyes at me. "Yes."

I fisted my hands on my hips and leaned toward her. "What?"

She sighed. "Life and the wonder that we have it."

"It? What is 'it'? Life or the wonder that we have it?" She was making me mentally tired. I had the greatest urge to reach out and shake some sense into her, which was disturbing to me since I abhorred violence, especially against women.

"Both."

I leaned against my doorjamb, trying to calm down. "That's a beautiful sentiment, but beautiful sentiment and French cops probing your life don't make for a happy combination."

She shrugged. "Enough, Paul! Enough! Let's talk about something else, something worthwhile. Look, I bought a bottle of wine and a slab of blue cheese today. If you'll come up to my place, I'll be happy to share both with you. Besides, there's something I need to ask you."

"Wine and blue cheese? Blue cheese is my favorite. Lead the way." Maybe after sharing some wine, I could make her understand the seriousness of her situation I thought, as I closed my door and followed her up the steps.

It was my first time in her studio, and I found it tastefully decorated, more so than my studio, to say nothing of the neatness factor. Her space reflected her in every way: warm, dazzling, cheerful, and vibrant.

On the wall over her red sleep sofa hung several paintings, originals she told me, bought from street artists on Boulevard Saint Michel. All were examples of descriptive art. Not my style, but knowing Bonnie as I did, I could see what drew her to them.

There were two framed pictures sitting on the stand next to her sleep sofa: one was a black and white wedding picture of whom I assumed were her parents and the other photo was of her and her friend, who lived the next flight up, Betty Jean Greenlee. I suddenly wished I'd thought to pack a few pictures of family before I'd left home. That thought tugged at my heart; I'd never been so far from family before for such an extended period of time.

A yellow bowl full of fresh fruit sat centered on her small, wooden dining table. In a corner stood a statuette crafted from brass tubing and horseshoe nails. Below the windows, she had placed a bookcase: three tiers of pine boards topping several cinder blocks. She'd painted the cinder blocks sky blue and the boards sun yellow—much like her personality, I mused.

About twenty volumes lined each shelf. Most were biographies of famous men and women: among them, Abraham Lincoln, Albert Einstein, and Johann Sebastian Bach. In addition to the works of nonfiction, there were several novels, two of whose titles I remember, *Madame Bovary* and *Look Homeward, Angel*. I smiled when I saw those titles for I'd read both books twice. Obviously we shared the same interests in literature.

She stepped into the kitchenette, through strands of brightly colored glass beads that hung from the top of the doorway, and seconds later reappeared carrying a tray on which rested an opened bottle of wine, a wedge of blue cheese, a baguette, and two wine glasses.

We sat at the table, sipping and chatting. Halfway through the cheese, she said, "Paul, remember I told you that I wanted your opinion about something. I suppose by now you're wondering what I had in mind." She looked into her glass of wine as she spoke. "Before I tell you, you have to promise you won't laugh at me. OK?"

"OK." One thing for sure, I'd come to expect the unexpected from Bonnie.

Those aqua blue eyes zeroed in on mine. "Are you sure?"

"Positive." What was the big deal, anyway?

"Well, if you're *really* sure, because I—"

"Wait." My patience was growing thin. "What're you going to tell me, Bonnie? That you hijacked the Mona Lisa and you're holding her for ransom, or that you plan to convert the Notre-Dame Cathedral into apartments? All joking aside, the way you're talking, makes me think you're hiding something that's really bad. Are you?" I was just starting to relax from our earlier conversation in the hallway outside my studio, but the worried tone of her voice had me tensing again. Did she have something bad to tell me?

"Nothing bad, my friend. Relax."

I tore off a chunk of bread from the baguette and spread it with blue cheese, afraid that I might need fortification for what she was about to tell me. "So, what's the problem?" I popped the morsel into my mouth.

"Well, it's just that I don't want you to think I'm some kind of nut. If others think that, I really don't give a damn, but I wouldn't want you to think it." She slowly ran her index finger around the rim of her wine glass as she spoke.

"Bonnie, listen. Unpredictable I know you to be, but a fruitcake I know you ain't."

She nodded. "OK, thanks." She took a deep breath almost as if to bolster her courage. "Anyway, a couple of nights ago I had this dream, see."

"A dream or a nightmare?"

"A dream—a pleasant one." She smiled, but it didn't reach her eyes.

I reached across the table, laying my hand on hers and intertwining our fingers. "So why are you so uncomfortable talking about it?"

"Because the dream was…well, kind of odd. Do you ever have odd dreams?"

"Sure, all the time."

"Me too, but this one wasn't just odd, it was grand slam odd, off the charts. When I woke up, I wondered what it meant. Paul, I didn't have the foggiest."

"So tell me, what happened?"

She picked up the bottle of wine and topped off our glasses. "Well, in the dream I was buck naked, nothing on but my birthday suit."

"Whoa! Wait! Are you sure you want to discuss your X-rated dream with me, a guy?" I was working hard at not getting a visual. This was Bonnie, after all...

"It was un-rated," she laughed. "Anyway, there I stood without a stitch on. Then, suddenly, in the wink of an eye, and for no apparent reason, I was airborne, winging like an eagle, helium-light. Up I soared, up above snowcapped peaks and beyond the highest clouds. Below me were vast expanses of oceans and mountain ranges that seemed endless. I was so high the earth looked like a tiny marble cast in a sea of purple. I felt lighter than a dream. Finally, I landed on the moon and, joy-filled as a child, I frolicked over the moonscape.

"Soon I was airborne again," She waved her hands in the air as she spoke. "I was ascending near the speed of light and tingling with euphoria. Then, something in me suddenly uncoupled. 'Snap,' it went, and instantly my flesh vaporized. It was then I saw things that once were invisible."

"Like what?"

"Oceans that talked and told tales of the nothingness that existed before the birth of time. I saw an endless line of bloody warriors who, since the beginning of organized civilization, had been slaughtered in countless battles and an equal number of slaves dragging leg irons. Suddenly, I felt a lurch and something catapulted me into the silence and darkness of time and space and..." She paused. "Paul, who knows?"

"Knows   what?"

"Perhaps one day my dream will come true; I'll soar like an eagle, mountain high and at last be...free."

"You'd like that, would you?" She smiled slightly and nodded. "What happened next in your dream?"

"I don't know. I woke up." She took a sip of her wine. "What do you think the dream means?"

"What makes you think I'd know?"

"Well, you write a lot, and people who write have to do a great deal of thinking. After all, writing is nothing but thinking on paper.

So I figured with all the writing you do, you might be able to figure out what the dream means."

"Okay, I'll give it a shot. Let me see if I can summarize what you told me. In the dream, you soared the heavens naked, frolicking among constellations and stars, and while doing so you felt liberated from the prison of earth and flesh. Is that a reasonable summary?"

"Close enough." She pulled a grape from the fruit in the bowl and popped it in her mouth. "So what do you think the dream means?"

"That's simple." I emptied the wine in my glass.

"Well?" she asked, reaching for another grape.

"It means that you are who you are, Bonnie Silver. And, if the world is lucky, you'll continue to be just that...who you are...always."

"And *that's* your interpretation?"

"Yeah." What more could I say without getting myself in trouble?

"To be honest, I don't think you've helped me very much." She yawned, obviously tired and sleepy from the wine.

"Sorry, but I have to call them the way I see them. Look, we're both tired. Time for me to head down to my place." I walked to the door and stopped. "Bonnie, you mind stepping over here?"

"Why?"

"I want to touch you, so I can verify that you're not an illusion, whimsy, the product of some fantasy."

Shimmering a smile, she wafted over and caressed my cheek with a kiss. "Paul."

"Yes?" I ran my hands up and down her arms, feeling very mellow for the first time that day.

"You gotta be mad. Me, an illusion? A whimsy? A fantasy? That's laughable."

"Is it?" I ran a finger down her cheek, gazing into those fathomless blue eyes of hers.

"Of course. Anyway, good night, my friend."

I walked out into the hall, glanced over my shoulder at her. "'Night, dream girl," I whispered.

"What did you say?"

By then I was feeling heat creep up my neck and face; I was glad my back was to her for a few seconds until I reached the shadowy staircase. I cleared my throat and turned. "Ah, I said 'night, *queen* girl."

"Oh. I thought you said dream girl." She twinkled a smile as she leaned out her doorway.

I started to descend the stairway to my studio. "Dream girl? Now *why* would I say a thing like that?"

Chapter 7

I had never met Bonnie's friend Abdul Bushaeve, the man Inspector DeMure implied was a person "of interest." I'd heard Bonnie speak of him, and I often saw her with him—at least, someone resembling him—as they sat on the terrace of a café or strolled up or down Boulevard Saint Germain. And always when she spoke of him, it was as if he were a family member or a close friend.

Often at around eight thirty in the morning, I saw Abdul—tennis gear bulging from the scuffed athletic bag he always carried and tennis racket in hand—darting into the Metro stop at Place Monge. In early evening when I sometimes sat on the terrace of a café near the intersection of Rue Monge and Saint Germain, I'd again see him, as always with his tennis gear, exiting the same metro station. He would then walk up to Rue Des Ecoles where, I later learned, he rented a room in one of the little mom-and-pop boarding houses that dotted the street.

Like many Algerians and Moroccans, Abdul migrated to Paris to find work so he could send money home to loved ones. Most of what he earned, Bonnie said, he mailed to his parents. I also learned he had a fiancée in Algeria, and she too received a portion of his pay. At the time, life in Algeria was harsh. Few jobs were available there, and those that existed paid miniscule wages, even lower than what migrants doing low-level jobs in Paris—street cleaners, garbage collectors, etc—could earn.

Soon after speaking to Inspector DeMure, I, quite by chance, met Abdul. I happened upon him the day I went to Bonnie's studio to tell her I was on my way to the outdoor market near Place Monge and to ask if she wanted me to purchase anything for her. Entering her studio, I saw Abdul, outfitted as usual in tennis garb, sitting on Bonnie's sofa with a mug of coffee in hand.

"Sorry, Bonnie, I didn't realize you had a guest. I'll come back later."

"Don't be ridiculous. You don't have to leave just because I have a visitor. Come in. Join us. Trust me, you shouldn't apologize just because Abdul's here. He's not that kind of guy. If he were, I wouldn't have him here to begin with." Bonnie's friend stood. "Paul, I'd like you to meet Abdul Bushaeve. Abdul...Paul, Paul Lasser."

"Pleasure, *mon ami*," he smiled, pumping my hand, exuding genuine warmth as he referred to me as his friend.

"No, the pleasure's mine."

"Paul," Bonnie said, "have a seat. Please?"

"Look, I don't mean to impose." I felt like a fifth wheel for some reason.

"Will you stop with that nonsense?" She reached out to touch my arm. "Sit. Coffee?"

Not wanting to appear impolite, I told her I'd be delighted. She disappeared through the strands of beads hanging in the kitchenette doorway; their tinkling played a tune in the quiet studio. I sat at the table, looking at Abdul. He stared at me and smiled, probably assessing me as I was assessing him. Perhaps he was wondering if I was a man worthy of Bonnie's friendship, just as I was wondering the same about him.

Rugged, I judged him to be in his mid-twenties. His leathery skin was that of someone who spent considerable time outdoors. There was a scar running down his chin form the corner of his mouth. I noticed his Nike tennis shoes color-complemented the sweat jacket and athletic trouser ensemble he wore, both in blending shades of burgundy. Gold stripes ran along the outer seams of his trousers. In soft disarray, his hair, rich ebony, was fluffed and curly. Like his skin, it had the parched appearance of overexposure to sunlight and wind.

Bonnie returned with a mug of coffee, telling me it was dark and sweet, the way I liked it. Abdul and I exchanged a few pleasantries as we enjoyed our java; Bonnie's easy banter and infectious laughter putting us both at ease with one another. I found him easy to talk to and very interesting, as well. Ten minutes or so later, I apologized for having to leave. "You see, I need to get my shopping out of the way. Is there anything you need, Bonnie?"

"Nothing, well, maybe a couple of oranges. I wish you could stay, but I guess if you must go, you must."

"My cupboards are bare, Bon, and I have a yen for some baked macaroni and cheese tonight. Homemade like my momma taught me."

"Ahhh!" she exclaimed, waving her arms and doing a few dance steps. "The man cooks, too. A wonderment." We all laughed at her gentle ribbing. Her joy and love of life always touched something in me and warmed my soul.

Abdul stood and extended his hand. "I look forward to our next meeting. And when we get together, let's chat about some of your

American tennis stars."

"I'd love that." It was easy to see why Bonnie liked him; he was very personable. We shook hands.

"Do you follow tennis?" he asked.

"In a casual way, yes. I played some in high school and college. Poorly, I might add."

"What about Arthur Ashe? Are you familiar with him?"

"Sure. Isn't everybody?"

"And then, of course, there's Althea Gibson."

"An all-time great," I added.

"And I shouldn't leave out Dr. Walter Johnson of Lynchburg, Virginia, who mentored both Gibson and Ashe and also provided funding, plus the use of his home tennis courts for practice. As you know—or perhaps you don't—Arthur was not allowed to play on the segregated public courts in Richmond, Virginia, his hometown."

"As a matter of fact, I did know that. I also know of the many other hardships he endured because of racial discrimination. Being from Hampton, a city in eastern Virginia, I'm familiar with Dr. Johnson. But I'm surprised you have such detailed information about the lives of these players and their benefactor. I mean, they being Americans, and you, Algerian."

"You shouldn't be surprised, Paul. You see, tennis is my passion, my life, so naturally I learn everything about the sport I can."

"Do you play professionally?"

"In a way of speaking, yes, but I don't play in tournaments, which I'd love to do. You see, unlike Ashe and Gibson, I have no Dr. Johnson to bankroll me. For a player to be ranked, you must play the tournament circuit and doing that requires a sponsor, someone with deep pockets, patience, and a love of the sport.

"So yes, I do play professionally, in the sense that I teach others to play. I'm a tennis instructor. I give lessons to a bunch of damn colonialist French bitches." He paused and quickly reconfigured his lips into a lemony-sweet smile, his scar more pronounced. "Forgive me. I should have said I give tennis lessons to French…ladies…on their exclusive courts out in Neuilly, where only filthily, wealthy snobs can afford to live."

"So, you give tennis lessons." Obviously he had little regard or respect for his students.

"Yes, but not to tennis players, which none of my students will ever be. I give lessons to dabblers, those with more money, free time, and colonial bigotry than…talent."

"I see," I remarked, feeling scalded by the acidity of his remarks.

"Ah, anyway, Abdul, I look forward to our next meeting."

"And I also, Paul."

My thoughts flashed images of the many Abduls I'd seen in Paris, and there were thousands—men who migrated from Tunisia, Algeria, Morocco, from hamlets near Tangier, villages bordering Port Etienne or Tindolf. Paris teemed with them, workers crammed into the poorer neighborhoods of The City of Light (for most of them, Paris was not the City of Light, but the City of Dreariness), eight or ten squeezed into a twelve by fifteen overpriced room, a firetrap waiting to ignite into flames...and kill.

These were the "invisible" Parisians. Their faces were never seen in travel brochures. They were the dark-suited little men who loitered on side streets and alleyways where native Frenchmen dared not venture. They were the cheap laborers who swept streets, scoured toilets and subway walls. They bused dishes, collected garbage, and did the other thankless drudgeries necessary so that the city of art, beauty, and culture would not choke on its own waste.

On street corners in Paris *arrondissements*, or neighborhoods, like Montmartre and Monparnasse, they loitered, hands stuffed in pockets, chatting, watching, waiting, as if anticipating a celestial phenomenon to descend, but none did; and so they continued standing, chatting, and waiting, they, the wanted-unwanted of Paris. Paris, their Promised Land, the anticipated heaven that for them was far less. With my writer's imagination I could almost hear conversations between loved ones as they separated in hopes of a better life.

"I'll write. Shutanda, I'll write. And money for the children, God willing, I'll mail it. Remember, while I'm away, the little ones are depending on you, so you must remain strong for them."

"I will, my husband, I will. I have faith in you, and I am certain all will go well. Soon the darkness of our needs will see light. As you know, much work is in Paris. There you will earn many francs so our children can have proper nourishment, and I, the operation so long delayed."

"Dear wife, God willing, all will go well...all."

"May the mercy and goodness of All Mighty Allah be with you. Farewell, dear husband...farewell."

Abdul's remarks jarred me from my reverie of imagined conversations. "Been a pleasure meeting you, Paul," he said as we stood near the door.

"Same here. I enjoyed our chat."

"Until the next time then." He held out his hand again.

I shook it and smiled. "Yes, until then." I hugged Bonnie and told her I'd return in an hour or so with her oranges.

As I walked out of Bonnie's studio, I recalled how Abdul, in speaking of his French female students, labeled them "colonialist bitches." Weeks would pass before I'd realize what a crucial role his hatred of the French would play in his life...and his death.

Chapter 8

Once again, The Phantom Lady disappeared. This time her absence came as no surprise to me. I'd grown accustomed to the fact that she, without rhyme or reason, would simply vanish for days—as if sucked into a black hole—and then, again without rhyme or reason, she'd reappear, seemingly from nowhere. I decided to do what I didn't do when she vanished the last time: go to her studio and knock on her door. I did. The trip was a waste of time. No one answered.

Thinking perhaps she was asleep, or worse, I rapped harder but got the same results. Twice a day for the next week, morning and evening, I trekked up to Studio 4-B, knocked, waited, knocked again. Not a sound.

Several times, I thought about going to the concierge and talking her into opening Bonnie's apartment. That way, I'd be sure she wasn't inside ill. I was hesitant to make the request because Bonnie's absence for a few days was becoming an ordinary occurrence. Besides, had the concierge opened the door, it might have been just my luck that Bonnie at that exact moment would come fluttering up the stairs, effervescing as usual, and wanting to know why I was so upset. I would have ended up looking like a paranoid jackass and the concierge, a patsy for listening to the ramblings of such an idiot. I decided not to ask the concierge after all.

After a little pondering, I came up with a better idea. If the concierge couldn't help in one way, maybe she could in another. I went to her apartment and knocked.

"Ah, pardon my intrusion, but—"

She was holding her door open about six inches as she gave me a thorough once-over. "Yes?" The tiny black poodle she embraced yapped at me as if to ward off any danger I might bring its owner.

"First, let me introduce myself. I'm—"

"You're *Monsieur* Paul Lasser from Studio Three-A."

"Oh, I see you remember my name. I'm impressed." Actually I was impressed she allowed me to finish a sentence. The poodle snarled. "Anyway, I was thinking that perhaps you might be able to help me."

"Help? How? Did you lock yourself out of your apartment?" The door opened a little wider. The dog bared its teeth and growled.

"No, not that." Maybe I should make friends with the curly-haired mutt. I extended my hand. "Nice doggie." The dog snapped at it, and I snatched my hand back to the safety of my pants pocket.

"Perhaps you wish to lodge a complaint against a neighbor?" "Nothing so simple." But I wouldn't mind lodging a complaint against the *damn* dog.

"Is your apartment too cold? Too hot?"

"Not that either." The woman was wearing me out trying to catch her rapid-fire questions.

One of her finely plucked eyebrows arched. "So, how then may I help you?"

"The tenant who lives in Studio Four-B is a friend of mine, and I'm a little concerned about her. I haven't seen her in a while."

"Oh?" Her door opened wider.

"I was just wondering if—" The dog's yapping intensified.

"Hush, my darling Fifi." She kissed the dog, nuzzling the fur ball. "Yes, *Monsieur*?"

"Well, first of all, are you familiar with the tenant of Studio Four-B? She's an American. Her name is *Mademoiselle* Bon—"

"Bonnie Silver." Now she was finishing my sentences.

"Yes, Bonnie Silver."

"Don't look so surprised. You see, I know all my tenants by name, first and last. And I have also memorized their birth dates."

"I see you are very competent at your job, no doubt the best in Paris." Her door opened all the way in response to my compliment. "Anyway, I was wondering if *Mademoiselle* Silver left a message with you saying she would be away for a few days and where she could be reached in case someone wanted to contact her?"

She smiled. "Sorry, I can't help you. She left no such information."

"I was hoping for a better answer."

Her finely manicured fluttered to her throat. "Are you concerned about her safety?"

"No, not really, it's just that—"

"Because if you are, perhaps you should contact police authorities."

"I don't think that'll be necessary. Anyway, *Madame*, let me thank you for your time." I turned to leave.

"Wait," she said, snapping her fingers, "I just remembered something."

I stopped and turned. "Oh?"

"*Monsieur*, several days ago, having sat up with a sick cousin who is dying of cancer, I entered the foyer at, oh, I'd say the time must have been around three in the morning, quite early. Yes, now I recall clearly; it was at about three. Unlocking my door, I saw *Mademoiselle* Silver as she was leaving the building, and in her right hand I noticed she carried a black leather bag."

"A bag, you say?"

"I recall the incident quite clearly because I was surprised to see a tenant leaving at that hour. Returning? Yes, quite common. But *leaving?*" She slowly shook her head and clucked her tongue. "Most unusual."

"Ah, this bag you mentioned, had you seen her carry it before?"

"Now that you mention it, no, and I run into her quite often. As a matter of fact, I'd never seen *Mademoiselle* Silver carry a bag, except for that single occasion. "

"Interesting."

"And something else caught my attention."

"What?"

"As you know, *Mademoiselle* Silver is quite friendly, a bubble of sociability."

"Without a doubt." The fact was Bonnie had tinted my world a golden hue with her bubbly personality. When she was gone, the glow seemed to go out of my world, and I was unsure how I felt about that.

"Always when she passes me in the hall or I see her at the market, she blossoms a smile, which is immediately followed by a cheery greeting. But this time, no smile, no greeting. Nothing. It was as if I was invisible. What's more, I detected a certain uneasiness in her eyes, as if her thoughts were on some disturbing matter. At the time, I assumed her silence was because she didn't see me, but looking back, I don't think that was the case at all—not unless she was totally blind and deaf."

"Why do you say that?"

"Because she was so close to me, and my little Fifi was barking in excitement at my arrival home." The concierge was known to dote on her tiny French poodle, which was not unusual in France. Their pets were loved and pampered, and unlike America, these pets were even allowed entrance to cafés, bistros, and stores. In Paris eateries, it was not uncommon to see a waiter bring two plates with a meal—one for the customer and the other for the customer's dog.

"Was there anyone with her? A friend perhaps? Someone who might have been, say, Algerian or an American black?"

"No, no such person. She left the building alone."

"What about outside the building? Did someone meet her there? A taxi perhaps?"

"Again, no. After she stepped onto the sidewalk, I watched her for a moment or so. Now, *Monsieur*, don't get the wrong impression. I am *not* a nosy concierge. Sadly, there exist such people who are forever prying into the private affairs of their tenants. No doubt, you have heard this charge against concierges before?"

"I must confess, *Madame*, such accusations have crossed my ears."

Her face took on the expression of someone smelling rotten fish. "Those who spread gossip about us concierges are disgusting. They give the entire profession an undeserved bad name. But I am *not* such a person, trust me." She placed her hand to her chest, and Fifi licked her face.

"Not for one second did I entertain the idea that you were. The thought was the furthest from my mind, *Madame*...believe me, the furthest." I bit the inside of my cheek to keep from laughing.

She nodded. "Good, good. At any rate, I watched *Mademoiselle* Silver as she hailed a taxi and entered it. Then, she was gone. And that was the last I saw of her. I'm sorry I don't have more information for you."

"Quite all right, *Madame*. You have been of great help."

"I take it that *Mademoiselle* Silver is an acquaintance of yours?"

"No. By that, I mean she is not *just* an acquaintance, but an acquaintance who is also a treasured friend and, at the same time, more than a treasured friend. Do you understand?"

"Yes." She smiled broadly.

"Again, I thank you for your time. *Au revoir, Madame*."

"*Au revoir, Monsieur*."

So, what had I learned from the conversation with the concierge? I learned that a few days earlier for some unfathomable reason, Bonnie left Twenty-One Rue Galande at around three in the morning. But why? And why so early? And if she had to leave at such an hour, you'd think someone would have accompanied her. But no one did. Where could she possibly be going before the sun rose? And what about her demeanor? For Bonnie not to smile or speak to an acquaintance was unusual.

And the black leather bag she carried? What did it contain? Neither the concierge nor I had seen her carry it or, in fact, any bag before except for her green, net shopping bag. Was Bonnie trying to hide something? Something illegal? Was she concealing the thing

Inspector Demure alluded to? Why hadn't she carried the bag during daylight hours? If she had, certainly the nosey concierge—her denials that she wasn't a prying busybody notwithstanding—would have noticed it. As would I.

As days passed and I struggled to make sense of Bonnie's disappearance, her mail continued to pile up in the mailbox. Finally, thinking she was not going to return anytime soon, I collected her mail, circled a rubber band around it and carried the bundle to my studio where I stored it until the prodigal returned—if she ever did.

Among the letters was one postmarked "Goode, Virginia," Bonnie's hometown—probably from some friend or maybe her father.

Another was from a Doctor Quinten Pilton, internist, of Johns Hopkins University, Baltimore, Maryland. Judging from the fancy print in the forwarding and return addresses, and the spare-no-expense quality of the envelope, the sender had to have been a big-time medical man, either that or he wanted to impress others that he was. And I, for one, was impressed. Originally, the letter was sent to Goode, Virginia. Someone crossed out the Goode address and penned in "Twenty-One Rue Galande, Paris, France, Arrondissement V."

In addition to several business-size envelopes, Bonnie received a large Manila one with a return address of "Mr. Joseph H. Benson, 1293 K Street, Washington, DC." From its appearance and feel, the envelope contained a book of some kind.

As days passed, Bonnie's absence grew more agonizing. I began to miss her, missed the way she, like wizardry, could enter a room and fill it with luminosity. I missed the music in her laughter and the vitality of her walk. Simply put, I missed her.

Without Bonnie, I seldom had an opportunity to converse with someone whose native tongue was English—American English. For an American in Paris, speaking from time to time in his mother language is as necessary as breathing. Soon after I arrived in The City of Light, I met a Baltimore reporter who'd lived in Paris for years. He assured me that if I remained there long enough, I too would begin to forget the most common English words, while instantly able to rattle off their French equivalents. I pooh-poohed the idea. Me, forget English? Absurd.

But soon, I discovered that the reporter was right; that the longer I heard and spoke only French—and I did while sitting daily at sidewalk cafés for five to seven hours—the more uncomfortable and less proficient I was speaking *Anglais*. Sounds absurd, especially since I taught English and had a Masters in English literature, but it was true.

I recalled vividly the many afternoons Bonnie and I relaxed on the terrace of a Boulevard Saint Germain café, basking in sunlight and savoring warm cappuccinos and even warmer conversations in American English.

There were times we walked along the Seine, often entering Shakespeare and Company, a famous bookstore run by an American, George Whitman. Books were shoved and crammed into every dusty nook and cranny, and we spent hours browsing the huge and varied collection. The business was more than a bookstore and reading library. It was home to struggling writers and poets, called "tumbleweeds," who stayed there for free for a week or a month in exchange for working in the bookstore a few hours a day.

Bonnie and I once attended a poetry reading there before strolling to our favorite café for French onion soup, the café we visited in the predawn hours of that first night of our friendship.

These were good times. But now the good times were gone, as was the Phantom Lady. And I had no idea when either would return…or *if* they would return.

Chapter 9

That evening I walked down Boulevard Saint Germain to a little café I'd discovered and fell in love with a few days earlier. Unlike most, it had tiered terraces and from the higher of the two, the view was excellent. Looking down on pedestrians allowed you to see without being seen, or at least without being noticed. The sense of anonymity made people-watching at that café an exceptionally pleasant way of relaxing away time.

I enjoyed people-watching and doing it at that café was quite enjoyable. From the flow of pedestrians, I'd focus on one and study his dress, stride, gestures, etc., all the clues appearance provided. Then I'd try to divine what kind of person he was, that is, what kind of person he *truly* was beneath his exterior. Did his smile signify genuine joy or was it masking some ominous inner turmoil? Did his sad expression indicate a wish to terminate his grief forever? Or was it a prelude to joy?

About each pedestrian who passed, I had questions. Who was he? Was he a native Parisian? If not, what brought him to The City of Light? From where? I'm sure those promenading by probably raised similar questions about me. Studying Left Bank pedestrians could teach one more about the nature of humans than a Shakespearian play. For in the Latin Quarter sidewalk parade of mini dramas—each pedestrian was a drama—the performers were real, not paid actors and actresses, their roles cast, not by a casting director, but by fate or genes. Their interactions followed a script only heaven could revise. And the knowledge gained about people and the human condition was accessible for a pittance, the mere cost of a cup of coffee and a little time at a Left Bank sidewalk café.

That evening after people-watching for a couple of hours, then heading back to my studio, I bumped into Abdul as he stepped out of a sporting goods store on Boulevard Saint Germain.

"What a nice surprise meeting you!" I smiled, shaking his hand. "Look, since we're going in the same direction, mind if I join you?"

"Be my guest," he stated with a wave of his hand and a broad smile.

As we walked, we chatted and after a couple of minutes, the conversation turned to his favorite subject, tennis. He continued to amaze me by rattling off minute details about American tennis players.

But soon it became obvious that he knew far more about black American tennis players than white ones. I asked him why the disparity.

"By raising the question, *mon ami*, you're forgetting one important fact."

I stepped aside to allow a woman pushing a baby stroller to pass. "Which is?"

"That I am Algerian. As an American, you can never fully understand the consequences of what being an Algerian means. You see, at one time my beloved country was a French colony."

"I'm aware of that. In college I did a research project on the relationship of France and Algeria." I'd carried a minor in French so my interest in their history and literature was strong.

"That's good, but research can only reveal, at best, surface facts. It can never make known the human, hidden costs of mental and physical agony colonialism inflicts."

"You think not, huh?" Obviously he'd never had to research a college project, especially for Professor Sinclair, whom I'd had for French history of imperialism. He was a stickler for details and not above double-checking your references to see that you'd cited sources correctly.

"Not just think it, Paul; I'm as sure of it as I am that we speak. It is impossible for mere research to address the pain a colonized people suffer. But forgive me, I prattle on and on and, sadly, I stray from the subject." He gave a wave of his hand.

"Allow me to go back and answer the question you raised. Why do I know more about American black tennis players than white ones? It's because, like me, American blacks have felt the sting of the oppressor's boot and they too have tasted the bigots' scorn. Oh, the tales I could tell you about my life in Algeria and here in Paris would astound you.

"You see, American blacks and I are members of the same fraternity, a brotherhood united through suffering. That is why I study black American tennis players, for in studying them I study *myself*. When I read that an American black has won a tournament, I rejoice. It is as if I had won. When I hear that one loses, I anguish. Their victories bring me hope, their losses, sadness. Do you understand what I'm trying to say?"

"I think I do. When I say 'I think I understand,' I mean, not having lived the life you, an Algerian, lived under colonialism, I understand as best I, an American, probably ever will."

He clasped a hand on my shoulder. "I can ask for no more than that, *mon ami*."

"Abdul, would you mind if I asked a personal question?"

"Of course not."

"Do you hate the French? I ask because of something you said about your French tennis students the first time we met. You called them 'colonialist bitches.'"

He stopped walking. "I did." He glanced around, and although his voice was barely above a whisper when he spoke, it shrieked with rancor. "Yes, I *hate* them."

"Judging from your tone of voice and expression, the hatred is more than skin deep."

"It's far deeper than words can say. For it is a hate riveted to my gut." He put a clenched fist to his midsection.

"If that's true, I can't help but wonder—"

"Yes?" His bushy eyebrows furrowed in question.

"I can't help but wonder if the hate you nurture—"

"And have for years."

"I stand corrected. The hatred you have nurtured for years, I wonder if it does more harm to you, the hater, than to the French, the hated?"

His dark forehead wrinkled into a scowl. "Harm me? I don't get your point."

"What I mean, Abdul, is does your hate infect your *own* mind, blinding it to all else, eating away at it like a disease?"

He pinched his lips and fingered the air, searching, it seemed, for words potent enough to convey his rage, which now seemed about to explode. Finally, he seemed ready to speak. But he didn't. Instead, he shrugged and continued walking.

Abdul didn't realize it but in those few seconds of conversation, he taught me more about French colonization and its aftermath than I'd learned during my yearlong research on the subject.

As we crossed an intersection, Bonnie's name somehow entered the conversation. "I suppose you know," he said, "what's happening with her?"

"Know? Know what?"

"Oh, come on, Paul," he smiled, the lilt in his voice insinuating that I knew far more than I was willing to admit. "Of course you know."

"Abdul, take my word, I don't have the faintest idea what you're talking about."

"Oh-h-h," he sighed, eyes riveted on mine, "so you don't know after all. I can see that now. Perhaps I have spoken out of turn. Yes, I believe I have. Not only have I spoken out of turn, but also I have spoken foolishly. For how could you have known? How could you or anyone have known?"

"Known what?"

"Never mind, it's of no consequence. Forget what I said. You see, I assumed you knew about Bonnie. I made that assumption because you seem so close to her, and, in my stupidity, I thought she had told you. I forgot that about this matter, Bonnie tells no one, and I do mean no one."

"Obviously, Abdul, she told you." I hated to admit the degree to which it galled me that Bonnie had kept me uninformed as to what was happening in her life. It rankled even more to hear Abdul prattle on about it, stumbling and bungling over his own words.

He took a deep breath, probably noting the irritation in my voice. His tone when he responded was soothing. "Not so. It was quite by chance that I stumbled upon the truth. And she becomes quite angry with me whenever I mention that part of her life. But, if it were me, Paul, if I were the one, and not Bonnie, I would tell the whole world so that all would understand, and I'm sure, if it were you, you would do the same, but not Bonnie Silver. It's just not her way."

"And why does she refuse to share this information—whatever it is?" At this point I'd decided to do my best to find out. I cared for her, after all; we were close friends.

"*Mon ami,* if you asked her that question, I'm sure she would give another answer, but I think the real reason, the true reason, is that she is too noble a person, too compassionate and does not wish to burden others."

"Burden whom? How?" I was losing my cool, my frustration was showing.

"Burden those she has told. At any rate"—he shrugged his shoulders—"this is what she thinks."

I put my hand on his arm, and we both stopped walking. "This *thing*, whatever it is she's hiding, is it something illegal?"

"Of course not." The tone of his voice was indignant.

"Can I tell you something in confidence?" I asked.

"Certainly."

"And will you promise that it will go no further than this place and time?"

His open hand went to his heart. "On that you have my word."

"Would you be surprised to know that French police are investigating Bonnie?"

He sneered and started walking again, as did I. "Not at all," he replied in a voice filled with contempt.

"Why so?"

"Because French cops are brutal. As a member of the Algerian minority here in Paris, I see them as they truly are, not as tourist books paint them to be. Investigate Bonnie? I would not put that, or anything else, past French cops. As for me, I can't count the number of times I've been harassed by them as I made my way to or from my job in Neuilly. Why? Because I am Algerian. And for *no* other reason.

"When French cops see my face in that neighborhood, they tell me that I am not in the 'proper' context. 'Do you have business around here?' they ask. And always they speak down to me, as if I am subhuman. 'We are only doing our job,' they say. 'We must investigate all who are suspicious.' Me? Suspicious? Dressed in my tennis garb, with my athletic bag and racket in hand, and within blocks of twelve tennis courts, and they claim I'm suspicious. Suspicious of what? The truth is French police are bigoted. They will investigate *anyone*, for *any* reason, valid or invalid, and especially if the subject is Algerian or from a North African country."

"Possibly so, but you must admit that they also investigate those who are guilty."

Abdul grunted and shrugged slightly as he sidestepped a fly-covered masterpiece left by a dog. "Sometimes, yes," he begrudgingly admitted.

"Anyway, as you may or may not know, a few days ago Bonnie vanished, and nobody seems to know where she is. Do you?"

We stopped in front of a men's formal wear boutique. "Well tailored, aren't they?" Abdul said, pointing to the tuxedos displayed in the window.

"Yes, well tailored. Now, as I was saying, do you have any idea where Bonnie—"

"The cut of the shoulders is chic," he observed, "and note the sculptured look of the lapels. Formidable."

"*Tres formidable*. Now back to Bonnie." He continued his perusal of the tuxedos, or seemed to. "Abdul."

"Yes?"

"I withdraw the question." And *frustration* is my middle name, I thought as we walked on, the formal wear display forgotten. As we approached the intersection of Saint Germain and Saint Michel, I said, "Abdul, I can't help but worry about Bonnie."

He sighed audibly and cast me a why-can't-you-just-leave-it-alone look. "You shouldn't. She can take care of herself in spite of what she's going through now, in fact, in spite of...in spite of...everything. "

"I wish I knew what the 'everything' is that you refer to. That's the part that troubles me. The 'everything.'"

"Don't let it, *mon ami*. What I mistakenly said back there about Bonnie is nothing, nothing at all. Erase it from your thoughts. Why?" He said at my questioning look. "Well, because there are some things that simply must be accepted and ignored, like the rising and setting of the sun and the passing of time. They are natural things and deserve no notice. And what is happening to Bonnie is similar."

"If natural, why the secrecy?"

He shrugged. "Women, you know how they are." We stopped as a man was helping an elderly woman out of a car and into a wheelchair. The man thanked us for our patience as he wheeled the elderly woman through a gate into a courtyard adorned with trees and flowers in large pots. We nodded and walked on. "I wish I could tell you more." Abdul said. "Doing so would please me greatly and one day, take my word, I will tell you everything."

"One day?" I could feel my gut tightening. This was not a relaxing conversation.

"Right."

"Why not now?" This conversation was making less and less sense. I was more distressed than the day I left school only to find all four of my tires flattened on my Volkswagen Beetle sitting in the teachers' parking area. "Abdul, just tell me *now*."

He glanced at his watch. "The time! I didn't realize how late it is. You'll have to excuse me. I have to hurry to the little grocery store around the corner before it closes."

"I understand." I also understood that the conversation had ended ten minutes ago; that we'd been going on a merry-go-round ride since I asked my original question. I shook my head in bewilderment. *What* was going on in Bonnie's life? Why the big mystery? And why was I excluded?

Abdul gave a hurried farewell and turned the corner. "And *mon ami*," he shouted, turning around and walking backwards, "as I told you, don't give what I mistakenly said about Bonnie a second thought. What I said was nothing. It was a mere slip of the tongue. Did you hear me?"

"I heard you, Abdul." I stepped into the first café I found and ordered a shot of whiskey. The *hell* with it, I thought.

Chapter 10

I was restless one Sunday, so I decided I'd do something different to break up the sameness of my assembly-line writing days. Earlier in the week, I'd bumped into Roger, and he said he might stop by my studio Sunday. I tacked a note on my studio door telling him I'd gone for a stroll, and that I'd probably end up at the outdoor bird market.

Enjoying the faint nip of fall in the air, I walked to Notre-Dame Cathedral and then headed to Ile De La Cite, the site of the weekly bird market. Situated between the Left and Right Banks, Ile De La Cite—an island in the Seine River—joined Paris proper by the umbilical cords of bridges coupling it to the Right and Left Banks. Generally, the slow-paced life on the island contrasted with the blur and din of speeding traffic on either side of the Seine. Ile De La Cite was an oasis of serenity, except on Sundays when the outdoor bird market was held there.

A stroll through the market provided a free tutorial in both birds and people. So vast was the avian inventory, I'd spent the better part of a Sunday there and still wasn't able to browse all of the merchandise. Buyers and sellers from miles around converged on the site. As far as could be seen there were rows upon rows of tables and stalls.

Sellers were as diverse as the bird inventory was colorful and large. For the most part, vendors were matron types, bundled in knitted sweaters with kerchiefs circling their heads. All seemed gentle and free of avarice and deception. In reality, appearances masked the truth. With only minor variations, the following was typical of conversations I'd overheard between vendors and perspective customers.

"Perhaps you are interested in buying one of my birds?" asked the seller, a note of anticipation lifting her voice. She was wearing a brown dress and black sweater. A navy kerchief adorned her head.

"Not today," replied the dapper gentleman in a tan suit and brown paisley tie.

"How odd."

"Why so?"

"Because you have the appearance of a true bird connoisseur."

"Which is?" his eyebrows rose in question.

"One who is handsome and as intelligent as he is handsome."

"I'm flattered, but I still don't want to buy a bird."

"*Monsieur.*"

"Yes, *Madame?*" the gentleman smiled.

The seller's smile was suddenly gone having been replaced by a superior sneer and an imperial wave of the hand. "Move on. You're blocking paying customers."

With a polite nod of the head, he replied, "As you wish, *Madame* . . . as you wish."

A vast array of birds populated the market—some minuscule, scarcely larger than a whisper, while an equal number were jumbo size with bowed legs. Others were elongated, their tails seemingly without end. Dazzling, the multi-colored wings of some were the pallets of Picasso or Monet. Their plumes shimmered gold, lemon, and cinnamon. Feathers of tropical species were even more colorful, slivers of rainbows.

Attached to each cage was a little sign on which the name of the bird inside it was printed. There were bobolinks and rooks, thrashers and wrens. Though fewer of these, there were also cockatoos and doves and song sparrows and horn screamers. Present also were endless varieties of partridges, swallows, and the most popular bird of them all, parrots, enough to populate a rain forest. The market pulsed with a symphony of bird sounds: trills, warbles, carols, counter pointed by whistles, chirps, and tweets.

Bird sales were sometimes brisk, but always theatrical. Bickering over prices was common. Native Parisians haggled all the time. Tourists never did and for their ignorance paid dearly. There were no signs indicating prices. If you wished to know the cost of a fowl, you had to ask. The seller, after *guess-timating* the size of your wallet and the depth of your gullibility, plucked some arbitrary figure from the air--a price that was always outrageously high. Only tourists paid the quoted price.

To hagglers, the thrill of ownership came not in buying the desired bird, but in the verbal gorilla warfare that flowed back and forth. Each combatant entered the fray with caches of finesse and verbal booby traps, weapons needed in the take-no-prisoners warfare natives knew well. The following exchange was typical.

"*Madame*, certainly you jest in asking fifty francs for this puny fowl," the potential buyer would state with a curl of his upper lip, disdain fairly dripping from his every word.

"Puny? This is the rarest of birds, one whose genes go back to the age of pharaohs."

"The price, *Madame*?"

"Price? Well, because of my generous nature, and—"

"The price!" The no-nonsense shopper insisted.

"And because you seem such a Christian gentleman, a man of breeding and—"

"Get to the price, please."

"I am prepared to *lose* money by selling this rare bird for forty-five francs and not a centime less."

"Let's be serious, *Madame*." The interested party would puff up with indignation.

"I am. As I said…thirty francs, nothing less."

"You gave your word that you'd be serious."

"Indeed, which explains my price of…twenty-five francs."

"That is your final offer?" The man's voice rising with feigned astonishment.

The saleswoman would tug on the hem of her ancient sweater. "Absolutely."

"I'll give you ten francs, *Madame*, no questions asked, take it or leave it."

"Sold. *Monsieur*. It's been a pleasure doing business with you. We understand each other."

"Indeed we do."

Maybe I'd been swept up in the excitement of the moment, or having browsed so many birds, I'd somehow become disconnected from reality. But for whatever reason, in a moment of lunacy, I decided to buy a bird. Why? At the time, it seemed like a good idea. Being alone as much as I was, a bird, I reasoned, would make a fine companion. It was small, easy to care for, never gnawed furniture or nibbled the legs of guests, irrigated carpets, woke up the neighborhood at three in the morning, or needed walking in a blizzard. And unlike a cat, birds weren't snobs.

With images of a song sparrow chirping happily in my studio, I approached a middle-aged vendor.

"*Madame*, I'd like to buy one of your song sparrows."

A smile broadened on her wrinkled face. "Wonderful, wonderful! Happy to serve you."

"I'm new at this, so perhaps you can advise me as to which sparrow would be a good buy?"

"All my birds are excellent buys, *Monsieur*, *all*." Her hands swept out in the direction of her many bird cages.

"I hope you don't believe that," a female voice behind me whispered.

Without turning, I asked out of the corner of my mouth, "Why not?"

"Because the seller profits by *selling* birds," my advisor informed, "not by telling the truth about them. Take a look at 'em. Most are prime candidates for the ER." I turned, a smile already plastered on my face for I knew that voice.

"Well, I'll be damned. Bonnie Silver!" I gave her a hug, my spirits lifting at the sight of her. "What're you doing here?"

"Looking at sick birds and hoping I can talk you out of buying a big vet bill." She smiled and the sunshine came into my world. "I saw the note you pinned on your door and came over."

I ran a finger down her cheek. "You're as lovely as you were the last time I saw you."

"You certainly know how to make a girl feel good, don't you?" A flush rose on her pale cheeks. She wore bell-bottomed jeans and a grey turtleneck sweater topped with a denim vest decorated with various patches, mostly peace signs, slogans and flowers.

I laid my arm across her shoulders. "I meant every word. Why, just this morning I was thinking about—"

"Is *Monsieur*," the vendor interrupted, "ready to make his purchase? As I said, all my birds are exceptional."

"That they are," Bonnie said, winking at me. "Quite exceptional. My friend here has decided not to buy one of your birds after all."

The vendor planted her hands on her hips, obviously upset at the prospect of losing an easy sale. "But, *Mademoiselle*, he has assured me he'd make a purchase."

"I don't think you understand," Bonnie said. "You see, in The United States he's an English teacher."

"English teacher. French. Spanish. It matters not; my sparrows are certain to make him a fine pet regardless of what he teaches."

"You don't understand, *Madame*; I said he's an English teacher, not one who teaches veterinary medicine in English. You see, sadly, Blue Cross won't cover sparrows that are at death's door." I turned my back to the vendor so she couldn't see me laugh. Bonnie was being her delightful, cheeky self.

"Blue Cross?" the vendor puzzled. "What is this Blue Cross?"

"Never mind. Anyway, I hope you luck in selling your birds. My advice is to sell them within the hour. A few might live that long." The vendor scorched a dirty look at Bonnie. "Come on, Paul. We'd better get the hell out of here."

We did...fast. After crossing the bridge from the island to the Latin Quarter, Bonnie and I sat on the terrace of a cafe. Over espressos, we watched masses of pedestrians pass, a typical group of Left Bank Sunday strollers: couples pushing baby carriages, veterans, lapels festooned with medals, and young French women, hair fluffing as they bounced energetically along.

Later, I said, "Bonnie, I guess you know I've been concerned about you? Fact is, I've been, well, damn worried." More worried than that actually. I'd been frantic and at times depressed over the possibility of never seeing her again. Her friendship was my emotional anchor in this city—regardless of its beauty and interesting people, regardless of its daily events that captured my curiosity.

She lifted a shoulder in response to my remark. "Why?"

"I was concerned about your safety, wondering if you were OK, if you'd been in an accident, if you were alive or if—"

"That's very thoughtful of you, *mon ami*," Bonnie laid a hand over mine.

I turned my hand over in hers and intertwined our fingers. "So, where've you been?" I was hoping against hope that she'd give me a straight answer.

She raised her cup, sipped, and then returned it to the saucer with a slight clinking noise. Sidestepping my question, she asked if anything interesting had happened at Twenty-One Rue Galande during her absence.

"Nothing new, just the usual stuff, same-o-same-o. Chances are Twenty-One Rue Galande will never change." Again, I asked where she had been.

Bonnie gave the same answer. None. She wanted to know if I had picked up her mail for her. I told her I had, and that she could drop by my studio and I'd give it to her, or if she preferred, I'd bring it to her studio. She said she'd stop in for it later that evening.

I thought of asking her again where she'd been, but I decided not to. Why should I keep beating my head against a brick wall, I thought with a long sigh? All I'd succeed in doing would be to frustrate myself and to ruin a perfectly delightful Sunday afternoon with Bonnie. My eyes swept over her beaming face. Being with her was like a tonic to my nerves and outlook on life. Why not enjoy the day, enjoy my time with her, I reasoned. Still…I wondered.

For over two hours, we chatted and laughed about a variety of subjects. But not once, about the *one thing* I wanted to discuss, the matter that had weighed most heavily in my thoughts for days—her mysterious disappearances and the reason or reasons for them. Surprisingly, the explanation would soon come, and even more surprisingly, I would not have to seek it, it sought me.

Chapter 11

Four days after Bonnie reappeared, a party was held in Betty Jean Greenlee's studio. The party didn't start until after ten that night. Betty Jean lived on the fifth floor, on the landing above Bonnie. The two women were close friends. It was Betty Jean who hosted the party, and it was she who invited me.

"So why the *soiree*?" I asked.

"Nothing special," she shrugged. "It's just that, like man, I thought it'd be cool to put together a little something for Bonnie, 'a happening.' Know what I mean? I just want to show her how much I dig her as a friend."

"Great idea."

I didn't know Betty Jean very well, only on a brief-encounter basis. We'd chat after bumping into each other at the mailbox in the foyer. Sometimes as she passed my studio on her way to hers, she'd stop for a minute to inquire about my day or writing progress. I often left my door open as I pounded away on my Remington.

From our conversations, I was able to piece together a few facts about her. The daughter of a successful realtor, she was born in a little town in southern Georgia called Lakeland. A sociology major, she first dropped out of the University of Virginia and then the University of North Carolina. She then enrolled at Rutgers. It too became another in a list of schools she didn't attend very long. And though she never admitted it, I had the impression officials at Rutgers and UNC asked her to leave, but for what reason or reasons, I didn't know.

After returning to her home in Georgia and remaining there for over a year, she became active in several liberal groups. Disenchanted by the slow results from her protests and demonstrations, she finally faced the realization that The Establishment did not intend to relinquish one iota of political or social power to activists.

Her ramblings to me about her frustrations, first with her conservative parents and second with The Establishment, indicated that she'd evidently sunk into a deep depression. Soon thereafter, she'd left home. To, what I imagined, was her parents' consternation, she didn't tell them where she was going or when she'd return. The reason, she'd told me, was that she simply didn't know. The only comment she admitted to making when she left was, "It's time you people wake up. This town and those in it are artifacts. I need to find relief...somewhere, anywhere...but here."

In Washington DC, she lived on the streets of Georgetown during the day, sleeping under the bridges of Whitehurst Freeway at night. Later, in Baltimore she rented a room in a rundown boarding house near Charles Street and ate at a soup kitchen run by Bee Gatty, the city's "Black Mother Theresa."

After a year of wandering—never staying in one place very long—she ended up in Paris, thanks to her parents' generosity. Of all the cities on earth, why Paris? What prompted her to journey across the Atlantic Ocean to seek refuge in a locale so far from home? What missing part of herself did she hope to recover on The Left Bank that she couldn't find in Lakeland, Georgia, where, in all probability, she'd lost it? The answer to these and similar questions she never shared with me. I'm not sure she knew the answers—or ever asked the questions.

I'd seen scores of other Americans like Betty Jean whose odyssey brought them to the Latin Quarter. Most were battle-scarred veterans in the struggle against The Establishment raging in the States.

In conversations I'd had with various young adults in cafés or while riding on the Metro, I learned that many were members of a counterculture. They were participants in anti-Vietnam War and civil rights demonstrations in various American cities: Chicago, San Francisco, Birmingham, not to mention hamlets in the Mississippi Delta where they ventured as much to find and register unregistered voters as to find themselves. They shared their stories at length with me, eager to state their cause with another American. From our conversations, I learned a lot about the experiences and emotions of many within this counterculture.

One such person was Winfield Blair III, or Winn as he preferred to be called. He claimed that Winfield was too stuffy and establishment for him. Winn was a drop out from Michigan University who'd traveled to Paris to wage the war against all wars. In short, he was escaping the draft back home, his status now changed since he was no longer a student. Although Winn never hesitated to denounce his family and their money, he also had zero hesitation about cashing the checks they sent his way; checks that allowed him the luxury of living as he chose.

Paris had become a rendezvous site for disenchanted American "revolutionaries" like Betty Jean, Winn and hundreds of others. It was a place for recuperation. From what I could gather, it was here they hoped to regain their sense of balance and to bandage spirits wounded by the unforgiving Establishment. Yet I never saw much forgiveness in them either.

These revolutionaries could be found practically anywhere in The Latin Quarter. Walk up Boulevard Saint Michel or Boulevard Saint Germain, day or night, and you'd see them. At night, I often found them congregated at a large café near the fountain in Place Michel. I'd sit and listen as they conversed almost ceaselessly about how society "would change, and soon" and of the role they were destined to play in the transformation, a transformation they called "The Great Revolution."

Often they spoke to me, to each other, or to anyone who would listen of the coming of "The New Order." When it arrived, they said, there would be "pure" justice and all power would be wrenched from The Establishment and placed into the rightful "hands of the people."

Most wore tie-dyed T-shirts, bell-bottomed jeans, circular, granny glasses, headbands, and sandals. The women's hair, long and parted down the middle, cascaded over their cheeks, ending just below the shoulders. Flowers, usually daisies, their symbol of peace and love, they carried or pinned to their hair. Around their necks draped strands of brightly colored love beads, while their fingers sported rings handcrafted from copper or some other soft metal.

A few men dressed in World War II army field jackets or ponchos or some other castaway garment, turning each into a symbol of defiance and disdain for those with power and money. I suppose to them, I looked stiff and conservative in my oxford shirts and chinos. Nor could they understand how I could, in all good conscience, serve my country for two years. But I had, and with pride.

Strapped to many of their backs were guitars or banjos. These they took into subway stations where they strummed and sang, placing a hat, "the kitty," on the platform to solicit money for use in "The Revolutionary Cause."

I'd talked to a couple of these street musicians from time to time, always interested in what they had to say. All were eager to explain to anyone who'd listen how imperative victory was in the struggle currently flaring on university campuses and in metropolitan streets of America. It was, they said, a moral obligation for the masses to unite as "comrade-warriors" in the Revolutionary Cause.

But as they spoke so convincingly of these things, I often thought that they were not *in* America where the battles, they claimed, raged.

Instead, they loitered on street corners in The Latin Quarter or lounged at one of the sidewalk cafés, sipping espressos. They were also found in subway stations chanting "revolution songs" for the few francs passersby gave them.

Weary veterans of anti-establishment street battles, I felt most seemed content to be where they were, though all denied this when I asked them. So, they went on speaking of the Great Revolution and prophesying the coming of the New Order. And always when they spoke of these events, their words flamed with passion. However, as weeks passed, and the war in Vietnam dragged on as if it had no end, and body counts escalated, and police forces quashed anti-war and civil rights demonstrations in America with storm trooper brutality, the revolutionaries spoke with less fervor. For the delayed arrival of The New Order sapped much of their zeal, leaving many, in spite of their denials, drained and barely able to sustain their vision of a "brave new world."

Nevertheless, on and on they would talk into the wee hours of the morning, until their favorite café in Place Michel was about to close and the waiters counted their tips. It was then the Revolutionaries would leave the café and congregate in little groups on the nearby bridge, *Pont Michel*. I usually tagged along if asked. There they continued to speak of the monumental day when the New Order would finally arrive. They were quick to proclaim that the "golden hour" would surely come, that, in fact, it was "just around the corner." This they reassured each other over and over—"just around the corner...not long now." All believed what they said—at least, they told me they did.

And there was something else. Whenever a cynic among the listeners—like me, for example—would remind them that countless revolutions had proceeded theirs, and all had fallen short of expectations, their vehemence for the cynic's remarks was palpable.

The cynic went on to say that once these rebels from an earlier time became disenchanted, they abandoned their ideals and ended up in collusion with their sworn enemy, The Establishment. In an act of irony, these aging rebels often joined the cause they once fought against, becoming more despotic than the oppressors they once despised.

When told of these things, the young revolutionaries were quick to point out that their revolution would "never" fail. "Never...never," they reassured us all, adding that nothing could entice them "to sell out to The Establishment"—Swiss bank accounts, luxury automobiles, palatial homes, nothing. This too, they believed—or said they did.

I wasn't sure how Betty Jean supported herself—like Winn, her father probably footed the bills. She always seemed to have enough money to keep her eyes glazed, and usually they were. It was obvious she was on drugs and had been for most of the time I knew her. Seldom did I see her when her eyes were bright and lucid, like those of most twenty-two year olds. Marijuana, I later learned, was her favorite means of "getting in touch" with herself, though more and more she turned to other drugs.

The first indication she was making the transition came the night she showed up at my studio door to borrow an electric converter. American-made appliances wouldn't work in Paris without one.

"A converter? Sure, I have one. Why don't you step inside?"

"Thanks, but no thanks." She stood in the hallway, jittery as though her whole body were one big nervous twitch.

"Well, suit yourself. But you're certainly welcome to come in."

"Nice of you to invite me, but—" She shrugged her shoulders and glanced away, her body bouncing and swaying as though in time with some internal, silent rock beat.

"Maybe I can change your mind. Earlier today I bought a bottle of wine. So why don't we pop the cork together?"

"Wine, you say?" She bit at a fingernail, spitting it out after she'd chewed it off.

"Yeah. Red wine. It's not expensive, but decent stuff."

Betty Jean scratched her shoulder. "Well, I mean, like...you know, man, to be honest, wine ain't my speed."

"What is your speed?"

"You said it."

"I did? What'd I say?"

"The magic word." Her expression turned dreamy.

"Which is?"

"Speed, man...speed. Speed and horse, but speed on a horse is outta-sight, man."

"Betty Jean, why are you doing this to yourself?" I stopped searching for my converter and looked at her.

"It's the solution, at least the one for me."

I stepped closer. "Solution to what?"

"To the nightmares I've been having, nightmares about that damn Vietnam War that slaughters Americans, as well as Vietnamese—they're human too, you know—a war that's maiming young men right and left. Add to that the countless injustices taking place worldwide, especially in Alabama and Mississippi. This topsy-turvy world gives me wake-up-screaming-in-a-cold-sweat nightmares, and I have them all the time. Really bad ones with horrible images of brown babies napalmed in Vietnam and black ones with bloated bellies starving in the Mississippi Delta." She inhaled a long breath and shook her head.

"And in the nightmares, amid all the carnage and death, The Establishment, the damned U.S. Government, what does it do? Closes its eyes, plugs its ears, and issues eloquent platitudes about freedom and the preciousness of human life. And all the while, the American war machine darkens skies over Vietnam with squadron after squadron of B-52s dumping fiery cargoes of death. Life is a bitch, ain't it? And this crazy world gives me nightmares. Speed makes them more bearable." The young woman seemed obsessed with the war and society in general.

"Betty Jean, folks tell me hard drugs erase one nightmare only to replace it with a *million* more. So what's better? One or a million."

"Worse? Better? These are relative terms, man. What's worse? What's better, huh? Who's to say? At least with speed, the new nightmares are…different, and that in itself is a relief."

"I hope you're right." Although I really doubted my words.

"Me too, because about a thing like that, I wouldn't want to make a mistake." She crossed her arms over her stomach and hugged herself.

"No, you wouldn't, Betty Jean"

A motorcycle raced down Rue Galande, the roar of its engine reverberating throughout the hallway. When the echo subsided, Betty Jean said, "Paul?"

"Yeah?"

"The converter, remember?"

"The converter? Oh! How silly of me. The converter, of course. I'll get it for you. Won't take but a second." I'd gotten so caught up in her tirade about all the ills of the world that I'd forgotten.

That conversation took place a couple days before she stopped by my open door to invite me to the party she was throwing Bonnie the following weekend.

Chapter 12

There were about fifteen guests at Betty Jean's party when I arrived, which didn't sound like many, but considering the size of her attic studio, it was. At first, I wasn't sure I'd seen any of the guests before. Though I may have run across one or all of them prior to the party, it was hard to recognize anyone in the studio's muted lighting, for around the shade of the table lamp now sitting on the floor, someone had taped a strip of plastic that shrouded the room in anemic blue.

Most guests stood chatting in little groups. I circulated among them, tarrying long enough to say hello here, exchanging a pleasantry or two, and then moving on.

Judging from their dress—headbands, love beads, granny glasses, etc—most were flower children, members of the counter culture. After seeing all of them up close, I realized they were not strangers. At one time or another I had seen each walking up or down Boulevard Saint Germain or Boulevard Saint Michel, or panhandling at one of the neighborhood Metro stops or, in the wee hours of morning, standing on the bridge near Place Michel, debating some point or other about the Revolution and the "glorious day" when the New Order would arrive. Some of them I had spoken to, asking them questions fueled by my writer's curiosity.

Tonight with backs angled against the wall, a few sat on the floor sharing a joint, the sour-sweet fragrance of marijuana smoke spicing the air in Betty Jean's studio like cheap perfume.

"Hey, dude," a smoker greeted. It was Winn, once known as Winfield Blair III.

"What's the word, Winn?" I asked, approaching.

"The word, my man? That's easy. It's Mary Jane, mo-jo, grass, weed, the plant. Know what I mean? Call it what you will. So come on, join us? We're puffing fine stuff tonight, top-of-the-line, Grade A. Columbian Red. Groovy man."

He inhaled, held it for a few seconds, and then exhaled, his eyes squinted shut. "It's guaranteed to erase the world's hypocrisy from your mind, make you forget The Four Horsemen of Vietnam— napalm, herbicides, body bags, and Pentagon lies. It's great grass, man, *the best*. It'll make you realize that 'Bull' Conner and the KKK ain't nothing but bad dreams, not real at all. And that money and the pursuit of it do not rule the world; love does, man. Like I said, daddio, *premium* stuff. So come on, let Mary Jane unshackle your mind, turn you on, and elevate you to another time and place, a happier sphere, the new dimension."

"Thanks, but I'll pass." I could see the headline in the newspaper at home in Hampton, Virginia: "Man from local family arrested in drug bust in Paris, high as a kite." I rolled my eyes heavenward, my mother would disown me—*after* she killed me.

"Why?" Obviously Winn couldn't understand that anyone could pass on such *premium* stuff.

"Because my life has enough problems as it is. I don't need another one, especially some unpredictable slut named Mary Jane telling me what to do."

"Well, suit yourself," he grinned. "After all, it's your world, man. Me? I just live in it. But, dude, if this joint ain't *the* answer, the be-all and the end-all, lemme know when you find what is. OK?"

"You'll be the first to know."

Fingering the joint as if it were a priceless heirloom, Winn inhaled deeply. "Believe me, dude," he grinned, "after searching, you'll end up on the floor with the rest of us, blowing your mind. Then you'll see that I was right."

"Like I said, I'll pass."

"Hi!" a female behind me chirped.

It was Bonnie. "Hi, yourself. And happy birthday," I said, bear-hugging her. She smelled like roses, a welcome change from the other smells circulating Betty Jean's studio apartment. Her yellow t-shirt read, "Make Love Not War" and her bell-bottomed jeans were frayed at the bottoms.

"Birthday? Where'd you get that? It's not my birthday."

I slung my arm across her shoulders. "Well, happy Party-In-Your-Honor Day."

"Thanks. Tell me, Mr. Straight-laced-Paul, are you enjoying yourself?" She quickly glanced around the room. "This isn't exactly your kind of scene. Can you relax and enjoy it?" She playfully tugged on my navy necktie and winked.

"Sure." I loosened my tie a bit and cleared my throat, trying to cover my sudden embarrassment. Did she really regard me as straight-laced? "How about you? Enjoying the party? But that's a silly question. You always seem to enjoy yourself, always upbeat, radiating warmth like a binary star."

"Do I really do all that?" she asked, searching my eyes with those fabulous blue eyes of hers.

"Yes, in spades. May I pour you a glass of wine? After all, you're the honored guest." When I returned with a couple of glasses of wine, I handed one to Bonnie. "You know, judging from the number of people here tonight," I observed, "you have quite a few friends."

She shrugged. "The truth is, some of these guys I've never seen before. Many are probably just party crashers and/or freeloaders. To me, most are strangers."

"Which ones do you know?"

"Um-m-m," she sighed, scanning the room. "Let's start with that guy near the record player."

"The short one?"

"That's Larry Gibson. I met him at another party a few weeks ago."

"And what's his story?" I took a sip of the wine and found it lacking.

"Well, back in The States, he was a scholar, and a damn good one too—Harvard, MIT. Here in Paris, though, he's just another sidewalk café philosopher. The city has scores of them, as you well know. But philosophizing isn't his full-time occupation these days."

"What is?"

"Draft-dodging; he's been doing that almost since the war started. Like a nomad, he wanders throughout Europe. I doubt if he'll stay in Paris much longer. He's been here over six months. That's two more than his usual stay in any one place. Next, he'll flee to Amsterdam or London or Lisbon or some such place. Terrified at the thought of going to jail, he stays on the run. Lucky for him, his father's bankroll is large enough to support his son's odyssey. Larry is really a great guy, but as you can imagine, not a contented one.

"Constantly looking over his shoulder has drained him. The result? What you see before you now: a man teetering on the brink of a breakdown. But, as fearful of jail as he is opposed to the war, he continues to run. Meanwhile, his ulcer goes on bleeding." Bonnie paused and took a deep breath. "Anyway, see that heavyset woman by the window?" She jerked her head in the direction of the woman.

I turned. "Yeah."

"That's Roberta."

"Who's she?"

"Larry's wife. Roberta is a Kansas-born girl, homespun and down to earth; she's got domesticity and the open plains in her DNA. She hates Paris, too glitzy for her. Do you know what she'd like to do more than anything on earth?"

"What?"

"Return to Kansas and live on a farm. But, of course, she can't because her husband is afraid to. So, here the two remain, trapped in Paradise."

I ran a hand through my hair and shook my head. "What a helluva life."

"It is, but it sure beats being behind bars."

"Does it?"

Bonnie waved her wine glass in Larry's direction. "Ask Larry, he'll say it does."

"It seems to me, Bonnie, that in a real sense Larry's already behind bars, isn't he? Wonder what answer he'd give if I asked him if he's not already a prisoner?"

"Probably none."

"No doubt you're right." Turning, I said, "Bonnie, see the guy sitting in the corner strumming a guitar and mumbling? For some reason, he looks familiar. Do you know him?"

"Sure. And so do you."

"I do?" My eyes traveled to the bearded man again, and my memory drew a blank. I shook my head. "No, I don't think I do."

"Sure ya do. Tell you what: try to picture his face without the heavy beard and sunshades. Do that and you'll recognize him. That's Steven Leftowich."

I squinted my eyes in his direction. "Hey, you're right."

"Remember the bombing of the ROTC building on Michigan State's campus?"

"Doesn't everybody?"

"Four students were blown to hell that night. What was left of them was so mutilated it took a team of coroners a week to identify the remains. Steve was the bomber. He thought the building was empty. It wasn't. A couple of guys had sneaked their dates inside. One was Steve's brother. The other, Steve's dearest friend."

"Are you saying he blew up his own brother and a close friend? What a heavy cross to carry." How does the guy live with himself, I thought. His pain—pain he'd created himself—must consume him night and day.

"You're right, my friend, it is a heavy cross to bear. And Steve doesn't carry his very well. Since the bombing, he pops tranquilizers and sleeping pills like they're M&Ms. But the pills don't help. With or without them, he doesn't sleep much. If you go up to Place Pigalle, the red light district, at two or three any morning, you'll find him leaning against the bar in some all-night joint, nursing a high voltage cocktail. He just stands there and stares at the door as if expecting someone he knows to come bursting in."

"Wonder who that *someone* could be?"

"Only Steve can answer that," Bonnie stated as she tipped her glass to her lips.

Chatting with a couple of guests, Betty Jean stood on the opposite side of the studio, and when she saw Bonnie and me, she gushed over. Squealing, the two women hugged and then began prattling, each tripping over the other's words. "So kind of you to have the party for me, Betty Jean. Real neat, and I wanna thank—"

"You don't have to thank me. There's no need for that. We're *friends*, remember? And friends don't have to thank each—"

"I know, but still...I mean, you went to a lot of trouble to—"

"Not another word. You hear? Not another word."

My glass was empty. While Betty Jean and Bonnie chatted it would be a good time, I thought, to go for a refill. When I returned, Betty Jean was standing in the far corner talking energetically to a man I'd never seen before. The stranger seemed out of context, being older than other attendees—in his early thirties, at least—and, unlike other guests, he didn't wear love beads. Instead, a thick gold chain draped his neck. He was decidedly different. However, on the Left Bank, being different was not a novelty. There the unconventional, even eccentric, was not only tolerated, but applauded.

"You know, Bonnie," I said, "you and Betty Jean are uncommonly close, more like sisters than mere friends."

"We are, and that's the hurting part." I could see pain in her eyes as she spoke.

I rubbed her arm. "What do you mean, sunshine?"

"Well, in case you haven't noticed, Betty Jean is strung out; she a top-of-the-line junkie. Her life is more mixed up than an overturned eighteen-wheeler of Grade A eggs. She's got it bad. You'd have to be blind not to know she's hooked. So, I'm assuming that you—"

"Do I look blind?" I glanced over at Betty Jean when I spoke.

"No." Bonnie's voice held great sadness.

"There's your answer. Of course, I knew. But I get the feeling you're blaming yourself because Betty Jean's got the monkey on her back."

"Yea, guess I do feel guilty about her problem."

"But, Bonnie, you've got it all wrong. You're her friend, not her guardian."

"My brain tells me that my concern and empathy for her can only lead to grief—*my grief*. But I still love her, love her as if she and I had the same blood in our veins. I want to help her, and I believe I can, if only I can chip away that protective wall she has erected around her."

"Doesn't she open up to you, a close friend?"

"About certain things, yes, but about the one thing that *really* matters, she's a mute. If she'd only talk about what's bothering her, I feel I could help. Meanwhile, she continues to be an idealist with endless compassion for the world's oppressed. She hemorrhages countless tears over every injustice she hears about. She's a dreamer, and for her, being one isn't good."

"Why? Without dreamers, Bonnie, we'd all still be barbarians cowering in caves, paralyzed by superstition and fear. In your own endearing way you're a dreamer."

"Yeah, guess I am to a degree."

"So, what's so bad about Betty Jean being a dreamer, one who envisions a kinder, gentler world?"

"I'll tell-ya why. It's because Betty Jean is Betty Jean. Look, it's nineteen sixty-eight. Or have you forgotten? Today confrontations are commonplace, demonstrations and riots as numerous as flies at a church picnic. In America, those favoring the war, hawks, attack those opposed to it, doves, whites assault blacks, visionaries assail those who have eyes and cannot see, and the old order combats the new. Trapped in the middle of the conflicts, dreamers are the first to bleed and more often than not, the first to die, sometimes the *only* ones to die. Wanna be an idealist and a dreamer today? You need the hide of an alligator and the patience of Job. And Betty Jean, as you and I well know, has neither."

Bonnie shrugged and stared into her wine glass. "You see when it comes to Betty Jean, my brain recognizes the truth, but my heart won't accept it."

"And the truth is?" I rubbed a hand up and down her back in a soothing motion.

"Betty Jean is a good-hearted woman in a bad-hearted world. But what the hell," she sighed, "enough. Why don't we pick another subject?"

"Good idea. Why don't we dream up a Utopia? And then we can pretend the *real* world doesn't exist."

She shrugged, her mouth a grim line. "Okay, you've made your point. Would you do me a favor?"

"Sure."

"My glass is running on empty. Mind pumping me a refill?"

"You got it." I started for the refreshment table.

"And this time, Paul."

I stopped and turned. "Yeah?"

"I want something a little stronger than wine. Make it high test."

"Sure thing. As a matter of fact, I could use something stronger, too. So, two high octanes coming up."

Once more I headed for the table. On the way, I stepped over Winn who earlier invited me to share a drag. Now on his back, eyes glazed, and a smile curling his lips, he appeared to be in another dimension, one in which body bags and napalm bombs were irrelevant.

I fixed Bonnie's drink, vodka and tonic, and I mixed one for myself, topping mine with a wedge of lemon.

Returning, I handed Bonnie her glass, then began sipping as I scanned the room. Winn, the marijuana smoker I'd stepped over was still on the floor, now babbling to someone in the ceiling that only he could see. "I don't wanna deal with it," he mumbled. "Life's too ugly. There's gotta be something better...just *gotta* be. Otherwise, what's the point, man?" Those near the speaker ignored his monologue and continued passing around a joint. "Where's the answer? There ain't none, man. It's all lunacy, absolute lunacy. "

Meanwhile, Betty Jean remained in the far corner still talking to the man sporting the gold necklace. Occasionally he shrugged and, as if it were a strand of prayer beads, he fingered the rope of gold circling his neck. He was calm, Betty Jean, edgy.

When she reached out to grab his arm, he turned his back to her. When he did, she circled to his front and spoke with frenzied urgency, her nose within an inch of his.

It was then that Roger Anderson, Bonnie's black American friend, entered the studio. Seeing Bonnie and me, he smiled, waved, and walked to where we stood. After the three of us exchanged pleasantries, and he'd poured himself a glass of wine, he, fidgeting, said, "Ah, Bonnie."

"Yeah."

"I got something I need to talk to you about."

"Sure. And judging from the look on your face, Roger, I'd say it's something *serious*."

"It is."

"Look," I said, "if you guys need privacy, I'll be happy to—"

"That won't be necessary." Roger ran a hand over his face. "What I have to say, I don't mind if you hear it. Stay, man, no big deal. It's cool." He turned to Bonnie. "Bon, I don't have to tell you that you're my ace-boon, my best friend, and because you are, I figured you should be the first to know."

"You're so sweet. I'm flattered."

"Bon, I want you to understand that what I'm about to say isn't a spur-of-the-moment thing. I've given it lots of thought. For a long while the matter has been bugging the hell outta me, causing countless sleepless nights."

Bonnie reached out to touch Roger's arm. "What's the problem?"

"I've finally made up my mind. I'm gonna return to Flatwater, Mississippi, my home."

"You're gonna do what?" she gasped. "Go back to...Flatwater? Come on-n-n, you gotta be puttin' me on, Roger. You're kidding, aren't you?"

"Am I?" Both his face and voice were somber.

"Of course you are. Look, ever since I've known you, you've told me how you hated Flatwater, Mississippi, hated the ways bigotry there marred you mentally. Do you remember saying that?"

"Of course I do, and I meant every syllable because that's how I felt. And *still* do."

"So you're kidding about going back? It was a put on, right?" Bonnie smiled, obviously expecting Roger to do the same.

He didn't. "No, I wish it was a joke, God knows I do, but it's not."

Her voice softened. "Have you run out of money?" She took his hands in hers. "Is that why you want to return to Flatwater? If so, my friend, I could help you a little."

"Who said I want to go back, Bonnie? Not want *to*, but *have* to. Anyway, the answer is no, I haven't run out of money. Money's not the issue. Thank God for my uncle in Chicago. He sees that money is never an issue."

"So, why are you going back? Is your brain firing on all cylinders tonight, Roger?" He didn't answer. "Come on, talk to me, Roger. She grabbed the front of his tunic. "Talk. Help me make sense out of it. What would make you go back to a place you hate, where hooded men hate you more than you hate the place? Why would you want to return to the cesspool of your life, Flatwater, Mississippi? Is somebody in your family ill? Is that it? Your mother? Brother? Uncle? Who?"

"No one." His sad eyes shifted from Bonnie to me to his shoes.

"Roger, I'm at my wit's end," Bonnie sighed, shaking her head. "I give up; I just don't get it."

"I didn't expect you to. I'm not sure I fully understand it myself.

Calvin Davis

Like you, I'm confused, maybe even more than you."

Bonnie placed a hand on her hip and leaned in close to Roger. "At least try to explain it to me, because I sure as hell would like to know."

"I'll try, I'm just not sure I can." As if fingering through a scrapbook of blurred memories, Roger, brow furrowed, paused. Finally, closing his eyes, then reopening them, he said, "Look, ah, what I'm fumbling to say is something I've been grappling with for months. I told myself it was all in my imagination, that it wasn't real, but, sadly, it was and is, and I knew it. I was hoping it'd go away like a head cold or a bad dream.

"Later, I tried telling myself that this thing had finally disappeared. Believing that it had was wishful thinking, for there it was, where it had always been, in the middle of my gut. You're right, I have no love for Flatwater because of the unspeakable cruelties I've suffered there."

"Yet," Bonnie whispered with tears in her eyes, "you're returning."

"Yes, I am." Roger's eyes were now locked on Bonnie's.

"Roger, I wish I could tell you that what you're saying makes sense, but it doesn't. I'll be so worried about you."

He took her hand. "Don't misunderstand; I'll always love Paris. This city welcomed me when my birthplace vomited in my face. It rolled out the red carpet, treating me as if I were a returning prodigal, a treasured human being, while in my hometown I couldn't have a Coke at a lunch counter without facing a lynch mob. But now that I've been in Paris a while, I've learned a valuable lesson, one that saddens and delights me at the same time."

She placed her palm on his chest. "Which is?"

"I learned that though I love Paris, and it loves me, this city is not my home. My deliverer, yes. My hope, that too. But my home? No. For a while, I duped myself into believing I was not born with Mississippi Delta clay in my veins. The bond to my birthplace is like a Frenchman's attachment to wine. Bonnie, I *have* to go home again. Home, where I can hear, smell, and touch familiar things.

"I need to feel the fellowship of family and friends, to see graying old men on street corners singing gospel songs, to feel the electricity and energy in a 'holy-roller' church, to hear the congregation's clapping hands, and the jangle of tambourines, and the sound of worshippers 'moved by the spirit' squealing, 'Thank you, Lord, you done brought me a mighty long way.' These are the things that make me who I am. And nothing in Paris, as beautiful as

88

The City of Light is, *nothing* in it—including the Louvre, the Sacre-Couer, The Eiffel Tower, Luxembourg Garden, even the Mona Lisa itself—nothing can replace these things. Nothing." He paused. "Bonnie?"

She blotted the tears on her face. "Yeah."

"I feel trapped. Paris is where my body is, but my soul never crossed the Mississippi State line, and probably never will."

"So, you really intend to go back."

"I have no choice. Look, my stay won't last forever. Maybe only a couple of days, a week or even as little as a day might do it. Just long enough to regenerate."

"I understand," Bonnie said, caressing Roger's cheek with her hand. "At least I think I do. When do you plan to go?"

"I'm not sure. Perhaps one day I'll just pack my bags and hop the next flight. The whole thing could be over so fast you won't even notice I was gone."

"What bothers me, Roger, is the time between now and when you depart, because during that intermission you'll be in agony, feeling, as you put it…trapped."

As if hoping vision could penetrate floorboards, Roger stared down. "Anyway," he said, counterfeiting a smile, "I wonder if you guys will excuse me? I need a refill."

Bonnie and I watched as he nudged a path through clusters of guests. Glasses and cigarettes in hand, some chatted quietly, but a few were now loud and vociferous, debating and sawing the air with clenched fists. As they did, a female walked to the phonograph, turned down the volume, then changed recordings, flipping on Joan Baez's "Amazing Grace."

"A-a-a-ma-a-zing grace, ho-o-w sweet the sound, that saved a wretch li-i-ike me. I once was lost, but now I'm found, once blind but now I..." The coloratura's voice wafted through the studio like an enchanted perfume, transforming the area into an oasis of serenity. But the serenity was short lived, as two male voices exploded.

"Damn!" one boomed, "you got it wrong, man, all wrong!" His blond bangs swayed back and forth as he spoke.

"Look!" his adversary shot back, "you know what your problem is? You got a bad case of perverted patriotism."

The blond guy did a twisting motion with his hands, as if he were wringing out an invisible sponge. "There you go again, twisting my words!"

His verbal opponent, with brown hair curling on his shoulders, leaned in as he spoke. "*Bullshit!* Whether you know it or not, you're contaminated with the right-winger's disease, a misguided love of the Fatherland. Why the blind devotion to flag and country? Why?"

The sound of his voice rose as he continued his invective. "Why so loyal to a government that lies about its role in the Vietnam War, one that preaches 'thou shall not kill,' then arms its youths and ships them to foreign lands and orders them to kill, pinning metals on those who murder the most, calling assassins heroes? The casualties of the misadventures are then shipped in flag-draped coffins to their parents. And what did these soldiers die for? To validate the egos of gray-haired old men in the Senate and White House.

"And I mustn't leave out Pentagon officials, who are past masters at choreographing news conferences, they with their pointers, charts, rigged statistics, and oily tongues."

Saliva sprayed from both debaters. Each seemed determined to shout louder than his opponent, spewing words like fifty caliber rounds from a machine-gun. "Okay, okay, so you disapprove of the war. That I can dig," yelled the blond.

"Not disapprove. I loathe the damn thing!" seethed the one with the long brown hair.

"Then that gives you options. You can be a conscientious objector, serve in a medical unit and *save* lives, not take them. You don't have to flee to Canada. Why not be like Gandhi or Martin Luther King—go to jail for your convictions. I'm just as opposed to the damn war as you, but hiding in Canada, as I see it, is not a moral option, but a copout." The blond pushed his long blond bangs from his eyes.

"What the hell does morality have to do with it? What?"

"Everything!" The blond waved his arms in wide arcs. "Hiding in Canada is a gutless way to face a problem. Running there solves nothing."

"I agree. And what you say would be true if we were dealing with an honest government. But from our government we've heard only lies." The dark-haired speaker's voice rose a few decibels.

"Look, all you're saying is that the ends justify the means, exactly what Hitler preached. And that way of looking at things is wrong. Dead wrong!"

"You wanna know who's wrong, Blondie? I'll tell you. Flag-wavers and my-county-'tis-of- thee-ers like you. That's what's wrong." The combatants inched closer, noses now separated by the thickness of a paring knife blade.

"Back off!" Gasps rippled through the room when the blond pushed the other guy.

"Look man, don't you ever put your damn hands on me again! You hear me?"

"Back off!"

Streaking like a major league fastball, the fist of the long-haired guy pounded the jaw of the blond debater. "Smack!" The legs of the targeted man buckled. Like a tiger pouncing on a sheep, the aggressor attacked; both pugilists kicking, clawing, and punching, their bodies a blurred orb of flailing arms and legs.

"Stop 'em! Stop 'em!"

"They're gonna kill each other. Won't somebody help!" The female speaker backed up against the wall out of harm's way.

Two brawny men shot forward, clamping their arms around the brawlers, tussling to separate the pair.

"Quick, grab the other arm!"

"I got it, I--"

"Okay, hold them. Ah-h hell!" The interventionists' efforts were futile. Both combatants wrenched from the intermediaries' grasps, and once again punches rained.

"They'll kill each other," the female against the wall shrieked. "Why won't somebody do something!"

Several guests scampered into the hall, and from there, seconds later, a female shrieked, "Oh my God! Call an ambulance! Quick!"

I glanced at Bonnie, then quickly scanned the room. Where was Betty Jean and the stranger she had been talking to? Both were nowhere in sight. "Bonnie?"

"Yeah?"

"We got a problem!" My intuition had kicked in. "Just follow me, okay?" She did as I headed for the door.

In the hall, several partygoers circled Betty Jean who, face up, lay twitching on the floor, her eyes focused on some invisible thing in the ceiling. A syringe, half filled with blood, angled from her arm. Where the needle punctured flesh, a trickle of crimson circled her arm, narrowing into drops that dripped into a little puddle under the elbow. I held Bonnie to my side, trying to step in front of her so she couldn't see.

Suddenly, all movement stopped. A woman knelt beside the motionless body and pressed her index finger to Betty Jean's wrist. Seconds later, the Good Samaritan glanced up, paused, frowned, and then placed an ear to Betty Jean's lips. "Too late," she sighed. "Too late."

"Betty Jean!" Bonnie shrieked. "Oh no! Not Betty Jean!"

Quickly I led Bonnie back into Betty Jean's studio. A couple of men had finally separated the brawlers, who, panting, stood on opposite sides of the room, each firing fusillades of scowls and curses at the other. "Someone get those two out of here," I barked in my no-nonsense teacher voice. I pulled Bonnie close, encircled her with my arms, and held her as sobs racked her body.

With Bonnie's head pressed against my shoulder in a protective gesture, I tried to make sense of what had just happened. Where was the stranger Betty Jean talked to most of the evening? Obviously he and Betty Jean had earlier slipped into the hall. Now she was lying on the floor, dead. And he was missing. What exactly had happened?

Shortly past four in the morning, after the police arrived and asked a thousand questions, they allowed the ambulance to take Betty Jean's body away. Guests were finally allowed to leave. In the ensuing quiet, I switched off the lights to Betty Jean's eerily silent studio and closed the door.

Bonnie and I stood in the pre-dawn stillness of the hall. She raised her tear swollen face and whispered, "Paul, it's hard to believe my friend is dead. Gone. Forever. My Lord, what a night this has been."

"To say the least. What a waste for a human being to die like that."

"I'll have to call her family." She put her fingertips to her eyes. "What do I say to them? How can I possibly help ease their grief when I feel the pain so deeply myself?" She choked out a sob. "Betty Jean. How I'm going to miss her. I just can't believe she's gone."

I wrapped my arm around her narrow shoulders and led her down the stairs to her studio. She was visibly exhausted. "What a hellacious night, Bonnie. Betty Jean overdosing. Roger going back home to face Jim Crow's racist cronies. And that awful brawl between those two guys. You know, I couldn't help but get the odd feeling I was back in America caught in the middle of two polarized activist groups battling over the war."

Bonnie looked up at me. "You, too?" She shook her head. "I had that same feeling."

"I wonder if here on the Left Bank in Paris, far removed from America, I wonder if we can ever escape the political and social turmoil that's ripping the States into shreds." We reached her landing, and I leaned against the wall next to her door.

Bonnie reached in the back pocket of her jeans for her key. "What happened up there tonight proves we can't. The conflict in the States follows us to Paris. There is no hiding place. Not on this planet. Do you think that years from now when the war's over and monuments are erected to honor Americans who died in it or because of it, do you think they'll chisel Betty Jean's name on one? Caught up in the war's aftermath and all the problems it spawned, she's as much a casualty of that conflict as any GI killed in Dien Bien Phu."

I reached out to touch her face and sighed, wishing I could take on some of the pain she was feeling. "No, they won't. But that doesn't make it right. In the past they've excluded countless others deserving recognition, and my guess is they'll do the same for Betty Jean."

"For sure."

I took her key from her trembling hand and unlocked her door. "Anyway, 'night, Bonnie."

She gave me a quick hug. "'Night, Paul."

"Are you going to be all right?"

She nodded and choked out a sob. Her hand trembled as it rose to cover her mouth. Large tears crawled down her cheeks.

I reached out with the pads of my thumbs to wipe them away. "You know where I'm at if you need a shoulder."

"Yes, my friend. You're right here." She placed an open hand to her heart and whispered, "You'll always be here." Another sob escaped. "And so will Betty Jean."

Days later I happened upon the stranger Betty Jean talked to that night at her party. Entering a little café, I saw him leaning against the bar. He recognized me, and after waving a greeting with his glass, he nodded and smiled, as if nothing had happened, as if Betty Jean had never existed, as if she had not overdosed, and he had not supplied her with the merchandise of his trade that enabled her to do so. Appearing as relaxed as he was the night he talked to Betty Jean, he looked over the bar and quietly contemplated his drink. Smiling, he seemed pleased with his cocktail, with himself, and with the universe in general, as if convinced that all in it was as it should be.

A waiter approached my table. "Would *Monsieur* like to order now?"

"Well, when I got here, I intended to order something, but I've changed my mind." My eyes slid to the guy from the party. "I'm not feeling well."

"Perhaps I can assist *monsieur* in some way."

"No, I'm afraid not. But thanks for your concern." I hurried from the café and when I reached the curb, I bent forward, clutched my stomach, and heaved. A second later, vomit spurted from me like water from a garden hose.

Several times during the following week, I returned to that café. But I never stayed over a second or so during each visit. The reason? Though the man with the golden chain was never physically present, nor was Betty Jean, each time I returned, I saw both of them, clearly, and though I tried to, I couldn't stay.

Chapter 13

For three days it had rained in Paris—soaking, gloomy rain. I'd sought out cafés nearest Rue Galande, seeking tables in the heart of the café rather than along windows. In a creative state of denial, I felt if I didn't see the rain, then it didn't exist. I'd returned to my studio about thirty minutes earlier, hung up my rain poncho, changed into a pair of dry shoes, and started pounding on my old Remington when Bonnie fluttered up the steps.

As usual, my studio door was open, and she stopped in the hallway outside my door. "I think I just saw Noah and two elephants float by. Can ya dig it?"

I leaned back in my chair and smiled for the first time that day. Bonnie was wearing a water-soaked, orange flowered scarf tied around her head, raindrops were resting on her long, dark eyelashes, shining like diamonds, and a puddle of rainwater was materializing at her feet. "Yea, sunshine, I can dig it. The paper says the rain is supposed to end tonight."

I removed the pencil from behind my ear and tossed it onto my desk. "I need a fresh supply of composition books, so I was planning on shopping tomorrow. It would be nice to walk to Gilbert's instead of having to swim there."

"What's the matter, tiger, is your breaststroke a little weak?" She untied her scarf and took it off, shaking out her hair. "Man, I am so sick of this rain. Want some company tomorrow? I could use some stationery. My supply is low. I've been doing a lot of writing these last few weeks to Betty Jean's parents."

"I'll take your company any day—rain or sunshine. Have you heard from Betty Jean's parents? How are they doing?"

Bonnie shrugged. "They're doing like one would expect. They're struggling, trying to make sense out of something that'll never make sense."

"I'm sure your letters help." I hated seeing her depressed, and memories of Betty Jean and her senseless death always depressed Bonnie.

"Help who? Them or me? Can you believe it's been a month since that horrible night?" She gave an audible sigh. "Life can be a blessing and a bitch, and often, at the same time." She shook her head almost as if shaking away negative thoughts, then she snapped her fingers. "Enough! Enough complaining. What time are you going to Gilbert's tomorrow?"

We decided to leave at ten the following morning to purchase our needs, and Bonnie continued upstairs to her studio. I turned back to my typewriter, feeling warmer after my brief dose of sunshine from the lady who brightened everyone's world. Within minutes I was lost in the imaginary lives I was creating on paper.

The sun was shining the following morning when we headed off to Joseph Gilbert Libraire et Papeterie, on Boulevard Saint Michel. Our spirits were light and buoyant as we walked along, holding hands and laughing at nothing and everything. Being with Bonnie did that to me.

For Sorbonne students, Gilbert's was a Left Bank iconic institution that needed no description, for it was as essential to their academic and social life as the ubiquitous leather briefcases they carried or the spirited gait at which they hurried along Boulevard Saint Michel en route to classes. On my earlier visits to Gilbert's, I found it packed with customers. Most were students browsing textbooks or buying compasses, rulers, artist brushes, easels, or other related school supplies. The store catered to every conceivable scholastic need, from paper clips to art portfolios. On the sidewalk fronting Gilbert's, male students often congregated and flirted with coeds, most of whom were strikingly beautiful—skin, spring-breeze fresh, and hair, like silk.

Bonnie and I stopped at a café a couple of blocks before reaching our destination. The sun was slowly drying up the mud puddles; the air was fresh smelling. It was a day to enjoy the outdoors, I thought as we sat on the café's terrace and chatted over Cokes. "When's the last time you saw, ah, what's his name? It's on the tip of my tongue."

"The guy you're trying to recall, what does he do for a living?"

"Oh, you know him, Bonnie, I pointed him out a couple of weeks ago, that French detective who's been asking questions about you. Wait, now I remember. His name is Charles DeMure. Yeah, that's it, Inspector Charles DeMure."

Her eyebrows knitted in contempt. "You mean that *nut*."

"Yeah, him. So, when was the last time you saw him?"

"About a week ago at Galeries Lafayette, the big department store in what was once an opera house."

"I know it well. What were you doing there, shopping?" That thought surprised me since Bonnie's wardrobe tastes ran more to the eclectic than the haute-couture styles I'd seen while browsing the few times I'd been there.

"No, I went to browse the window displays. They're always fantastic. Oh, wait until you see them at Christmas. The French are masters at decorating, especially department store windows. Even Left Bank mom-and-pop boutique windows can become works of art. It's amazing how a roll or two of aluminum foil, crepe paper and infinite imagination can turn drabness into fiestas for the eyes. And nobody does that better than the guys who decorate windows at Galeries Lafayette."

I placed my hand over hers. "You were about to tell me what happened the last time you saw Inspector DeMure."

"Yeah. Like I said, I was at GL's admiring the window displays when I saw the inspector on the other side of the street staring at me like he was the Grand Inquisitor and me, The Supreme Antichrist."

"So what'd you do? I mean, did you try to shake him, duck around the corner, wait until a crowd happened by, then blend into it? What?"

"Why should I do any of those things, Paul? I continued looking at the windows, what I'd come to do. But after about ten minutes of his gawking at me, he was beginning to wear on my nerves. I had had about all I could stand of the guy, so I stomped across the street to where he was. Seeing me barreling toward him, he took off in the opposite direction, but I blocked him."

I set down my glass of Coke. "You're kidding?"

"No, I'm not! 'Hello,' I smiled. 'Ah...ah...ah, hi,' he stammered. 'Galeries Lafayette window displays are beautiful, aren't they?' I said. He muttered that they were."

"Then what happened?"

"I told him that, at his age, his eyesight probably wasn't what it used to be and that he could see the windows much better if he crossed the street and joined me."

"You *actually* said that?"

She smiled from ear to ear and tucked her hair behind her ears. "Every word. And you should have seen his face turn fire engine red."

I chuckled and shook my head. "Did he join you?"

"No. He glanced at his watch and said he'd just remembered an engagement. I insisted that he join me."

"What'd he do?"

She shrugged and tried her best not to laugh. "He crossed the street and joined me."

"You're kidding! And while you two were looking at the

windows, did he pepper you with questions about your activities and those of your friends?"

"Not a word."

"That's strange. When he talked to me, he had *endless* questions about you, but none, you say, when talking to you. Wonder why? Maybe his dossier on you was complete."

"I doubt it. Want to hear what I think the real reason was?"

"Yeah."

"Well, as we stood admiring the windows, I started yakking, ooh-ing and aah-ing, and squealing about how lovely the decorations were. Like man, I really poured it on, big time, talking so fast he couldn't get in a word edgewise. I think I frustrated him. After about ten minutes of listening to me go nonstop, he was finally able to wedge in a word."

I leaned toward her. "What word was that?"

"'Good-bye.' But I'll bet he was thinking, 'Good riddance.'"

I laughed some more as I choked out, "It was charitable of you to give him equal time. Well, almost equal time."

"He told me he enjoyed my company and looked forward to chatting with me again. I don't think he really meant that. Anyway, after giving me a funny look, he left—walking quite fast for a man his age."

I laughed, raising my glass to my lips and wiggling my eyebrows. "Poor guy."

"What-cha mean, *'poor guy'*?" Bonnie slapped my arm. "If you have any sympathy, it should be for me, not him. I was the one being harassed. So why'd you say, 'poor guy'?"

"Bonnie, you're even cuter when you're provoked. You know that was just a figure of speech." A blush kissed her cheeks at my words. After we ordered a couple more Cokes and an order of French fries—*frites*—to share, I asked, "Have you seen Roger lately?"

"Yeah, he stopped by my place a couple of days ago."

"Remember at Betty Jean's party he said he planned to visit his hometown, Flatwater. Did he go?"

She shrugged her shoulders. "If so, he didn't tell me about it."

"Did you ask?"

Bonnie shifted in her tiny café chair. I couldn't help but notice how the sunlight brought out shades of auburn in her dark hair. "No."

"So why didn't you ask?" I'd have asked, I thought, but then I was known for asking too many questions. How many times had my mother warned me about "curiosity killing the cat"?

"For three reasons, Paul. One, it was none of my damn business.

Two, if he'd wanted me to know, he'd have told me. And three, I didn't need to ask."

"Why not?"

She sat back and crossed her arms over her chest. "Because I already knew the answer. Listen, to me Roger is an open book. Even if he wanted to, he couldn't hide anything from me. And the reverse is true. He and I are transparent to each other. Maybe that's why we're such good friends. So, though he never told me he did or did not return to Flatwater, I knew the answer, and the answer is he didn't. And if you want my opinion, he won't *ever* go…nor should he."

"But he vowed he would return. Remember? He said he had to go back, that he needed to reconnect with his roots. So why do you say he won't go back?"

She sighed and glanced momentarily at the couple kissing at the next table. "Because I don't think he has it in him to return."

"Not even after vowing he would? Roger had seemed pretty determined when he'd spoken to us at Betty Jean's party. Without a doubt the guy had a severe case of the "homesick blues.""

"Listen, since Roger made the promise to return, I'm sure he's had time to consider the reality and consequences of the decision."

"And what is this 'reality' you speak of?"

"That you can't go home again. In Roger's case, he wants to relive the few good times he had in Flatwater, good times that were indeed few. At least from what he told me."

"Don't we all long to do the same—to rediscover our roots, to go home again? What's wrong with Roger doing what everybody wants to do?" The waiter returned with our *frites* and drinks.

Bonnie picked up the salt and doused the fries. "Nothing. It's just that after having time to think it over, he'll come to see that you can't split memories like you do a six-pack. It's an all or nothing deal—picking and choosing is not allowed." She waved a French fry as she spoke. "The bad memories Roger has about Flatwater, Mississippi, I don't think he can handle. The last thing he needs is one more nightmare about that damn place. He's suffered more than enough of those already. I know because he's shared them with me---horrible images of castrated bodies swinging from tree branches and armed, hooded men lurking in shadows."

I swirled a fry in a puddle of ketchup. "You could be wrong, Bonnie."

"True, but I'd hate to think of what'll happen to Roger emotionally if I'm right and he does return to Flatwater."

Later, when Bonnie and I approached Gilbert's, a larger group than usual congregated on the sidewalk fronting the store and, oddly, all loiterers were silent and solemn-faced, as if awaiting the commencement of some grave event. Looking back on what happened next, if I had been more intuitive, I might have realized that their expressions were prophetic of what was to come.

"Bonnie?" I asked, taking her arm and peering around.

She stopped and looked up at me. "Yeah?"

"Do you notice anything strange?"

"Like what?" She glanced around, her curiosity obviously peaked now, by the crowd's strange behavior.

"Like the people in front of Gilbert's, just standing and staring, silent as tombs."

"Gee, maybe it's some sort of college prank or a fraternity initiation ceremony. They do have fraternities at the Sorbonne, don't they?"

My eyes were slowly assessing the crowd. My teacher radar was picking up some bad vibes as I absently answered her question. "As far as I know, yes."

"So, that might be it."

"Might be." But, somehow, I didn't think so.

Bonnie and I entered Gilbert's. There were only four customers in the store, fewer than I'd ever seen there before. One was a middle-aged woman who, face blanched, stood nervously in front of a clerk at the checkout counter. Instead of waiting on her, as she obviously wanted him to do, he stared out the window at the crowd now dallying on the sidewalk.

"*Monsieur*," she said, "would you kindly take my order? Like you, I don't want to be in this place any longer than necessary. So, if you don't mind!"

"My apologies," the clerk said, "but under the circumstances I'm sure you understand."

"Of course I do. That aside, I'm anxious to get out of here as quickly as possible."

"I understand."

After ringing up her sale, the clerk disappeared behind a display rack, scooped up a leather bound notebook and handed it to the jittery woman who, her purchase in hand, walked briskly toward the door.

"*Madame*, your receipt, don't you want your receipt?" He frantically waved some paper money at her. "What about your change?"

"Keep it. And good luck to you, young man. You'll need it, I'm sure." The woman quickly exited.

"Bonnie," I said, "what's going on? Where're all the customers, and why's everybody so--"

She was peering around the store, rubbing her arms as though she were chilled. "Edgy, Paul. Edgy. I've got a bad feeling about this."

Like the buzz of an approaching swarm of giant bumblebees, and, at first, barely audible, a droning noise sounded, "Hum-m-m." Soon it was apparent from where the din originated—the sidewalk fronting Gilbert's.

"There he is," someone outside yelled.

"Hum-m-m." The drone continued, steadily growing louder.

"Where?" another inquired.

"Hum-m-m-m. . . "

"There!" came an excited cry.

Bonnie and I rushed to the window and stared out. Atop the shoulders of two muscular males sat a gaunt, longhaired man dressed in black. The two men transported their passenger across Boulevard Saint Michel toward Gilbert's. Protesters swarmed around the elevated figure as a sea of hands reached out, fingers extended, straining to touch the object of the adulation, to make contact with any part of him: his sweater, trousers, shoes, *anything*.

"Bonnie, who's the guy everybody's so worked up over?"

She glanced at me briefly before turning her eyes to the spectacle on the street. "Don't tell me you don't know?"

I glanced down at her. "OK, I won't, but I still don't know."

"That's François, François the Incendiary. I thought everybody knew him."

"Call me Mr. Nobody, because I don't."

"He's the leader of the student protest movement in Paris. When that guy speaks, demonstrators listen and *act*. Let's go outside and see what happens." She headed for the door.

I grabbed her arm. "Why? To get caught up in the middle of a riot?"

Suddenly, store lights flickered.

"Ladies and gentlemen, Gilbert's is now closed," a clerk shouted. "For the safety of all, management requests that you vacate the premises." What few customers there were inched toward the door, then stopped. "I *must* insist," the clerk added, "all must leave."

"Why not lock the door and allow us to stay here?" an elderly gentleman asked.

"I have my orders, sir. Management insists that everyone vacate. Now!"

"But I see no harm in allowing us to stay," remarked a mother pushing a child in a stroller. "We'd be safer in here. Don't force us out in that mob. My baby…"

"Please, *Madame*, don't make my job more difficult than it is."

Seconds later, the other customers exited along with us. Outside, Bonnie and I filtered into a mass of chanting demonstrators. "François! François! François!" Voices were tides of sound, echoing up and down Boulevard Saint Michel. "François ! François!"

Chapter 14

"Bonnie, What the *hell* are we doing here in this mob? Let's get out, while we can."

"Ah, come on, Paul." She craned her neck to see over the people standing in front of us. "Don't be such a stuffed shirt. What are you so afraid of? I've always wanted to hear François speak, just to hear for myself why students get so enthused by what he has to say."

"François! François!" Herds of demonstrators swarmed down the boulevard. Others emerged from intersecting streets. "François!" Sidewalks fronting Gilbert's now overflowed. Necks craning, protestors clogged the street, backing up traffic and enraging motorists.

"Have you people lost your damn mind? What's gotten into you?" one motorist yelled, leaning out his car window.

Horns honked.

"Move! Move!" another driver ordered.

"Bonnie," I said, "let's leave." My heart was pounding in my ears. I'd never seen a crowd so worked up before.

"Too late unless we can bulldoze through that wall of people in front of us."

"Fat chance," I growled, growing more uneasy by the minute.

François dismounted from his porters and, amid choruses of cheers, leapt onto a vendor's table where, arms raised, he signaled for silence.

"Quiet!" someone yelled.

"Yeah, knock it off."

"Bonnie," I whispered in her ear, "now's our chance." I really wanted to get out of there and pronto. I had a real uneasy feeling about all of this.

"Isn't this exciting?" she smiled. About as exciting as being tied to the railroad tracks, I thought, and with a runaway locomotive barreling down on me. I laid my arm across her shoulders and drew her near, hoping to protect her from the inevitable. She looked up at me. "I wonder what he's going to talk about."

"Hey, you!" The man to our left was speaking to Bonnie. "Knock it off. OK? Quiet!"

"Yeah. Why don't-cha?" someone added. "François is ready to speak."

One of the leader's aides handed him a bullhorn, and he pressed its mouthpiece to his lips. Immediately, Boulevard Saint Germain transformed into a sepulcher: total silence. "Fellow revolutionaries," the Incendiary bellowed, "patriots of France"—he paused, the intermission accentuating silence like an exclamation point—"hear my words."

Cheers exploded, followed by a chain of chants: "François...François...François!" The speaker once more signaled for silence.

"Comrades," he continued, "comrades." Again, an explosion of cheers.

"Quiet, let 'em speak," a man yelled.

"The time," François said, "has come, the day, the hour; the *moment* is at hand! Not tomorrow, as the bureaucracy would have you believe, nor some unnamed future date. Fellow revolutionaries, *now* is the time when we must end once and for all the university's inequalities, dismantle its archaic bureaucracy and curricula and make known to the world our grievances." With a raised fist, he shouted into the bullhorn, "*Now! Now! Now!*"

The crowd responded: "Now! Now! Now!" Beneath the din of the throng edged another sound, the wail of police sirens, but the resonance of approaching sirens didn't deter François. "We have not gathered here," he extolled, "to capitulate!" His words were now fireballs of passion. "*We shall not be moved!*"

"Never!" demonstrators responded. "Never!"

"Nor shall we cower," intoned the speaker.

"Never!" protestors replied.

"Or be intimidated by billy clubs."

"No."

"Or tear gas!"

"No! No!" The crowd chanted louder and louder.

The screech of police vehicles slamming to a stop punctuated protesters' chants as officers with shields, nightsticks, and gas masks, poured from vans. "Form ranks!" barked the commander. "Double time!" Like automatons, lawmen scurried.

"The presence of policemen will not weaken our resolve," François the Incendiary orated.

"No!" responded a chorus of frenzied voices.

Officers formed lines on the sidewalk across the street from Gilbert's. "This demonstration," the commanding officer bellowed, "is unauthorized. You have sixty seconds to disperse." No one moved. "Fifty-nine seconds."

"Comrades," François said, "our right to protest is written not on paper, but in the *justness* of our cause."

"Speak the truth," a demonstrator yelled. "Speak the truth."

"Because of the nobleness of that cause, we are justified in using *any* and all means necessary. Any and all!"

"Right on, right on!"

"Too long we have begged for, not the universe, but mere tidbits of quality in education, properly heated classrooms, updated textbooks, and accessible professors. And too long our supplications have been ignored. But no more!" François insisted.

"Speak the truth...speak it."

"If we must paralyze traffic on Boulevard Saint Michel, indeed, tie it up in every arrondissement in the city in order to secure what is *rightfully* ours, we will!" Cheers, followed by more cheers. "If we have to obtain justice through the barrels of guns, *it...will...be...so!*"

"Yes, guns! Guns!" Several chanted.

"What must be, must be. Comrades, do you follow my meaning?"

"Yes, we follow! Yes! Yes!" Clearly they would have agreed to anything—legal or not—that François would have suggested. He was in complete control of the crowd.

A protestor pried a cobblestone from Boulevard Saint Michel and heaved it at the line of officers on the opposite side of the street. As if guided by radar, the missile found its target striking the shoulder of a policeman and toppling him. Hailstorms of cobblestones now arched across the thoroughfare.

"Attention!" the police commander bellowed. "Attention!" Troopers froze. "Prepare!" Helmet visors flipped into place, the collective snaps audible to onlookers. Officers raised shields and nightsticks. "Advance!" The line of troopers stepped forward.

"Comrades," François shouted, "remain calm. We will *not* be moved." The followers heeded the leader's instructions and froze. "Our unborn will long applaud what we do here today. So, freedom fighters, memorialize the moment! *Stand firm!*"

"Detail," the assault team commander barked, "halt!" Officers stopped. "Prepare." A pause. "Ready." Another silent pause. "Launch." Waves of tear gas canisters sailed across the boulevard. Near Bonnie and me, a container skidded, spraying streams of gas. I grabbed Bonnie by the arm and led her further up the street, trying to escape the gas.

As I glanced back to where we'd stood, I saw a protester retrieved the cylinder and launched it at the officers. Seeing the arching missile, demonstrators cheered, but their jubilance quickly aborted, as troopers launched squadrons of canisters.

"Freedom fighters, stand fast!" François bellowed. "Stand fast!"

Canisters clanked over cobblestones and skidded, hissing billows of choking vapor. "We will *not* be moved. The hour of our destiny is upon us," François raged to the crowd. "Stand fast!" Protesters scattered like deer in a forest fire. "Stand firm, hold steady." Demonstrators did neither.

Amid the pandemonium, the two men who transported François across Boulevard Saint Michel wedged through the tangle of bodies and reached the orator, then escorted him through a labyrinth of protestors. François and the bodyguards bolted down a side street, leaving behind clouds of eye-smarting gas and demonstrators bolting helter-skelter. Blinded, some staggered into policemen who hammered them with hails of nightsticks. The flailing lawmen were gender-neutral, bouncing nightsticks off the skulls of males and females with impartiality: "Thump! Thump! Thump!"

A contingency of officers surged forward, while smaller groups moved in from the flanks, blocking protesters on either side. Intersecting streets were impassable, obstructed by police cruisers and vans. There remained only three means of escape. One: bore through buildings, which was impossible. Two: scale them—also impossible. The third: the only achievable one was to confront the line of riot policemen and somehow make it to the opposite side of the boulevard and to safety.

"Bonnie, let's face it; we don't stand a snowball's chance in hell of getting out of this mess alive, if we don't make it to the other side of the street and fast."

"I agree with you, but the question is how are we gonna do it?" Fright was obvious in her voice. Evidently she'd finally seen the seriousness of the situation, for her enthusiasm at witnessing something exciting had morphed into fear.

Stretching a city block, a line of French riot police stood poised between Bonnie, me, and the opposite sidewalk of Boulevard Saint Michel. Troopers were swinging truncheons so rapidly they blurred. Like a tide, the lawmen waded into screaming and scurrying student demonstrators. Batons ricocheted off skulls, others landed squarely on them, thudding like lead pipes pounding water-soaked two-by-fours. The lawmen seemed obsessed with cracking skulls and flattening bodies. I noticed that some policemen smiled as they clobbered, apparently delighting in the orgy of brutality.

Seeing the flailing batons, I knew that nothing short of a miracle could get Bonnie and me to the other side of the street safely.

"Paul, are you seriously suggesting we walk into that buzz saw of baton-swinging French cops?" Bonnie's voice rose with apprehension.

"Right. Unless you have a *better* idea." I peered up and down the street, frantically searching for an alternative.

"I think I have a better one. Why don't we...why don't we...ah." She looked around, wide-eyed with fear. Her shoulders slumped. "On second thought, that wouldn't work. The entire area is crammed with protesters and police as far as the eye can see. I thought maybe we could go further down the street and go around this mess, but the crowd's too thick to walk through. Every one's acting crazy. So, I suppose we'll have to do it your way—face the nightsticks."

"It's our *only* option. Granted, it's a gamble, like it or not. What choice do we have?"

Bonnie and I moved toward the officers who continued to pound, flatten, and stride over fallen bodies. I imagined that her heart was pounding in triple-time, the same as mine.

Clenching my hand, she cried, "Paul, what are we getting ourselves into?"

"I wish I knew, but we've got no alternative. Stay close to me."

Our chances of reaching the opposing sidewalk were as murky as clouds of tear gas now hovering above Boulevard Saint Michel. What happened next made those chances even murkier. About 5'2", the protester beside me lowered his shoulders and, legs churning, charged bull-like toward the police line. His shoulder and an officer's shield collided with a loud, clunking noise, stopping the would-be assaulter as if he had slammed into the Great Wall of China. A trooper, his weight compacted into each blow, repeatedly pounded the demonstrator. Blood spurted. Other officers joined the spectacle of violence.

Bonnie and I continued walking. "Paul, when we get to the line of cops, what'll we do?"

"There's only one thing we can do: play it by ear. But remember one thing, Bonnie."

"What?" I could tell she was frightened near tears.

"We still have a trump card. The fact that we're Americans. French higher-ups don't want to rock the diplomatic boat, and certainly not over a couple of Americans trying to cross a street in the Latin Quarter. It wouldn't be worth the hassle. Anyway, you got your passport with you?"

"Sure. As always."

"You'll need it. Me too. Are you ready?" I put my arm around her and drew her to my side, hell-bent on protecting her with my body as best as I could. We inched toward the melee of officers and students. When we were within a yard of the line of officers and standing face to face with two officers, both stopped and zeroed their fierce attentions on us. We stopped, too.

The lawman fronting Bonnie was in his early twenties, about the same age as most of the protestors. His partner was older, graying, probably in his late fifties. The younger policeman slowly and methodically raised his nightstick, aligning it with the crown of Bonnie's skull.

"No-o-o!" I blurted. "No! She's American! American!" Neither lawman seemed impressed. "*American*," I repeated. Nearing its apex, the cop's nightstick slowed, then started its descent. I lunged, clamping his arm in a vise-like grip. "American, *damn* it. American!"

"Stop!" Bonnie screamed, joining the tussle.

I faced the older officer and drew myself up to my full height, hoping that alone would be an intimidation factor. Standing tall and wearing my stern teacher's expression, I asked, "Do you want your retirement benefits? Harm us, and the American ambassador will see that you won't get a single centime."

"Bertrand!" the older man bellowed.

"Yes, sir."

"Enough!" Bertrand lowered his arm.

"You're Americans, you say?" the senior cop asked.

I nodded, thanking God that I'd been able to break through the officer's mental barrier of official wrath. "Yes."

"If American, then you won't object if I examine your papers?"

"No problem."

Bonnie and I whipped out our passports and handed them over. The senior officer studied each, looking first at the attached photographs, then at us, repeating the sequence several times. Finally, he flipped the documents shut and returned them. "I want you two to listen and listen carefully. Leave this street, leave it immediately. Do you have any questions?"

We both shook our heads. "So what are you waiting for?" The older officer bellowed. "Go! Now! And I do mean...*now!*"

Bonnie and I didn't tarry. Instead of walking to Boulevard Saint Germain, our usual route, we headed west on Rue Des Ecoles. A block later, we could still hear canisters clanking over cobblestones and hissing gas, punctuated by the shatter of glass and female screams.

When we reached Twenty-One Rue Galande, we turned and looked in the direction of Boulevard Saint Michel. A ribbon of grayness hazed the horizon, amid intermittent burst of yellow and ruby as flames from torched vehicles flared, punctuated by the booming explosions of gas tanks. The sky was a canopy of colors, beneath which, I later learned, lay shards of glass, scattered cobblestones, charred autos, pools of blood, and the lifeless bodies of three Sorbonne coeds.

The next morning Bonnie and I walked over to Gilbert's again, hoping this time to get our needed items without further incident. Neither one of us was prepared for the sights we saw or the whiffs of tear gas that still lingered at the foot of Boulevard Saint Michel.

We held hands in comfort as we viewed the vestiges, the residue of the student riot. Spent canisters dotted the sidewalk. Near Gilbert's, a scarlet-stained jacket draped the curb; beside it, a tennis shoe was also splattered with dried blood. About a yard from the sneaker lay a pair of wire-rimmed spectacles, lenses cracked and frames twisted. The type popular with Sorbonne students, a leather briefcase rested a few paces beyond, and next to that, several crumpled sheets of notebook paper soaked in dried blood.

The vendor's table on which François stood the previous day was upended. Where two of its legs once were, only splinters remained. On either side of the street there sat, like tombstones, the charred carcasses of several Renaults and a Citroen, their quarter panels crushed and windshields shattered. Cobblestones lay everywhere; once they paved the street, a remnant of an earlier time in history. Yesterday, they'd become impromptu weapons that now littered the streets, sidewalks, and the interiors of buildings where they'd been hurled through windows.

The damage seemed too much to take in. I must have repeated myself a dozen times, saying, "Bonnie, I just can't believe it. Look at all this destruction. I just *can't* believe it!" My mind couldn't seem to wrap itself around the sights my eyes observed.

After making our purchases, we strolled toward *Pont Michel*. Along the way we stopped at a vendor's stand, and she bought a bag of roasted peanuts. Munching and chatting, we walked to the middle of the bridge and, leaning over its railing, watched barges and tourist boats glide by.

I tossed a couple peanuts into the water. "It's kind of funny once you think about it, isn't it?"

She turned to me. "What's that?"

"I mean, what happened to us yesterday was funny, as in…odd."

"How so? I didn't think it was so funny, if you want my opinion." She looked off into the distance, her eyes squinting into the sunlight reflecting off the Seine. "I thought for a minute that we were going to be bludgeoned to death by the authorities."

"Well, while we were nose to nose with those two truncheon-swinging cops—*and very near death*—I wasn't half as frightened as I thought I'd be in a situation like that. But after lying awake most of last night, thinking about how close we'd come to dying, I got scared as hell, for it dawned on me that death was but the mere swing of a cop's nightstick away."

Bonnie put her hand on my arm, her voice gentle, yet sad. "I know. But being in the presence of death is something you get used to. Kind of like an eccentric friend."

"What do you mean?" I looked at her and saw an incredible sadness in her eyes.

"Nothing," she murmured, tossing a couple of peanut shells into the Seine. "Nothing. That was just one of the many flippant remarks I sometimes make. I'm afraid that after my mother died, I became rather dismissive about the subject. It used to upset my father terribly, but we were each mourning Momma in our own way."

I brushed a strand of hair away from her cheek. "How old were you when your mother died?"

"Almost sixteen. She went so quickly once we learned her diagnosis—pancreatic cancer. Mere months, really. How can you say good-bye to your momma in two months? I was so angry over losing her. She filled our house with love and then, pouf, she was gone. I'm afraid I became an angry, sullen, dark teenager for a while. Poor Daddy. He was lost. I was lost." She exhaled a long sigh. "And Momma was lost to us."

"I'm sorry you went through that pain—losing your mother." She looked away, blinking rapidly as if to fight off the tears. I rubbed her back for a minute, and then whispered, "Are you ready to go?"

Bonnie briefly laid her head on my chest and sighed. "Give me a second, please?" I wrapped my arms around her, enjoying once more the faint smell of roses that she wore. We stood there in an embrace for several minutes For some reason I sensed that she was grappling with more than the death of her mother. Was it Betty Jean's untimely death, I wondered, or something else. I felt her give a shaky long sigh. She pulled out of my arms. "Now I'm ready."

"Good. Tell me, are you OK?" She nodded, although she avoided eye contact with me. "I only ask, because a few minutes ago you seemed…oh, I don't know, distant, as if groping through the fog of a distasteful thought."

"That was nothing, *mon ami*. Nothing at all." She still wouldn't look at me. "Sometimes I allow things to get to me." She sighed. "I guess we all do that, huh? Sometimes the consequences of things we do or things we experience cover us with a kind of melancholy, like an avalanche of desperation. Eventually we're able to dig our way out from under, but for a while it becomes all-consuming."

"What are you talking about? Tell me. Your load might be lighter if you'd share." I reached out and tucked a curl behind her ear. "You know I'd do *anything* to help you."

She swiped at a falling tear. "I know," she whispered.

I put my arm around her, drew her close. "Talk to me, sunshine." I didn't like that she kept so many secrets from me. We were friends who could talk about anything, share anything, including pain. Or were we? My mind was being plagued with doubts about her. And I didn't like it.

"Just believe in me, please." Her eyes were still focused on some far-away object. She'd shut herself off form me, that much was clear.

I wanted to believe in her. Oh, how I wanted to. I glanced at my watch. "It's getting late." I took her hand, and, silent, we walked on.

Chapter 15

At around three the following afternoon I sat in my studio proofreading what I'd written that morning. I was enjoying gusts of cool fall air as it flowed into my studio through the open window, relishing its crispness before it swept out through my open studio door.

I heard the front door to the apartment building suddenly burst open. Someone gushed into the foyer, slamming the door shut. Bounding several steps with every stride, the person raced to the fourth floor, stopped, and rapped on a door. No answer. Again, he knocked and evidently got the same response.

Seconds later, someone descended a flight of stairs and strode down the hall, tapping on my door frame. To my surprise, there stood Roger. "Of all people!" I beamed. "Come in. Come in."

"How've you been, Paul?" He was out of breath.

I slipped my pencil behind my ear and leaned back in my chair, locking my hands behind my head. "I'm great. And you?"

"Still hangin' in there."

"Long time no see. Well, don't just stand there. Come in, grab a seat, make yourself at home."

After hesitating, he entered and sat at the table across from me. "I should apologize; I didn't mean to barge in like this."

"Believe me, you're not. Here you're welcome anytime. Anytime."

He smiled, visibly relaxing. "Thanks. I'm looking for Bonnie. Have you seen her?"

"Not today."

"Man, I'm confused. A couple of days ago I told her I'd drop by this evening, and she promised she'd be home. I come and what do I find? No Bonnie."

"Maybe she stepped around the corner to the grocery; if so, she'll be back shortly."

"But not keeping her word is just not like her, not like her at all." His face was filled with concern.

"You're right, but as I said, there's probably some simple explanation. Unless she's gone on one of her disappearing jaunts again. Do you know where she goes when she disappears?"

"No. I wish did. I worry about her and I gather you do, too."

"More than worry, Roger. *More* than that."

"Anyway, like I said, man, I didn't mean to barge in on you."

"You don't have to apologize, but as long as you're here why don't you visit for a while?" I slid my composition book aside, promising myself I'd finish my rewrites later.

"Well, OK, but only for a minute or so, then I think I'll head to Café Deux Maggots and treat myself to a hot rum."

"Café Deux Maggots, you say?" I smiled. "That sounds good. Mind if I join you?"

"Hey, man, I can dig it. Let's split now, if you wanna."

Of all the cafés in the City of Light, most Parisians regarded Café Deux Maggots as the trendiest; "the in crowd" loved going there to see and be seen (emphasis on the latter). Once a gathering place for intellectuals like Jean-Paul Sartre and Simone de Beauvoir, to say nothing of writers like Hemingway and artists such as Picasso, the popular watering hole had recently become a magnet for social climbers and tourists. It was located on Boulevard Saint Germain in the sixth *arrondissement*. To reach it from Twenty-One Rue Galande you had to walk six or seven blocks east on Saint Germain, beyond where it and Saint Michel traversed.

As we walked down Saint Germain, I told Roger about the experience Bonnie and I had during the student riot a couple days earlier. Nearing the intersection with Boulevard Saint Michel, Roger and I were shocked, for as far as we could see, Saint Michel swarmed with construction workers. These workers were all busy digging up cobblestones, not torn up during the student riot, and pouring asphalt. Dump trucks, bulldozers, and earthmovers were everywhere. The putt-putt of engines and tattooing of jackhammers rattled the air.

"I'll be damned," Roger said. "Will you look at that? After the student riot, city fathers didn't waste any time paving over the cobblestones, did they?"

"None." I remarked, surprised that any government decision could be made and acted upon so swiftly.

"One thing is certainly clear now," Roger said in disgust. "From now on if protesters want to pelt cops with cobblestones, they'll have to bring their own weapons. Maybe at the next demonstration, Molotov cocktails will be the weapons of choice."

"If so, I wonder how cops will stop the protesters from acquiring them?"

"Simple. Outlaw the sale of wine in Paris. No wine. No wine bottles. Thus, no Molotov cocktails." Roger's hand moved in expression as he talked.

I laughed. "Outlaw the sale of wine in Paris? That'll happen when used car salesmen are nominated for sainthood."

A wooden barricade stretched the width of Boulevard Saint Germain, blocking pedestrians from crossing Saint Michel.

"Well, it looks as if we won't be going to Deux Maggots after all," I remarked.

"You're right. So where do you suggest we go?"

"I know a place we passed a few blocks ago. Want to give it a try?"

Roger turned to head back the way we came. "Sure. Why not?"

Minutes later, we sat on the terrace of Café Le Balkan. Usually the place was packed, with most patrons congregating at the bar where drinks were cheaper. The café sold more than its share of alcohol, though spirits weren't its sole source of revenue. In America, cigarettes were retailed practically everywhere: drugstores, supermarkets, vending machines, etc. Not so in Paris. There only a select number of government-licensed outlets traded in tobacco products. Le Balkan was one, a fact that accounted for a sizeable portion of its business.

In addition to cigarettes and pipe tobacco, you could buy telephone tokens, *jetons*, there. French pay phones at that time didn't accept coins. So, if you wanted to make a call from a public phone— and lucky enough to find one that worked, which was rare—you first had to purchase *jetons* from an authorized dealer such as Le Balkan. Thus, alcohol, tobacco products, and telephone tokens were the main customer-magnets at this café.

Roger and I had been sitting on the terrace for about fifteen minutes when I said, "There's something that has been bothering me. But I'm not sure I should bring it up."

"Why not, man? We are *friends*, and friends are free to discuss anything."

I sipped my hot buttered rum. "Doubting our friendship wasn't why I hesitate."

"So why do you?"

"Well, as crazy as it sounds, it's because I think I already know the answer to the question I had in mind; at least, I know what a friend told me she thought the answer was. It's just that I'm not sure she's right."

"Whatever is on your mind, man, feel free to let it out."

"OK, I will, but understand, I don't mean to pry into your business."

"For you, nothing is off limits."

"I'm flattered. Anyway, at Betty Jean's party you said you were going back to your hometown, Flatwater, Mississippi. Did you ever go?"

A cloud of pain floated across his eyes. "I'll answer that, but it may take a while because it's a long story."

"My ears are open for business."

He smiled faintly and glanced away. Then he looked at me and began talking. "A few days ago I packed my bags, stuffed in everything I figured I'd need for at least a week's stay. I told my concierge I was going stateside and asked if she'd pick up my mail for me. She said she'd be happy to. I then walked to the corner café and shared news of my departure with Jean-Claude, a waiter friend of mine. Hearing that I was finally returning home made him as happy as I was, for he knew I'd talked about making the trip for some time; my 'sentimental journey,' he called it.

"Around three that afternoon I hopped a commuter bus to De Gaulle Airport. My flight, Flight Twelve-twenty, didn't depart until eight that night, but I left early. I wanted to allow myself *more* than ample time to get to the airport, in case something unforeseen happened en route, like getting snarled in one of the city's infamous traffic jams." He paused and exhaled a deep breath.

"Wise move." I sipped on my drink, waiting for him to continue.

Roger shrugged, rubbed a hand across the back of his neck. "On the way to the airport, I was edgy. You'd have thought I'd overdosed on speed. Perspiration poured from me as if my skin was a sieve. Nervously I fingered my ticket. Images of family members flashed before me, as did visions of people I'd known in childhood; the resolution of the faces racing in my thoughts was sharp as Kodak prints. I saw Mrs. Ledbetter, the old woman down the street from my home who helped raise me, and Widow Stokes who ran the corner grocery, and Reverend Thornhill, the preacher who baptized me. I saw them all, as clearly as if they were sitting beside me.

"Finally, I arrived at the airport. The trip there seemed to last days, not the forty minutes it actually took. When the driver parked the bus, I grabbed my bags and hurried to Air France's boarding area, sat, and began what seemed an endless wait."

"So," I smiled, "let me be the first to congratulate you, Roger; you did return to Flatwater after all. I'm proud of you. It seems my source of information was wrong. She said you would never go back."

"Man, believe me, setting foot on that plane and on Flatwater soil was the most important event of my life. For months, I'd dreamed of going home. I'd lie awake nights imagining the trip. No one can know what the journey meant to me." Roger paused. After momentarily staring into space, he continued, "Soon, over the PA system, an Air France employee announced boarding instructions. 'Those scheduled for Flight Twelve-twenty bound for Atlanta, Georgia, report to Gate F-twelve; boarding for Flight Twelve-twenty now at Gate F-twelve.'

"Paul, I'll bet you can't guess what I did next?"

"Sure, I can. You boarded the plane. What else?"

"You'd think I would have, but I didn't. Instead, I…" He ran a hand across the back of his neck again.

"Yeah, go on." I leaned toward him.

He shook his head slowly. "Man, I just *sat*."

"You, what?"

"As if bolted to the seat, I just sat. A minute passed. Then two, then three and four. Finally, I heard the final announcement: 'Passengers boarding Flight Twelve-twenty please report to Gate F-twelve. Last call. Last call.' A half hour later, I was still sitting. Finally, I picked up my bags and headed for the bus parking lot. Shortly afterwards, I boarded the commuter bus and returned to Paris." He shook his head slowly again, as if unable to believe his own actions. "Paul?"

"Yeah?"

He lifted his dark soulful eyes to meet mine. "Have you ever heard of anybody doing a thing like that?"

"To be honest, no. So, as it turned out, Bonnie was right after all. She said that in spite of the promise you made at Betty Jean's party, she felt that you wouldn't go back to Flatwater. She said she *knew* you wouldn't."

He sat back, crossing his arms over his chest. "So she said that, huh? Did she tell you why she thought I wouldn't go home again?"

"Yes. She said because you…*can't*. But, of course, that was just her opinion. What about you? What do you think is the reason you didn't board that plane?"

"That's a question I've asked myself countless times and I always come up with the same answer: I don't know." He sighed and looked at me with a forlorn expression. "I just don't know. Maybe one day the answer will come."

"For your sake, I hope it does."

Minutes later, it began raining, a slow, constant drizzle that cascaded in waves down the glass enclosure surrounding the café terrace. Water carpeted the street, glazing its surface like sheets of ebony glass.On the sidewalk, little pools formed that mirrored globs of illumination from street lamps. Soon the rain stopped. Then, I thought, would be a good time to return to my studio. Familiar with Parisian weather patterns, I was certain another shower would soon begin, for expanses of leaden clouds now blanketed the early evening sky.

"Look, I think I'm going to leave now. I want to stop at the newsstand and buy a copy of the *Manchester Guardian*, go home, and read myself to sleep." Roger didn't respond. "Did you hear me?"

Roger was staring off into the wet darkness of the night. "Yeah, I heard. Sorry, man, my thoughts were elsewhere."

"Anyway, like I said, I'm going to leave now."

"Why so soon, man?"

"Well, I have a feeling you might need a little time to yourself."

"You're right. I do. Anyway, it's been cool seeing you." He focused sad eyes onto mine. "When you see Bonnie be sure to tell her I dropped by. And I hope she's OK. If anything were to happen to her I'm not sure what I'd do."

"I know how you feel, but try not to worry. She'll be fine, Roger, just fine."

I walked to the kiosk and bought a copy of the *Manchester Guardian*. When I returned to Twenty-One Rue Galande, I mounted the stairs to Bonnie's studio and knocked. No surprise, she wasn't home. Seconds later, I entered my studio, scanned the newspaper, undressed, showered, and then crawled into bed. Though I tried to sleep, I couldn't. Instead of drifting off as I usually did, I lay peering into darkness and there I saw an image of Roger sitting on the terrace of Café Balkan, sitting and gazing into the velvet Parisian night, gazing and dreaming of home.

As contradictory as it may seem, Roger was home, but he was not. He was where he wanted to be. He wanted to be where he was not. He was a Mississippi Delta born, Afro-American, but his heart was fabricated on the sidewalks and in the cafés of Paris.

He was the offspring of two parents.

Haunted.

Alone.

Lost.

Chapter 16

Two days later I stepped up to Bonnie's studio, and, no surprise to me, she wasn't home. She really *was* becoming the Phantom Lady of Paris, I thought. On her door, someone had taped a note. "Dropped by," it read. "Need to see you, but you weren't in. I'll try another time. Love, Abdul."

The following day Abdul placed another note on Bonnie's door. "Bon', do you *ever* stay home? A little help, please. Leave a note telling when you'll be in. Meanwhile, I hope to see you soon. Love, Abdul."

The memos were still on her door the following night. I left them there. I didn't have the right, I reasoned, to remove them. When Bonnie finally returned—and I assumed she would, eventually—I was certain she'd want to see Abdul's memos exactly where he left them; that way she'd know he'd repeatedly tried to contact her.

I came home a couple of evenings later, and, instead of going to my studio, I mounted the stairs to Bonnie's. The notes Abdul left were still in place. Obviously Bonnie hadn't returned. When I reached my apartment, I found a memorandum on my door. I immediately recognized the bold, slanting handwriting: Abdul's. "Paul," the note read, "I need to talk to you about something urgent. Could we meet? Would Café Le Balkan be OK with you? Say, at around nine tonight? Hope you can make it. I really need your help. *Votre ami*, Abdul."

So, he wanted to see me about, what he called, "an urgent matter." I wondered what "the urgent matter" could be. Maybe he needed a loan, was considering a change of jobs or had decided to return to Algeria. Or planned to do what, as he once told me, his "heart longed to do": enter professional tennis tournaments and dedicate his energies full time to his true passion, playing tennis for a living, not teaching it.

I reasoned that what was bothering him was probably the same thing he wanted to talk to Bonnie about, but unable to locate her and, weighted by the "urgent" matter, he turned to me. Perhaps he only needed someone to talk to, and I, he believed, was accessible. And why shouldn't he turn to me. From our first meeting, I saw him as a friend, and he seemed to view me as the same.

But what *thing*, I wondered, had become so imperative and pressing to Abdul? It must have been something quite significant, for he didn't seem to be the type who became disconcerted over trivialities. At the same time, there existed the possibility he was taking a matter that I would have considered miniscule—when viewed in a larger context—and given it more importance than it deserved. And I, not emotionally involved, could assist in putting it in its proper perspective.

On the other hand, there was the possibility all he needed was a sympathetic ear or a shoulder to lean on, or both. As I stood at my door rereading his note, a hundred "maybes" sprinted through my thoughts, speeded along by the winds of my writer's imagination. There, of course, was only one way to discover the truth—and that was, to meet Abdul at Café Le Balkan at nine that night.

I arrived a couple of minutes past nine. Abdul was sitting inside at a table almost at the extreme rear of the café. Surprisingly, he was not on the terrace where I expected him to be and where most customers usually sat.

I walked over to his table, smiling as I neared it. "It's a good thing I looked inside the café, Abdul. Not seeing you on the terrace, I thought for a moment, that you hadn't come and I was about to sit outside and wait. If I had, I might have missed you."

He stood and shook my hand. "I'm glad you didn't. Sit, please, *mon ami.*"

"Tell me, why are you sitting inside on such a pleasant evening?"

"Well, ah, I…I have my reasons. So if you don't mind, let's sit in here?"

"Fine by me. Anyway, inside or out, it's good seeing you, Abdul."

"Same here." A waiter came over and I ordered an espresso. Abdul smiled when he spoke once the waiter left us, "Tell me, how is your writing coming along?"

"OK, I think."

"Why do you say, you . . . *'think'*?"

"Well, it's like this. If you write every day as I do—for six, seven, or eight hours straight—you become like a doting mother about your work."

His forehead wrinkled in confusion. "How so?"

"A mother is so emotionally attached to her kid that she can never truly see her offspring as he *really* is; only someone else can do that. For that reason, I said I think my writing is going well. But I'm so involved with it that I'd be the last person on this planet who could give a true assessment. So maybe you should ask someone else how my writing is going. Such a person might be able to give a better evaluation than I."

He smiled and nodded. "I see your point."

"But enough about me, Abdul. Enough. Hearing about my dull life and what I write is certain to bore you to tears." The waiter brought my espresso and disappeared. I took a sip, setting the tiny cup back on its saucer. "So, tell me about yourself. How do things go with you? Are you still giving tennis lessons to French students in Neuilly?"

"Yes, still trying to instruct those with more money than talent, and, as usual, I have little success teaching them anything. But I shouldn't complain. The pay is good and the work, steady."

"Has your attitude toward French people changed since we last spoke?"

Again he nodded, only more slowly this time. "Yes, it's changed."

"I take it you've softened your contempt for them, that your outlook is less destructive to your own mental health, because hate can be a destructive thing, Abdul, a malady of the mind."

"Like I said, Paul, my feelings about the French have changed, but probably not the way you think or hope." He sipped from his wineglass. "You see, since we last spoke, my hatred for them has not decreased, but *increased*. Now I despise them with deeper passion. And because of this added hate, I've become concerned, no, more than concerned. I've become fearful."

"Fearful of what?"

"Paul, my rage now haunts me whether I'm asleep or awake. There was a time I wore it as you would a garment, something I could slip into or slip out of at will. But, now..." his voice trailed off.

"Now what?" I didn't try to hide my concern in the tone of my voice.

He shrugged and smiled. "Ah, on second thought, Paul, the matter is nothing. Not really. I shouldn't burden you with it. I'm sorry I brought it up. In fact, it's better that we don't discuss it any more. I regret I mentioned it."

"Was this thing you don't want to talk about the same matter you mentioned in your note to me?" Was he going to talk in riddles again, I wondered.

"Yes." He drank the rest of his wine and motioned for the waiter, signing that he wanted a refill.

I tried to read his expression. "This thing, does it interfere with your daily routine, your daily life?"

"For the most part no, but each day it grows more and more grotesque, assuming the proportions of a monster. Once I controlled it, but as time passes, I…" He shrugged and looked around the café, seeing nothing but his thoughts, I imagined. "Now…now I'm not sure who is in control—the thing or me." The waiter brought a glass of wine for Abdul. He quickly drank it and ordered another.

I was troubled by the rate he was consuming the wine. My friend was in trouble. His demons were gaining the upper hand. "Abdul, this matter you speak of—whatever it is—alarms me. Do you think in time it will pass?"

"I hope, but my fear is that it might overpower and force me to do some…*dreadful* thing."

I quickly glanced at the tables nearby to see if someone was listening. "Like what?"

He stared into his empty wineglass. "Something I'd rather not even think about, let alone mention."

A man approached the café terrace. After stepping over the threshold, he stopped, glanced about, and then focused on Abdul and me. Apparently recognizing the new customer, Abdul watched him as he walked to the bar and leaned against it.

Approximately 5'9", the stranger at the bar wore a blue suit, the kind popular with migrant workers from North Africa. His hair was curly and midnight black; his complexion was like burnished copper.

I continued talking to Abdul, but he, eyes fixed on the new customer, didn't appear to be listening.

"Paul," he said finally, "a friend of mine just stepped into the café. I wonder if you'll excuse me. I need to talk to him."

"Sure. Sure."

Abdul stood. "By the way, *mon ami*, I'd be honored if you'd accept an invitation to come to my place tomorrow night, say around eight. We can share conversation and a bottle of wine."

"Sounds great to me. I'll be happy to join you."

"Good. Here's my address." He scribbled on a napkin and then handed it to me.

"So, it's settled; tomorrow evening, around eight. I'll be there." I pocketed the napkin.

He grasped my hand and pumped it several times, then walked to the bar and stood beside his friend. Backs to me, both leaned over the bar, the stranger occasionally glancing at me. His hand now resting on Abdul's shoulder, the man spoke energetically, gesturing with the fervor of a used car salesman closing a deal.

To my surprise, Abdul, who was usually quite talkative, said nothing. Head slanted and brow furrowed, he listened intently, as if considering some tempting proposal his friend was making.

Chapter 17

I walked to Abdul's apartment the following night. It was in a building close to where Saint Germain intersected Montparnassse and just up from a nightclub featuring live Latin American music. A sign in the club's window announced that it opened daily at six P.M. and closed at three in the morning. Given the thump of bongos and the thunder of Congas in Latino music, I wondered how Abdul was able to sleep.

He lived in a rooming house. I later learned that about twenty other tenants, all common laborers from Algeria and other North African countries shared the building, sleeping two and three to a room. Abdul was lucky. He had a room to himself. It was neat, though sparsely furnished with a narrow bed, a small dining table with two mismatched chairs, and a chest of drawers with the bottom drawer missing. Pictures of whom I assumed were his family and his girlfriend sat on top of the chest of drawers. His lone window faced a brick wall.

"Thanks for inviting me to your place," I said as we sat at the little table on which he placed a bottle of red wine and a couple of mismatched glasses.

"I'm glad you've come. My room is far from luxurious, as you can see, but I feel it's adequate for my needs. And believe me, I know how lucky I am to have a place like this. Today it's difficult to find a decent apartment in Paris at a reasonable price. Rent is sinfully high. Landlords charge whatever outrageous figure pops into their heads, and they are certain they can get it."

"From what I hear, they usually do. The real problem is there are so few new apartment buildings being built in Paris today, making the city a landlord's Paradise."

"That's for sure. Would you like to hear how much I pay for this place?"

"I already know. Too much and rising."

His face was glum. "Exactly. Being Algerian, I have a very hard time renting a place at any price. Landlords take one look at my face and immediately jack up the price, or claim they have no vacancies. Such people are without conscience." He opened the wine and poured.

"You know, Abdul," I said after taking a couple of sips, "I've been doing a lot of thinking about something you said the last time we talked." At his raised eyebrows, I continued. "I've been wondering what accounts for your increased contempt for the French. Remember you told me your hatred of them has grown. Why?"

He shifted in his chair. "Because, not long ago I met some new friends, countrymen of mine. We have become like brothers, and they've removed the mental cataracts I had that prevented me from seeing things I should have seen years earlier. They've educated me."

"I take it that the man you left the café with last night is one of your new friends?"

"Yes, but there are others, and thanks to them I now see the truth. I've discovered what my attitude toward the French should have been all along, and with this new knowledge, I now have a mission in life—a *calling*."

"Would you mind explaining that?"

Before he could, someone tapped on the door, and Abdul's head whipped around. "Excuse me," Abdul said as he walked to the door and opened it wide, then, almost instantly, eased it partly closed. I wasn't able to see who his visitor was, and, to my surprise, Abdul didn't invite him in.

"Here. This is for you, Abdul," the voice in the hall said.

"But you were supposed to deliver it tomorrow." Surprise was evident in Abdul's voice.

"I know, but there's been a change in plans. He wanted me to give it to you tonight."

"But why? I mean, this is a bad time. I have a guest." He motioned toward me.

The man, his face shadowed by a hat pulled low, quickly leaned his head in and gave me a cursory appraisal. "Look, don't talk as if it's my fault. I don't give the orders. I merely carry them out."

"I understand that, and you don't have to apologize. So, OK...OK, I'll take it." The visitor handed something to Abdul. "Tell him he should stick to our plan. Otherwise, what's the purpose in having one?"

"I see your point, and I'll pass on what you said...for all the good it'll do. Anyway, I gotta run. Sleep well, Abdul."

"Sleep well? How the *hell* am I gonna do that?"

"I know what you mean, and you're right; sleeping well for you may be a hard thing to do. Anyway, good night, Abdul."

"'Night." My host eased the door shut and gingerly cradled a package wrapped in brown paper and bound with frayed twine that measured about a foot square and an inch or so in height. "Paul, you'll have to forgive the interruption."

"No problem."

"The fellow I just spoke to is one of the new friends I was telling you about. He wants me to store a package. It's for a neighbor who lives on the next floor. He doesn't want the neighbor to receive it until tomorrow."

"What is it, a birthday present?"

"Well, sort of." Abdul walked to the bed and slowly slid the parcel under it. When his hands reappeared, they trembled.

"Abdul? Are you...are you OK?"

"Of course. Why'd you ask?" He straightened and ran a hand over his head.

"Your hands, they're quivering."

He chuckled. "The wine explains that, Paul. You see, ordinarily I avoid red wine. I bought this bottle because I thought you'd like it. Most people prefer red wine. There's some ingredient in red wine, a doctor once told me, which does odd things to my nervous system. So, it's the wine that makes my hands tremble."

He returned to the table and sat.

"Abdul, I think I've figured out what that package is all about. I'll bet you and your buddies are planning a surprise birthday party for the guy who's getting it. Right?"

He lifted his glass, his hand still trembling, and emptied it. "Paul?"

"Yeah?"

"Mind if we talk about something else?" Abdul's eyes were expressive. Beads of sweat had popped out above his mouth. He pulled out a handkerchief and blotted them.

"Sure, if you'd prefer."

For the next hour, Abdul and I chatted about the Australian Open. I didn't mention the package again. After all, I was his guest. And it's not proper etiquette for a guest to raise a subject that makes his host uncomfortable, and it was obvious that any mention of that package made Abdul *very* uncomfortable.

A couple of days later, I felt ill when I woke up. My nose was clogged, and my chest ached with weighty congestion. It was as if my lungs had drowned. From the small of my back to my shoulder, there was a stinging throb. Maybe I'd caught a cold or the flu; at the time, both were raging in Paris. But whatever it was, one thing was certain, I didn't feel up to writing that day, so I decided I'd go to some quiet place where I could relax, people-watch, and read.

I walked to a small self-service cafeteria on Boulevard Saint Michel and had breakfast: yogurt, fruit, and an espresso. After eating, I stopped at a newsstand and bought a copy of the *Manchester Guardian*, boarded the metro at the Boulevard Saint Michel station, and rode to the De La Concorde stop. From there I trudged down Avenue Des Champs-Elysees to Jardin Des Tuleries, a sprawling park where I sometimes went to unwind. "Tuleries," as Parisians called the park, was just up from the Louvre Museum, the famous castle-like structure housing one of the world's greatest troves of classical art. The park was an oasis of tranquility, complete with chestnut trees and gravel paths for promenades.

Several vendors' stands dotted the recreational area, each offering arrays of sugary enticements, as well as little busts of Napoleon and Charles de Gaulle. Both these souvenirs, at the time, were very popular with tourists.

In the park was a small corral of Shetland ponies. Toddlers loved riding them. Uniformed attendants hoisted them into the saddles and led the animals around a circular course.

There was a calliope that sat not far from a carousel. The sound of the calliope punctuated the morning air like brass exclamation marks. "Um...paw...paw..." Nearby, young men and women played volleyball or badminton, and for those with no interest in athletics and didn't wish to be bothered, which included me, portable chairs were available. If you saw an attractive *mademoiselle* and wished to get closer to her, you—and your chair—could. On the other hand, she—with her chair—was free to move away or closer, depending on her desire.

After a visitor sat in one of the park chairs for about ten minutes, an attendant, most of whom were middle-aged women wearing blue uniforms, would approach. Her request, a polite ultimatum, never varied. "*Monsieur, s'il vous plait,*" she'd smile, extending her hand, indicating that all must pay tribute to enjoy nature, at least to enjoy it in that park while seated.

At around ten, I sat in one of the chairs and, as if scripted, within minutes an attendant sauntered over and reminded me that I was obligated to surrender unto Caesar his usual cut. So advised, I rendered to the emperor—his Parisian representative—the requested amount of what American gangsters called "shake down money." I then sloughed in my chair, snuggled into my heavy sweater, unfolded the newspaper, and began scanning it.

That day's *Manchester Guardian* bulged with news. At London's Tate Gallery, an exhibition of Picasso sculptures opened. Gerry

Dorsey, better known as Engelbert Humperdinck, topped the pop charts in England, while Tom Jones gained popularity in both America and the United Kingdom. A columnist hinted that dissension threatened to break up the Beatles. Police arrested several members of the Rolling Stones on drug possession charges, again, but the scandal, said the article, didn't appear to tarnish their popularity.

A London newspaper, *Sunday Citizen*, folded due to sagging circulation numbers. Meanwhile, the city's countless other tabloids continued to flourish, cranking out stories the American *National Inquirer* would have refused to print—"too trashy"—but not so London tabloids.

A couple of hours later I decided it was time to return to my studio. I'd hoped the fresh air would open my nasal passages and help me feel better. Unfortunately, all it did was make me sleepy, or perhaps my body was telling me it required extra sleep. In either case, I decided I had an urgent date with my bed, one that would start as soon as I collapsed onto it.

As I folded the newspaper, a tiny article on the back page caught my eye. "Bombers Strike Paris Café," read its headline. Someone, the piece stated, detonated a bomb in the lavatory of a café on the Right Bank, Café France. The blast killed two and injured five, three seriously, one not expected to live. The proprietor of the café reported that seconds before the explosion, two men, to use his words, "both looking as if they might be from Algeria or Tunisia," fled the scene. One wore a blue suit, the other, an athletic suit and a type of shoe popular with tennis players.

I finished reading the article, stood, yawned, and stretched. So, a bomb exploded in a café in an arrondissement far from where I lived. Of what concern was that to me? None. Sighing, I headed for the Concorde Metro station, not giving the news report much thought. Why should I? The incident cited was something I knew nothing about and, as far as I could determine, it had no connection to me.

Later, I'd discover that I was wrong. How wrong? In due time, I'd be able to answer that question, but not in time to prevent more bombings, more bloodshed…and more deaths.

Chapter 18

Two days later, I felt better, eager to be back in my comfortable routine. After six hours of writing, I left Café Le Balkan, where I usually wrote, and then strolled down Boulevard Saint Germain on my way to Twenty-One Rue Galande. Glancing over my shoulder, I noticed two men walking a stride or so behind me, one to my diagonal left, the other to my diagonal right. At the time, I thought nothing of it, that is, until I slowed and they did the same—at almost the identical instant. I walked faster, so did they. Soon they closed the gap and walked beside me, their shoulders pressing against mine.

The one on my right said, "*Monsieur*, if you don't mind, we'd like a moment or so of your time."

"What? Who...who are you?" I demanded.

"Our chat shouldn't take long, that is, if we get your cooperation, which I am sure we will."

"Are you two guys con men? Scammers? Or what?"

The man to my right was slender, angular, over 6', the other, shorter, around 5'9". Both dressed conservatively, their suits mirroring their expressions, somber and businesslike.

"We, con men? No, *Monsieur*," the taller man smirked. "Our concern is neither frivolous nor devious, but *serious* governmental business. So, if you would be so kind," he said, nodding toward the café on the corner that we were approaching.

"Perhaps we can find a booth inside where we can sit and talk." Their shoulders nudging mine, they directed me into the café. The taller man gestured toward a booth in the rear and there we sat. Both produced identification cards and badges, indicating they were police investigators. The taller man was Detective Louis Askivour, his partner, Detective Robert Russo.

"*Monsieur*, we have a few questions," Detective Askivour said. "And to assist your memory, this should help." From his coat pocket, he produced a brown envelope containing a little stack of photos.

"Shouldn't we show him the others first?" Detective Russo wanted to know.

"In time he'll see them. Just relax. Relax. OK?"

"Sure." A waiter appeared and Detective Russo waved him away.

Detective Askivour looked at the photographs, then at me. "*Monsieur*, shall we examine these." He angled the top snapshot so he and I could view it. "We have here a picture of you and *Mademoiselle* Bonnie Silver entering Gilbert's, the stationery and bookstore. I'm sure you recall the occasion. That," he said, pointing, "is you, the one with his hand on the door handle, right?"

"Yes. And yes, the woman with me is Bonnie Silver."

He slid the top photo aside, revealing the next. "And in this picture we see you and *Mademoiselle* Silver exiting Gilbert's. The two of you stand near the intersection, beside a young man waving a *Soviet* flag."

"Who took these pictures?" I asked.

"Irrelevant," he snapped. "The point is, do you admit that you are the person pictured participating in this anti-government uprising?"

"Anti-government uprising? Don't you mean pro-education protest? But either way, yes, that's me, but I wasn't participating. I was merely observing what was happening around me."

He flipped to the next print. "And this one shows you smiling and seemingly applauding as you gaze at the terrorist and communist agitator François Leguy. François Leguy, that's his legal name, though, of course, he's best known here in France as 'François the Incendiary.' Is that *not* you?"

"It is, but I don't think you understand. You see, I was *herded* into that crowd, not because I wanted to be there, but because I happened to be in the *wrong* place at the *wrong* time. I'm not a follower of François; in fact, I had never even heard of the guy until the day these photos were snapped."

Detective Askivour stared at me with penetrating eyes. "But the point remains, you *were* there, as evidence clearly indicates." His finger tapped on the photo as if to prove his point.

"Yes, but quite by accident. What the pictures don't show is how I got there, or if I wanted to be there. But you're right, if you only go by the photos, I was there. And by the way, why did you refer to François as a communist terrorist?"

Detective Askivour chuckled. "Because of comprehensive police investigative work, that's why. Our quest has produced an exhaustive dossier on François. The information it contains may surprise you. But on the other hand, perhaps you are already familiar with his biography. In any case, we know François for what he truly is."

"And what's that? An idealist who dreams of building a Utopia?"

"Idealist?" Both men chuckled. "For your information," the tall one continued, "communist leaders selected François when he was but a child. At the age of ten, they enrolled him in a special training institute for precocious youths. As a teenager, he was, to use your wording, 'idealistic,' and you might have added, ruthless, cruel, and pathological."

"Pathological? Cruel?" I repeated leaning forward in my seat. What evidence did these men have? What kind of man was François the Incendiary? I knew basically nothing about him, only what Bonnie had told me.

"Yes. For years, cadres schooled him in techniques for inciting civil disorder and promoting urban revolution. Tactics in guerrilla warfare constituted the bulk of his curriculum. He learned the art of pandering to the grievances of the masses, with the ultimate objective being the overthrow of democratically elected governments.

"*Monsieur*, I trust you understand that addressing the masses' legitimate grievances is *not* François' goal, though he professes it is. His real objective, as well as that of his fellow conspirators, is to achieve political domination, followed by the establishment of what his Bolshevik comrades euphemistically call 'The New World Order.' New World Order indeed!" He slapped the pile of photos onto the table in a demonstration of repugnance.

Detective Russo couldn't wait to chime in. "And this New World Order he plots to establish here in France. Our mission, of course, is to see that his plans are thwarted."

Askivour slid the top photo aside, revealing another. "Here you are again," he continued, "with *Mademoiselle* Silver, surrounded by fellow travelers."

"Student protestors," I corrected.

"Fellow travelers," he retorted, and then turned the photo face down, exposing another. "And this snapshot is perhaps the most intriguing. It shows a man dressed in all black about to enter an apartment building. The building should be familiar to you. Do you recognize the door, the filigree above it and the building number," he said, pointing. "Twenty-One, it reads. I think you're familiar with that dwelling."

A chill crept up my spine, clawing at the entrance of my mind for admittance. "Of...of course. It's where I live."

"Precisely." He slipped his hand into his inside coat pocket and produced a brown business envelope. "Here, *Monsieur*, is a picture I bring to your attention." From the envelope, he removed a photo. "This shows François the Incendiary exiting Twenty-One Rue Galande."

"So?" *Please* don't let it be so. My heart did a mean tap dance in my chest.

"Note that there is a young lady accompanying him. Do you recognize her?"

I peered at the photo. My heart sank. "It looks like Bonnie Silver."

"Precisely. Now the question becomes, why is *Mademoiselle* Silver, product of American capitalism and democracy, fraternizing with, of *all* people, François the Incendiary, a died-in-the-wool communist fanatic, sworn to dismantle both capitalism and democracy, a man whose sole mission is to create anarchy and deliver the French Republic into red hands? Why? And why is the couple so cozy? Note how they smile approvingly at each other, like a pair of veteran comrades and fellow travelers?"

"You're rushing to conclusions," I said. My mouth had gone dry. My stomach was clenched. "There could be a hundred perfectly innocent explanations why they're together. Maybe François was looking for a friend he thought lived in the building and didn't know the friend's studio number. Bonnie gave him the number, but the friend wasn't home. After finding he wasn't, François and Bonnie struck up a conversation as they left the building, chatting perhaps about something as innocuous as the weather.

"Or perhaps," I continued, frantically searching for excuses, "François entered Twenty-One Rue Galande in search of someone who didn't live there. He stopped Bonnie and—"

"Interesting scenarios. However, there is one you omitted."

"Which is?" I was afraid to hear what he was about to say. My logical, questioning mind was waging a brutal war with my heart.

"That there is a conspiratorial relationship between *Mademoiselle* Bonnie Silver and François the Incendiary and that the pair is, in fact, plotting sedition."

"What've you guys been drinking today?" I asked, "Jet fuel and antifreeze cocktails? Whatever it is, it must be powerful stuff because the accusations you're tossing around are ridiculous. Bonnie Silver, a terrorist Bolshevik? In collusion to topple the French government? Ridiculous! It's *beyond* ridiculous, in fact."

He looked at me with cold, steely grey eyes. "Is it?"

"Of course." Please let me be right, I thought frantically. Please let me be right.

Across the table, Detective Russo leaned in and stated in a voice filled with excitement. "*Monsieur*, we have in our possession additional evidence my associate has not mentioned."

I skewered him with my eyes. "Which is?"

"I cannot divulge it."

"At any rate," I said, "how do I figure in all of this?"

"We'd like you to answer a few questions. First, let me caution that at the risk of being charged with obstructing justice, it is in your best interest to respond truthfully. Question One: Have you ever seen François in the presence of *Mademoiselle* Silver—in her studio perhaps, chatting in the hall, at some café, at a soiree, at a bus stop, on a Metro platform? Anywhere?

"Question Two: did you hear *Mademoiselle* Silver speak of meeting this individual? If so, where was the rendezvous?" Before I had the time to draw a breath to answer his first two questions, he sped on with his interrogation.

"Question Three: Do you know of any collusion between the two, in *any form*? And finally, have you heard *Mademoiselle* Silver speak of a revolution in France?" He paused. "Before answering, *Monsieur*, I suggest you consider your responses…carefully."

"I have."

"And I must remind you again that there are legal and penal consequences involved here."

"I'll keep those facts in mind." As if I could ever forget it.

"And your responses are?"

"No to all questions." Detective Askivour frowned at my response. "You seem disappointed," I said.

"Not disappointed, but, in truth, your answer is not exactly what we had in mind."

"Tell me what you want to hear, and I'll give it to you. However, it won't be the truth."

"We seek *only* the truth." He extended his hands upward as if to lend credulity to his statement.

"And that's what I've given you." And in addition, I thought, I'd like to give you a punch in the nose for questioning me as if I were a criminal.

"We ask for no more," Detective Askivour stated, pocketing the envelope of pictures.

"Well?"

"Well, what?"

"Am I free to go?"

"Of course. Of course. You have been at liberty to do that from the moment we met." I stood. "*Monsieur*."

"Yes?" I asked on a weary sigh, ready to bolt for the door at any second.

"There is…there is just one…minor matter, before you leave."

I rubbed my hands over my face. I felt like I'd been beaten and I had—verbally. "Which is?"

"It concerns our just-completed conversation about *Mademoiselle* Silver."

"Let me guess: you don't want me to mention it to her, right?"

"No," he smiled. "To the contrary, I encourage you to do just that."

"You do?" I picked up my writing portfolio, eager to leave, yet wanting to ask an important question.

Detective Askivour nodded once. "Of course. I do hope you have a pleasant day, *Monsieur*."

"Thanks. And, by the way, I don't suppose I can get you to tell me what kind of trouble Bonnie is in? What has she done? After all, I've truthfully answered all of your questions. Surely you can answer one of mine." My eyes locked with his steely gray ones and held.

"*Au revoir, Monsieur*," Detective Askivour muttered, reaching for a cigarette. "*Au revoir*."

Obviously I'd been dismissed. I turned, stalked out and gulped breaths of fresh air once I reached the street. I was shaking and couldn't decide if I was shaking from panic or outrage.

Chapter 19

After my disturbing conversation with the police investigators, the walk home to my studio apartment was a long one in which I replayed the conversation over and over in my mind. When I stepped into the foyer, I checked through the mail in the building mailbox, hoping to find a letter from home. I needed the diversion—badly.

Instead, I found a letter with my name and address neatly printed on the envelope, no return address and no stamp. Not knowing what to expect, I ripped it open and looked inside. There I found a letter from the last person on earth I expected to write me—Bonnie Silver.

> *Dearest Paul,*
>
> *I'm sure by now you've called me a litany of bad names, some probably worthy of inclusion in the famed Barroom Dictionary of Cusswords. Among them, you no doubt included the ever-popular 'damn bitch'—or worse. I shudder to think what the 'or worse' was.*
>
> *I realize that you're peeved with me. I can understand your irritation. However, if you knew the reason I haven't been at Twenty-One Rue Galande lately and why I didn't contact you before now, you wouldn't be peeved. So much for my clumsy attempt to plea bargain, except to say I didn't want to disappear or to stay away as long as I have. If it were left to me, Paul, you'd see me much more frequently. But for now, what must be, must be.*
>
> *Trust me, the day will come (sooner than later, I hope) when you'll understand.*
>
> *Oh, before I forget it. Paul, I wonder if you'd do me a favor? I'm certain that by now my mail is piling up in the box, so I'd appreciate it if you'd pick it up and hold it for me. And when I say 'mail,' I include junk mail. It may surprise you, but I enjoy getting junk mail, too. Receiving it makes me feel important, feel that people care about me. Even if they only care commercially.*
>
> *And oh yes, there's one letter in particular I want you to be on the look out for; it'll be from Mr. William Wallace Jones of Chicago. I'm anxious to hear from him. Very*

important. So be sure to set his mail aside.

How are my friends coming along these days? Abdul, Roger, and the rest. I haven't seen those guys in a while, and I truly miss them.

Don't misunderstand me, I miss you also. Surely I don't have to tell you that. It's just that some of my friends need me more than others. Roger, as you know, tops my 'needs-me' list. He has carloads of needs, but that doesn't change the fact he's a great guy. Anyone can see that he is if one is able to peer beneath the facade Roger wears like a turtle wears a shell. I hope you understand what I'm trying to say, though I know I'm not saying it very well.

And while I'm on the subject of friends, I don't want to leave out Monsieur Galdan. You remember him, don't you? How is the old gentleman? He's the retired widower who walks his poodle, Jo Jo, each morning on Rue Galande, then mulls over an espresso on the terrace of Café L'amour as his pet snoozes at his feet. I sometimes wonder what the old man would do if his dog, like his wife, unexpectedly died. He probably wouldn't live much longer himself.

And Marcus Seldan, how's he? In case you've forgotten, he's the young waiter at the café across from Notre-Dame Cathedral. He works there to help pay his education expenses and to support his ailing mother. Marcus' face always glitters a quick and easy smile that brightens the days of his customers like morning sunlight, but few realize that beneath his smile lies heartache. The heartache's name is Maria DeClare. Once his sweetheart, she jilted him for a flashy-dresser and smooth-talking hustler named Louis-Jean Paul. Today Maria is a streetwalker at Place Pigalle. Marcus says you can usually find her working a corner of Rue Des Martyrs, while her pimp/boyfriend sits nearby in a Mercedes, a present from Maria to prove, as she put it, her 'eternal love for a great man.' Life can sometimes be a bitch, can't it?

Paul, I hope you'll forgive me for being so chatty. I didn't mean to. Anyway, tell Roger I haven't forgotten him. He needs to hear that. And tell him also that I still love him.

Let me see. Did I cover everything? I think I did. So, I'll be seeing you. Soon, I hope. Till then, a bientot. And as always, you, my dearest, have my love, too.

Eternally—The Phantom Lady of Paris

That was all there was to Bonnie's letter: two pages and a half, no return address, no date, and a sometimes-rambling text. It was obvious that someone other than the postman placed the letter in the mailbox, for there was no stamp or cancellation marks on the envelope, a fact I found odd—very odd.

So, what had I learned from the correspondence? Not much. In spite of its wordiness, I still didn't know *where* Bonnie was, *why* she left, *when* she'd return, or *if* she'd return. The answers to these and similar questions she obviously didn't want me to know.

Bonnie said she hoped to see me "soon." What did she mean by soon? The word could mean practically anything from, by earthly clocks, a millionth of a second or less, to, by heavenly timepieces, an eternity or more. Soon. The term was about as quantitative as the word "infinity," and as comprehensible as a black hole or an explanation of the String Theory at a theoretical physics convention.

I trudged upstairs to my studio, feeling the weight of the world on my shoulders. Between my encounter with the two police detectives and Bonnie's letter, I felt drained and unsettled. I closed my door, toed off my shoes, and stretched out on the sofa. My mind went over every detail of the interrogation session with the detectives. Irritation started chafing my frame of mind. I'd come to Paris to study French culture and to write. *Not* to be watched and photographed by the authorities.

If one were to describe a troublemaker or revolutionary, never, *never* would they think of me. I'd been an average, straight-shooting person all my life. Never broken a law or gotten a ticket. I was an Eagle Scout, as American as apple pie. In many ways, I was a momma's boy and damned proud of it. Now, I was being watched and interrogated. I groaned as the realization hit me—there was probably a file somewhere with my name on it. A file containing pictures and a list of my comings and goings and those with whom I associated. What a *fine* state of affairs!

And what about Bonnie? What role did she play in all of this? On one hand she seemed open and honest; yet on the other hand, she was definitely hiding something. Where was she going when she disappeared? So many questions.

Should I sever my ties with her? That would be the prudent thing to do, but I could no sooner do that than I could stop using oxygen to breathe or stop using my legs to walk. Somehow this woman had become a part of me, an important part of my heart—and my soul.

When I approached a little café on Saint Germain a couple of days later, I saw Roger sitting on its terrace pouring over the *Herald Tribune*. Even though the fall chill was in the air, the sun was shining making the day pleasant for sitting outdoors.

I joined him and after ordering an espresso, I remarked that I hadn't gotten a chance to read my paper that morning. Was there anything interesting in it today?

"Not much," he replied with a shrug, "but there is one article that caught my eye. It's about a disturbance last Sunday in the American Church of Paris. Have you heard about it?"

"What? The church or the disturbance?" I loosened the knitted scarf I'd draped around my neck before starting out that morning and stuffed in my coat pocket.

Roger was turning the pages in the paper in search of the article. "Either, man."

"About the disturbance, no, but the church, yes. That is, I know where it's located: on Quai d'Orsay, in a rather ritzy neighborhood. I've passed it a few times, but that's the extent of my knowledge."

Roger folded the paper so he could read me the article. "Well, the article says the church is popular with middle- and upper-class Americans. Anyway, that's where the disturbance took place."

"It's hard to believe anything out of the ordinary would happen in such a neighborhood or such a church."

Roger looked up from his perusal of the article. "Why would you say that, Paul? Today, disturbances and protests are common and can, and do, take place anywhere. If they can happen in front of the White House and the Pentagon, why not in a church?"

"True," I acknowledged as I leaned forward, folding my arms over the table. "So tell me, what happened?"

"Better still, I'll read you the rest of the article. It goes on to say, 'When the church pastor, the distinguished Reverend Willis Davis Stone, asked in his benediction for God to bless America, the land of the free, a black woman, later identified as Zelda Lou-Jane Adams from Greenleaf, Mississippi, instigated a disturbance.

"'What land are you talking about Reverend?' Miss Adams was reported to have shouted, popping to her feet, her voice slashing the Sabbath's stillness like a razor. 'Is America this land of the free to which you refer? If so, who is free there? Those with political power? The right skin color? The right-size bank account? Those who can influence draft boards so their sons won't be forced into uniform and shipped to die in some God-forsaken Vietnam hamlet? Are the free Americans those rich enough to beat the draft by enrolling their sons in Ivy League schools or bankrolling their flight to Canada?'"

When Roger stopped reading to sip his espresso, I said, "My goodness! What an outburst! No doubt those parishioners will remember *that* sermon for the rest of their lives. Read on, man."

"Reports say a chorus of gasps rippled through the congregation. The church leader then cautioned, 'I must remind you, madam, that you are in a house of worship, a consecrated site of dignity and protocol. Thus, as long as you are within these walls, I must insist you observe proper decorum.'

"Miss Adams was quoted as shouting, 'Decorum? Is there a proper decorum for the truth? I ask, can we Americans here in Paris insulate ourselves and our consciences from the inhumanity heaped upon blacks in the Mississippi Delta or the deaths of GI's in Dien Bien Phu? Is there so much light in the City of Light that it blinds us to the truth, especially the truth about ourselves?'

"Four ushers sought to remove the screaming woman from her pew. As they dragged her down the center aisle of the church, she continued her ranting. 'Throw me out, if you like, but try to evict your conscience.'

"Witnesses, who were interviewed at the close of the service, said the outburst was most disturbing. All expressed hope the woman would never darken the doors of their revered church again."

Roger folded the paper. "Funny thing is I once knew a woman with that identical name: Zelda Lou-Jane Adams. She was a classmate of mine at Mississippi State College for Coloreds."

"What happened to her?"

"She dropped out of school. Ran out of money, I was told. I later learned that Klansmen one night dragged her father, a small town preacher and president of the local NAACP chapter, from his home. The father was footing her college bills. That was the last anybody saw of him, until a few days later a vagrant found his bloated body floating in the Yazoo River, skull bashed, ribs crushed, and if that wasn't enough, they stuffed his testicles down his throat."

I hung my head. "Stories like that make me ashamed to be a human being. Why are we so cruel to each other, to those who are different, who don't look or sound the way we do? That poor man. His poor family." I exhaled a long breath. "So, the woman who created the disturbance in the Paris church, could, in fact, be the *same* Zelda Lou-Jane that you knew in Mississippi, the daughter of the man so brutally murdered?"

"Could be. But if so, I wonder how she ended up here in, of all places, Paris, France? On the other hand, maybe the real question is a broader one: Why are you, I, and so many other Americans like us drawn to this city?"

"Maybe to escape the social upheaval that plagues America, and now ripples across the Atlantic Ocean and echoes in a cathedral in this city. Or maybe to escape…"

"Escape what?" Roger looked earnestly into my eyes. "Escape what, man?"

"Ourselves."

"To date no one has found a way to do that."

"True." I acknowledged with a nod.

"Do you think anyone will?"

"No. But that won't stop folks from trying—if not in Paris, then somewhere else. But in spite of their best efforts, they'll all end up finding the same thing."

Roger's dark eyes bored into mine as if looking for an answer. "What?"

"Themselves."

Chapter 20

Finally, winter came to Paris. You could feel its chilling presence everywhere: in clusters of shoppers at outdoor markets, on café terraces, in Place de la Concorde, at kiosks, in neighborhood parks, and on sidewalks near Gilbert's where Sorbonne students gathered to flirt. Winter, the long awaited visitor—loathed and loved—had finally come.

Grayness draped the city like a pall. Wintry air tingled fingertips, stinging and reddening cheeks. Skies, once ablaze with splashes of amber and gold, were now leaden. A yellowish disk in an endless expanse, the sun was a lonely nomad in an odyssey across the firmament, occasionally peeking from beneath argosies of clouds. Winter had come. However, it had not come with raging fury as it does to Moscow or Alaska, where mercury plunges beneath freezing and for months hibernates there. Still, winter had come, and all in Paris knew it had.

There was only one snowfall in the city that year, less than two inches of powdery fluff, but it was enough to snarl traffic on side streets and bridges. Like a Pied Piper, the flurry lured scores of youngsters to Rue Galande and there they sweetened the morning air with the music of youthful laughter and volleys of snowballs. Their antics brought to mind cherished childhood memories of sledding, ice skating, and engaging in snowball battles. Winter had come.

Strolling down Boulevard Saint Germain, you passed scores of boutiques and brasseries, all with frosted windows. You saw swarms of Sorbonne students, bright, knitted scarves circling their necks, striding with the speed of youth. Winter had come.

Always at the intersection of boulevards Saint Germain and Saint Michel, a grey-haired vendor stood rubbing his hands over a steel drum brimmed with crackling logs, flames, yellow and amber, dancing like shimmering ballerinas. Through-out the nippy city, vendors roasted chestnuts in steel drums, selling bags of the fragrant, warm nuts to passersby. Winter had come.

Trees lining Saint Michel Boulevard stood as desolate as skeletons juxtaposed against winter's bleakness. When you saw the sun, which was seldom, it appeared to be not a yellow ball of blazing fire, but a gray disk drowning in oceans of tears. Winter had come.

Homeless men gathered under bridges and there built fires, then huddled around the flames, hoping light and heat would delay winter's debut. However their efforts were futile, for, like it or not, winter had come.

With its arrival—for reasons I didn't understand, and still don't—Roger spent more and more of his evenings sitting in a little café near the intersection of Saint Germain and Rue Monge, sitting silently and staring into the velvet Paris night. Far from the main flow of pedestrian traffic, the café was on a shadowy street, a desolate place for a business. I'd seldom seen more than six customers in it at any one time.

One Friday evening, I happened upon Roger at the café and joined him. I shared the news that Bonnie had returned from her mystery trip to some mysterious destination. "She's effervescent and charming as ever," I told him.

He nodded and smiled. "I'll have to hook up with her one day soon. Catch up."

"I have a message for you from her." His eyebrows shot up in question and I smiled in response. "Bonnie said if I saw you before she did that she has not forgotten you and that she sends her love."

A smile illuminated his face. "Did she really say that?"

"Every word. I meant to tell you the last time I saw you, but we got caught up in that newspaper article about the disturbance at the American Church of Paris. Frankly I forgot."

"Don't sweat it, man. You remembered it today and I certainly needed to hear something like that. I surely did. She's one fine chick, isn't she? Warm, caring. She's *real,* man; there's nothing fake or insincere about Bon. I needed to hear something upbeat for a change. I've been in a real funk lately." He exhaled a long sigh which spoke eloquently of his mood. "Listen, man, in spring, as anyone can tell you, and as you so well know, Paris is a glittering delight, but in winter the place is sadder than a requiem. Do you dig what I'm saying?"

"I think I do. You're saying what I've heard others tell me: Paris is as sad in winter as it is lively and gay in spring."

"Exactly. And when winter's bleakness settles over this city, I'm sometimes plagued by—how can I phrase this?—ah…strange thoughts."

"Strange in what way?" I asked. His eyes locked on mine, but he said nothing. "Strange in what way, Roger?"

He smiled a smile that didn't reach his eyes, for they were still filled with melancholy. "Could I interest you in another round of drinks? This one's on me."

"Well, if you're buying, why not? So, sure, another round."

I told Roger what I wanted, and he ordered. Soon the waiter returned and placed two cups of espresso on our table.

After a couple of sips, I said, "You were about to speak of the strange thoughts you've been having." He raised his demitasse to his lips and paused. After sipping, he lowered it. "What about the strange thoughts you've been having." Silence. "Did you hear me, man?"

"I heard." He continued sipping his espresso. In silence. His silence was protracted and weighty. Soon it transformed into an unspoken contract that stated that we would no longer discuss his "strange thoughts." And so we didn't. But that was of no consequence for I was certain I already knew what his "strange thoughts" were. And what they were troubled me.

That year, winter came early to Paris, bringing sunless skies and dreary days. When it came, Roger left. Not physically, but he left nevertheless. I wasn't sure where he went, but my hope was that he would return and soon, for I missed him.

Early the next morning when I came bounding down the steps of Twenty-One Rue Galande, I found Bonnie searching for her mail in the building's mailbox. "Good morning, sunshine."

She beamed me a smile, pulling a letter out of the box. "Morning yourself, tiger." She glanced at the return address on the envelope. "A letter from Betty Jean's mother. I hope she's doing better."

"Mourning the loss of a child must be never-ending. Every parent expects to die long before their child."

Bonnie leaned back against the wall next to the mailbox. "Yes, and to have Betty Jean die so far away from home and for no good reason. I mean, *how* can a parent come to grips with a thing like that? There must be so many self-recriminations. So many what-ifs. Ain't life a bitch?"

"I've never lost someone close to me. My parents and grandparents are still living. Guess I can't fathom the pain of losing someone I hold dear."

Bonnie opened the envelope and pulled out the letter. "Dealing is not easy. We all do it in our own way, mostly by holding the person we've lost close to our hearts. To do anything less allows death to claim another person. Those left behind have to engage in life, to feel, to enjoy everything and everyone around them. Otherwise they're as good as dead, too."

I reached out and ran fingers down her cheek. "You are a marvel, you know. Goodness just seeps from your pores."

"Paul, would you just get the hell outta here?" She playfully slapped my arm with her envelope. "Do you have a piece of the Blarney Stone in your studio that you kiss every morning?" She looked up at me, a flush on her cheeks and sparkles of humor in her eyes.

"Oh, well, if you want to hear blarney, how about joining me for lunch? I'll give you my full repertoire."

She thought for a second. "I could maybe fit that into my hectic social calendar. Will you be at Café Le Balkan writing? I could meet up with you there. Say twelvish?"

"I'll be looking forward to it. Maybe after lunch we could take a walk to Shakespeare and Company. See if he's gotten any new books in."

"You know how much I love that bookstore. Sounds great."

I started searching through the pile of letters and papers for my *Herald Tribune*. Finding it, I held it up and declared, "There must not be much to read in the *Tribune* today. You didn't steal it."

Bonnie was heading up the steps by then. She never slowed down as she barked, "I'll pretend I didn't hear that."

I chuckled as I headed out to the dairy and bakery for my breakfast. Twelve o'clock couldn't come soon enough.

Chapter 21

I didn't understand. The surface facts, yes, those I understood, but the more meaningful ones, those at the core, I didn't understand. In time, I would. However, when I did understand I wasn't prepared for what the facts turned out to be.

My tutorial began several days later when I had a chance encounter with Abdul at a drugstore on Boulevard Saint Germain. During the sixties, French businessmen introduced "American style" drugstores to Paris. The Gaulish version of a drugstore was not a place selling pharmaceuticals. A French drugstore vended sandwiches, salads, and sundaes that looked like Monet paintings and drinks, including, of course, a variety of thirty gourmet wines served in stylish flutes, but no drugs, not even an aspirin. French capitalists took the word "drugstore" to another level, creating something most Americans wouldn't recognize as a drugstore, but a café on steroids.

That day, I saw Abdul enter the drugstore as I sat enjoying a Coke. In Paris, for reasons I don't understand, Cokes are served with a wedge of lemon, but no ice. Request ice and the waiter will give you a condescending glance and a smirk, both of which say, "You must be one of these unsophisticated Americans."

"Paul," Abdul greeted when he came strolling over to my little table. "I'm so glad I ran across you because I wanted to share some joyous news, news about my recent good fortune."

"Well, I'm flattered you've chosen me to tell of your good fortune. And believe me, the good fortune you speak of—whatever it is—couldn't come to a more deserving guy."

"Kind of you to say that, *mon ami.*"

"I merely speak the truth." I motioned to the chair opposite me. "Won't you join me for a Coke?" He sat and I ordered for him. "It must be extraordinarily good news you have because I've never seen you look so happy. Your face glows."

"Does it?" he smiled.

"For sure. The good fortune you speak of, let me see if I can guess what it is. Are you dating a lady friend here in Paris?"

"Not that. I have a sweetheart in Algeria, and I could never be unfaithful to her. Never. *"*

"She means that much to you, huh?"

Genuine warmth torched his eyes. "She means everything."

"So, you say it's not a woman?"

"Right, not a woman." The waiter brought Abdul's Coke. I wondered if Abdul would get the same show that I'd gotten with my Coke. Sure enough, he did. With a flourish that only a French waiter could dream up, he laid a white towel over his shoulder, where he placed the bottle of Coke on his shoulder and secured it in place by leaning his head onto it. With a can opener in his other hand, he snapped off the cap, leaned over as he securely wedged the bottle between his shoulder and head, and poured it into a glass—all without spilling a drop. The waiter, who was obviously pleased with his performance, sauntered off.

We both shook our heads in amazement. "Only in Paris," I muttered. Abdul chuckled. "So tell me why you're so happy. Did you hit the French lottery?"

He snorted. "Me, play *that*? No, that's a fool's game. Odds are stacked too high against the gamer."

"OK," I said, enjoying my guessing game. "It's not the lottery and not a woman. Let's try this. You inherited a fortune from, say, a rich uncle or some other relative?"

"Paul?" He said with an indulgent tone to his voice.

"Yes."

"That would have been a good guess if you'd made it two years ago, for it was then my uncle owned a thriving expert-import business in Algeria. But sadly, French mobsters and oily-tongued lawyers armed with fraudulent contracts stole his business. Their deception left the poor man a pauper who, to survive, panhandled and slept on the street and in doorways. Not only did they rob him of his business, but they decimated his self-esteem. One day on the steps of the French Embassy, he put a bullet through his brain."

"Good God! I'm really sorry to hear that. What a pity."

"You should have no pity for him, *mon ami*, though I appreciate your sympathy, but pity is unnecessary."

"Why so?"

"Because the time for pity has long passed."

"Still, I feel it was *unfair* how your uncle's life ended so tragically."

"True. But the time for sympathy has come and gone. Now is the time for…"

"For what?" I held my glass in midair, halfway to my mouth. My eyes searched his.

"For justice. And after all this time, there *will* be justice, not only for my uncle, but for all my fellow countrymen wronged by Frenchmen profiting from the suffering of Algeria and her people."

"I can understand how you must feel. And you're certainly entitled to feel as you do. This brings us back to the starting point, namely, what has taken place in your life that gives you so much joy? I thought I could guess, but I see I can't, so I'm afraid you'll have to tell me."

Abdul stared at me for a moment, then shook his head. "I've had second thoughts."

"About what?"

"About sharing my news with you. You see, I think it's much better you don't know after all."

"Why the change of mind?" This man could talk in more riddles than anyone I'd ever met.

"Trust me, your knowing will only complicate matters, in ways you can't possibly imagine."

"Well, if that's how you feel, I suppose there's little I can do to change your mind, but I'm still disappointed that you—"

"Don't be disappointed," he smiled. "My friend, shall we share a toast? A toast to justice," he sighed as our glasses kissed, "to justice, which is always blind and slow, and though it creeps at a snail's pace, in time, will come...*and* come with vengeance. So, here's to justice. Long may it reign."

"To justice," I repeated. Then, in a manner my mother used to describe as a dog that can't let a bone alone, I said, "Perhaps I shouldn't be, but I'm still saddened that you won't share—"

Abdul raised his Coke glass again. "I propose another toast."

I mirrored his gesture by raising my glass. "To what this time?"

"To our friendship."

We drank. "This 'good fortune' you speak of, Abdul, it bothers me not to know what it—"

"Another toast," he smiled.

"Another?"

"Yes. This one to your wisdom."

"My—"

"Yes, your wisdom. Wisdom: that's the stuff that alerts one when one is asking too many questions."

We both chuckled. "OK, you've made your point. I am inclined to ask too many questions, aren't I? It's just that—" I glanced across the table at Abdul, taking note of his raised eyebrow and the smirk on his face. "I was about to do it again, wasn't I?"

His smile was warm. "With your questioning nature, you must be very hard on your students. I'm sure you give them no peace." The laughter we shared was affable, a sign of our deepening friendship. We were learning to accept each other, the good and the bad of each other.

Two days later, my life hit a speed bump. The jolt came the morning I sat in my favorite "writing café," unfolded the *Herald Tribune* and spread it across the table. Front-page headline: "Bomb Explodes, Café in Rubble, Police Probe." Unlike the last bombing, this one occurred closer to Twenty-One Rue Galande, in the thirteenth *arrondissement* in a café catering to upper-class, international customers. In choosing this target, perhaps the terrorist, I reasoned, wanted to send a message to not only France, but to the world, the message being that the stakes were now higher.

Following the bombing, top French officials announced an emergency meeting of ranking ministers for the following day, at the conclusion of which there would be a televised news conference.

When the waiter, Pierre, brought my order, he glanced at the newspaper. "A real shame isn't it?" he muttered. "A dirty shame."

"Yes, a shame."

"And all the victims were innocent; slaughtered because they were in the wrong place at the right time."

"Or, as the bomber saw it, in the right place at the right time."

"Either way, *Monsieur*, they're just as dead." He waved his hand in emphasis.

"No argument about that."

"You know," he shrugged in that way French men have. That eloquent shrug of the shoulders, a squint of the eyes, a sneer on the lips and a pair of up-turned hands that told more than mere words. "Ahh-h, but life is unfair, is it not?"

"Unfair? Who said life *had* to be fair? The only thing about life that *has* to be is that it exists, it is. And any other conclusion is not what life is, but what we humans *want* it to be, and what we hope and pray it will be, namely just. But life doesn't come with labels, though humans are forever trying to stick them on."

"True, but when you hear that innocent folks are blown to bits, it just seems that it's not right, not as life should be."

"Not the way you and I would like it to be. True. Morality and ethics have nothing to do with a café bombing. When a bomb explodes, it's a matter of physics and geography, not *philosophy*. It's where you happen to be when the blast occurs, because the bomb has no conscience. Only humans do. At least…*some* humans do."

"Even so, you have to ask yourself what kind of man would detonate a bomb in a café, knowing it'll snuff out the lives of fellow humans, people who've done him no harm; in fact, they don't even know his name?"

"True, that is a question you have to ask."

"And what answer do you get?" the waiter asked, balancing his serving tray on one up-raised palm.

"That the bomber is diseased with hate, which is the most charitable thing I can say about him. At any rate, Pierre, would you mind bringing me another coffee?"

"*Certainment, Monsieur.*" Again, he glanced at the newspaper. "A shame," he muttered, shaking his head. "A *damn* shame."

"And Pierre, about that coffee, hold the cream and sugar, will you, please?"

"Sure. One TNT coming up." He hurried off.

"Pierre?"

He stopped and turned. "*Oui.*"

"Here I sit in a café less than a couple of blocks from where one was blown to bits, and what do you do, you call my order a 'TNT.' Can't you think of a better name?"

"*Certainment, Monsieur,*" he smiled, bobbing his head in agreement. "*Certainment.*"

The following morning was especially cold with a bitter wind blowing off the Seine. I sat, embraced in the warmth of my writing café, perusing the *Herald Tribune*. The front page carried a headline reminiscent of one printed the previous day: "Blast Rocks Elysees Bistro, 50 Injured." I shook my head at the horror of another bombing.

"Unnamed sources," said the article, "reported that police were no closer to apprehending the bomber or bombers than they were following the previous attack. Investigators would neither confirm nor deny the allegation but did assure the public that the probe 'was ongoing.' Critics of law enforcement predicted that if someone didn't arrest the culprits soon, Paris would cease being a center of culture and art but would become a killing field where no one was safe, policemen included.

"The city's association of café owners predicted that if the devastation continued it would cripple the hotel, food, and drink industry, resulting in a loss of millions of francs and forcing the layoff of countless service workers. One economist foresaw that a national depression would follow, resulting in bread lines, civil strife, and, finally, anarchy.

"Meanwhile, a café on Saint Germain near Rue Monge posted a sign announcing that no one carrying a package would be admitted without having the parcel inspected. Civil libertarians were outraged." Pierre, my favorite waiter in Paris, set my coffee down and hurried off to another table.

I sipped at the black brew and continued reading the article. "At the largest café in Saint Michel Plaza, a customer left a paper bag on a table. Seeing it, the proprietor immediately notified law officials. The parcel turned out to be a prankster's idea of a joke. It contained a hamburger and a sheet of paper on which someone scribbled the word 'Bang!' The café owner didn't find the prank amusing, nor did his customers, who, seeing the bag, bolted like cornered rats. A middle-aged woman tripped and fractured her hip. Her husband, rushing to her side, suffered a heart attack and died."

All of Paris was on edge, I reasoned. It seemed from what I'd read and overheard on the streets and in cafés that just about everyone was a suspect, including Sorbonne students carrying briefcases, doctors carrying medical bags, and postmen, mailbags. Café patrons didn't feel comfortable sitting beside anyone who looked suspicious, and to many, everyone did.

Has the whole world gone mad, I wondered? Would calmness and normalcy of a gentler time ever return? War demonstrations, student riots, civil-rights demonstrations and now this. The entire world seemed on a collision course with itself. Man's inhumanity to man, I supposed. Yet, was this current epidemic of social sickness a rarity or the natural ebb and flow of civilization?

The next time I saw Abdul, I asked, "This 'good fortune' you mentioned a few days ago, did it turn out to be all you thought it would be?"

"More, Paul," he smiled, "much more."

"I see. By the way, I suppose you've heard about the café bombings?"

"Hasn't everybody? It's the buzz of Paris. And the bombings make the rich very uncomfortable, at least those in the neighborhood where I work. There I hear fear in their voices. It's as if at *last* they confront something their wealth and power can't buy or control."

"The fear is not restricted to the rich. A few days ago, a waiter friend of mine told me he doesn't allow his wife in cafés anymore. He said if he didn't make his living as a waiter, he wouldn't go into one himself. He and I tried to figure out what could possibly take place in the mind of a man who commits such cruel and egregious crimes."

"And what answer did you two guys come up with?"

"None. I mean, none that made sense."

"Maybe the bomber, whoever he is, sees himself as the administrator of a long-delayed and much-needed *justice*."

"By killing innocent people?" How could Abdul possibly believe such a thing?

"Paul, justice is blind. Remember, she is always shown with a cloth covering her eyes."

"True, but with *nothing* covering her ears. So she is quite able to hear the screams and wails of those injured and killed in the bombings."

Abdul sighed. "There is an old adage in my country that goes like this: retribution is inherited like genes, especially bad genes. Therefore sons and daughters are doomed to pay for the father's sins."

"And you think the bomber might be guided by such a belief?"

Abdul shrugged. "Might be. But I, of course, have no way of knowing for sure. Only the bomber knows. I merely speculate, in a kind of mental exercise."

"As you say, for you it's only a mental exercise and nothing more."

"Right...nothing more."

Chapter 22

Two weeks after our luncheon date where I displayed my "rotten line of blarney," as Bonnie called it, she went missing again. By now I was becoming acclimated to her unannounced and unexplained disappearances, or so I liked to think. Still, every time she went away, the color went out of my life; I felt as if I were living in shades of grey. Perhaps it would be better said to say I existed in a world similar to a song I enjoyed hearing on the radio—"A Whiter Shade of Pale."

Every afternoon, I'd climb the steps to her studio to see if she were back. Two minutes later I'd return to my studio, lonelier than I had been the day before and swearing that I wouldn't look for her anymore, yet knowing full well that I would.

One afternoon, after finishing my self-required hours of writing, I stepped up to her studio again. I didn't expect to find her home, but out of habit, I mounted the stairs anyway. When I reached the fourth floor, I was surprised to see that the door of her studio was partly open. Could she have at last returned? Was the prodigal finally home? Sure, she *had* to have come back. I rushed toward the half-opened door.

"Bonnie," I blurted, "man, it's good to..." Just over the threshold, I stopped, as did my greeting, though snippets of it continued dribbling out. "...have you back..." Someone was in the studio, but it wasn't Bonnie Silver. Instead I was looking at two males in dark business suits and even darker expressions. The glowering duo stood in front of Bonnie's sleep sofa, each glaring fusillades of question marks at me.

"Oops, sorry," I said. My eyes did a quick scan of the room. The studio was in a shambles. Several empty dresser drawers leaned against a wall. Two wastepaper cans sat upside down on the floor near the window, their contents dumped on the table. Helter-skelter, several pairs of blue jeans lay on the sofa bed amid piles of books, some of which were lying open.

"It seems I entered the wrong studio." I leaned around the open door to look at the brass number and letter on it. My inner self told me I was sounding and—worse—acting like an idiot. After all, I certainly knew which door was Bonnie's.

"Perhaps not." The tallest of the two slowly walked toward me.

"Obviously I have. You see, I'm looking for—"

"*Mademoiselle* Bonnie Silver?"

"Right." What in the world was going on here? Who were these men? What had they done to her cute, well-kept apartment?

With a smirk he looked at his companion, a bald gentleman. "It seems we're not the *only* ones in search of her." The older, bald man quietly stared at me.

"Does she still live here?" I asked.

"From what we can determine, yes," the taller one replied.

"I see. You mind telling me why you're rummaging through her things?" I asked, eyeing the disarray. My common sense and irritation were beginning to override the confusion I'd had seconds earlier.

"Because we're looking for something. Isn't that obvious?" barked the bald man.

"Of course. And what is this *thing* you're looking for?" I glared at the rude, obnoxious man.

"Naming the object, or objects, would benefit neither you nor us. So I'm afraid I can't reveal that information."

"I see. Well, perhaps there is a question you *can* answer. Who and what gives you the right to rifle through *Mademoiselle* Silver's belongings?"

"*Monsieur*, your questions are endless, aren't they?" interjected the taller of the two. "Suppose we back up. First of all, you are someone who barges into this studio unannounced. Right? Right. So, I'd like to know just who *you* are."

I gave him my name. He asked to see my passport. After handing it to him, I said, "I live downstairs. I'm Bonnie's neighbor and friend, and, I might add, an unofficial guardian of her interests and rights in her absence. Now, perhaps you can answer my questions. *Who* the hell are you, and *what* gives you the right to rummage through the property of an American citizen?" I was in full-blown irate teacher mode.

Almost in unison, they replied that they were investigators, though neither produced a badge or an identification folder. "So, as we said, we are investigators," declared the taller of the two.

"Yes, so you *said*." I folded my arms over my chest. I wasn't sure I believed a word that tumbled out of their mouths.

"Knowing who we are, does that finally answer all your questions?" The tall one asked.

"It *might* answer one."

He crossed his arms over his chest in a mirror stance of mine. "There are others?"

"Yes. The most important being, does the concierge know you're in a tenant's studio going through her things?"

"She most certainly does," the older, balding man insisted. "We have her full cooperation, not to mention that of the building's owner. Being good French citizens, they are anxious to assist authorities in any way possible in this investigation." He paused. "*Monsieur*, do you have anything else you'd like to know?"

"Yes. Your badges and ID folders---you produced neither. Do you mind if I see them?"

The tall one chuckled. "*Monsieur*, do I have to remind you that you are merely a neighbor of *Mademoiselle* Silver and a friend? Or so you *say*. At the risk of being rude, which I don't wish to be, the answer is no, you may not examine our credentials." He glanced at his watch. "I do hope you'll excuse us. We have duties to perform."

"Of course. I wouldn't want to stand between you and the performance of your duties." I glanced around the shambles in Bonnie's studio and then shot them a telling glance. "The two of you have a lot of work to do before you leave. I assume you'll exit the premises with the apartment in the same pristine condition it was in upon your arrival?"

The taller of the two gave the French shrug. "Ah, but of course. Have no fear. You are most understanding; we do appreciate your cooperation. And I wish you a pleasant day, good fortune, and God's speed."

"To you, the same." I walked to the door and stopped. "I hope you'll find what you're searching for."

He shrugged, picking up a shoe with two fingers as if it were toxic waste. "Sometimes I think we will, and at other times I think not. I often wonder if what we're looking for really exists, or if it's the product of someone's imagination." He smiled. "But raising such questions is not my job. I'm paid to follow orders. At any rate, I appreciate your good wishes."

"With my compliments. Good day." The French were not the only ones who could sarcastically drip with honeyed manners, I thought.

As I stepped into the hall, the door in the foyer gushed open, followed by an explosion of children's laughter and the tattoo of little feet bounding stairs, sounds frequently heard at Twenty-One Rue Galande. A young couple from Vietnam living on the second landing had three small children who often, as they did now, frolicked in the hall.

I was sure the men in Bonnie's studio couldn't hear my footsteps over the children's din. They would assume I'd gone downstairs, which I hadn't. Instead, I pressed myself flat against the wall, near the door of Bonnie's studio and listened.

"About how long would you say we've been here?"

"Around three hours, more or less." I recognized the voice as the taller of the two men.

"That sounds about right. And for all that time, what do we have to show for it?" OK, I was getting a take on the balding man's voice. It was deeper, more nasal than the taller guy.

"You know the answer to that question as well as I do. A big fat zero. But of course, that's not the results the chief is looking for." The taller man was speaking again. His voice was higher in pitch, kind of on the squeaky side.

"No, it's not. In spite of the fact that we've gone over every inch of this place with a fine tooth comb, from top to bottom, we got nothing."

"What do you say we go back to headquarters and explain the situation to the chief?" Squeaky asked.

"We? What do you mean we? I'll let you explain it to him. I don't want to be the barer of bad news to that guy. I'm still in one piece, and I'd like to stay that way," Old Baldy stated.

"Good point. We both know what a nut he can be. Believe me, if he was just a bad administrator, I could live with that. I've worked under some terrible asses in my day, but this guy goes beyond bad to sickeningly bad, with an ego as big as his brain is small."

"That's the understatement of the year. I often wonder how he got to be a department head anyway"

"You know how the game is played—politics," Squeaky whined. I stifled a chuckle. In the middle of this mess, I was amusing myself by nicknaming the two so-called investigators. One was now thought of as "Squeaky," and the other as "Old Baldy." Maybe I was losing it.

"Right. And he's a maestro at playing politics. Nobody can kiss an ass with more style and finesse." Oh, I smiled. Old Baldy has a bit of a jealousy problem regarding his superior.

"Nobody. Add to that the fact that when he latches on to one of his crazy ideas, nothing on this planet can make him let go," Squeak stated with authority.

"Right, nothing—especially the facts." Baldy was speaking again. I was beginning to enjoy my eavesdropping.

"Facts would be the last things that'd get him to change his mind. But still, maybe we should go back and tell him what we've found, anyway," Squeak said.

"If we told him, he'd just order us to return. 'And don't you show your faces in this office again,' he'd bark, fists pounding the desk, 'until you find it! And that's a direct order. Disobey and I'll have you bums walking the worst hellhole beat in Paris." I smirked; Old Baldy was a real character.

"That's a good imitation of the way that arrogant son of a bitch talks! You have him down pat. Well, anyway, let's get back to work." Noises filtered out of the open door.

"Might as well," Old Baldy said. "And though I hate to admit it, maybe the old bastard is right after all. It could be that what we're looking for is right under our noses, and somehow we've overlooked it."

I tiptoed to my studio and eased the door shut, all the while scouring my thoughts to see if I could figure out what the strangers in Bonnie's apartment were searching for, and if they, in fact, were who they claimed to be. If they weren't, just who were they? And in what way were Squeaky and Old Baldy connected to Bonnie? At this point, I had loads of questions and very few answers.

Chapter 23

The following day I met Abdul at his favorite café. I immediately told him about the men who'd searched Bonnie's studio. "What do you make of it?" I asked. Having not slept well the previous night, I was eager to get yesterday's events off my chest. Three times I'd been approached by police regarding Bonnie: once in the foyer of Twenty-One Rue Galande, the session with two detectives in a café where they showed me photos, and yesterday's run-in with Old Baldy and Squeak. Things like this didn't normally happen to me and, frankly, I was unnerved.

"Paul, there's one thing you gotta keep in mind; you're not in America now, but in Paris. Stateside you're accustomed to the professionalism of the FBI and many other large urban police departments. Police in France don't always measure up to such standards. More often than not, they're inept at what they do. Case in point, not too long ago, French police investigated a friend of mine."

"Why?"

"He says that to this day he doesn't have the *faintest* idea. Your asking why implies that they had or needed a reason for the probe. Many from my country believe that often French police randomly select a foreigner and investigate him."

I certainly hoped this was the case with Bonnie. "Was your friend frightened when he learned they had him on their radar screen?"

"For a while, yes. But as time went on, and he learned more about how French cops operate, their methodology—or lack of it—he was less frightened. In fact, most times he was just puzzled and sometimes amused."

"In Bonnie's case, the investigators—at least, that's what they called themselves—seemed to have been searching for something specific. I wonder what? They'd completely torn apart her studio and went through all her belongings." I leaned forward in my seat, glancing around to make sure we weren't being overheard. "I'm telling you the place was in a shambles."

Abdul gave a dismissive wave of his hand. "Finding the answer to that is like identifying your Uncle Lou's voice in a two thousand-member choir."

"I get your point."

So, Abdul was as mystified as I about what the "investigators" were looking for in Bonnie's place. What were all the secrets about? Why couldn't the police tell me why they were investigating Bonnie? And where was Bonnie going on these mysterious jaunts? Secrets, I was sick of them.

Still, having unloaded my chest about the men in Bonnie's apartment the day before, I felt my appetite return. I ordered a hamburger. As usual, it arrived French style with a fried egg—sunny-side up—on top of the meat patty.

As I ate my hamburger and *frites,* Abdul and I talked. We spent the better part of an hour exchanging stories about our families and friends remaining in our respective countries.

With Christmas around the corner, I was feeling nostalgic for my family's traditional preparations for the holidays. Mother would have the house decorated inside and Dad would be on a ladder, grumbling and cussing as he strung lights across the porch roof. Smells of homemade cookies would fill the house and the pile of presents under the tree would mysteriously grow every few days.

Abdul, a Muslim and therefore not a believer in Christmas and all it stood for, was homesick for his girlfriend. However he refused to bring her to Paris where she would suffer more bigotry.

He teased me about not having a girlfriend, suggested that having one would cure my inquisitive mind. "*Mon ami,*" he said, "you'd be too busy trying to figure out the woman in your life, so much so that you'd stop prying into others' affairs."

"Is that what I do? Pry?" I swirled my last French fry in the ketchup.

Abdul slapped me across the back and laughed until he wiped tears from his eyes. I soon joined in the laughter, admitting that he might be just a tad correct in his assessment.

Later I left the café and headed for my studio, walking down Boulevard Saint Germain and turning left onto Rue Anglais. Exiting Rue Anglais, I approached Rue Galande, which was more crowded than I'd ever seen it. Hordes of spectators lined both sidewalks, some spilling into the street. Obviously, something extraordinary had happened—or was about to.

In the center of the street, demonstrators marched, some waving banners and placards, others pumping the air with clenched fists, all chanting and exhorting those on the sidewalks to join the march. "Yankee murderers," demonstrators chanted, "go home…go home… Yankees murderers leave Vietnam…leave Vietnam."

A tall, broad-shouldered man led the marchers. Arms flapping, he entreated those on sidewalks to lend their voices to the chorus of protestors: "Yankee murderers, go home...go home...Yankee murderers, leave Vietnam...leave Vietnam..."

Additional voices from the sidewalks gradually blended with those of the marchers. The chants now echoed, no doubt heard as far away as Notre-Dame Cathedral.

I wedged into a narrow space behind two spectators, a man and a woman. In their mid-fifties, both were dressed conservatively. The man, spectacles straddling his nose, carried a briefcase, the woman, a copy of *Le Monde*, the most respected newspaper in France, was neatly tucked under her arm.

"I wonder," the woman said to the man, "at what point did they lose their humanity?"

"Who are you talking about?" her companion asked, turning to glance at her.

"Why, the Americans, of course. Gaston, I ask, is there a difference between Nazi genocide in the furnaces of Dachau and the massacres by American carpet-bombing in Vietnam? Hitler killed crudely and savagely. Americans kill with sophistication and scientific refinement, employing the latest in the innovative technology of death. I wonder when it will all end...or if it will *ever* end."

"The Vietnam War, you mean? Or war in general?"

"Both," she insisted.

"Why don't you ask an easy question, like where was time before time began or what is at the bottom of a black hole? The answer to both these questions and to yours is, only God knows."

She nodded. "Yes, only God."

"What has America gotten itself into in Vietnam?"

"Something that is almost impossible to get out of, like crawling out of quicksand. The more you struggle to get out, the deeper it sucks you in," the woman stated. "Meanwhile, armies on both sides of the conflict march lock-step into slaughter machines, ending up corpses piled like cords of firewood."

"Nicole, why are you getting so upset? You and I have nothing to fear. We are French citizens, living here in Paris, far from the Vietnam killing fields and the violent street demonstrations in the States. This is America's war, America's problem...not ours."

"Not yet, for as surely as the sun sets, Gaston, the Vietnam War, in some form or other will come to France."

He put his arm around her slender waist and drew her close.

"You believe it will, my love?"

She gave a wave of her leather-gloved hand. "Look about you; the advance party already enters Paris. It marches down Rue Galande as we speak. And there is other evidence. You see it in graffiti on toilet walls, bridge buttresses, and the fountain in Saint Michel Plaza. 'Americans napalm Vietnamese babies,' the graffiti reads. Soon rabble-rousers will be among us, along with terrorists carrying briefcases of explosive death. Whether we like it or not, French sons stand a good chance of one day marching into the jaws of war."

"Yankee murderers, go home…go home…Yankee murderers, leave Vietnam…leave Vietnam…" protestors continued chanting, voices louder, reaching a thunderous crescendo.

Exhausted and weary of the America-bashing, I turned away from the chanting throngs and headed for my apartment building. Granted I often had the same sentiments voiced by the crowd, but like siblings who constantly fought, yet banded together when attacked by someone outside the family, I felt that I—as a taxpaying American—had the right to criticize my country, not them.

I mounted the two flights of wooden stairs to my studio. The tides of demonstrators' chants flooded the apartment. "Yankee murderers, go home…go home." I wrote a letter to my mother, telling her of the demonstration and thanking her for the two packages she'd sent me for Christmas. As always, they were packed with love, for that's what my mother did—she spread love. I was the youngest of three and the only boy; therefore I was indulged and fussed over. And I loved it.

Missing my family, missing the holidays as I'd always known them, and missing Bonnie, I got ready early for bed. Sleep would not come, for though the windows were closed, the voices of protesters continued to filter into the studio. "Yankee murderers, go home…go home." After much tossing and turning and staring at the ceiling, I finally dozed off. I dreamt of Bonnie and Christmas trees and Vietnamese babies.

Abdul once hinted that he not only knew where Bonnie disappeared, but also why. He made it clear however, he would not share that information. The conversation I had with him on the subject took place weeks earlier, and since then much had changed in his life, and mine. The most significant change was that he had acquired a group of new friends from Algeria, people I knew little about and he avoided discussing in detail. When they came up in conversation, he seemed uncomfortable and usually parried the subject. Whether they were or were not his *true* friends, one thing was certain, they consumed a great deal of his time and energy.

Due to the influence of his recently acquired friends, Abdul said his "outlook on things" was now different. Because this transformation occurred after our last conversation about Bonnie, I thought he might now tell what he knew about her disappearances. I had nothing to lose by asking, so the next time I saw him at a café on Boulevard Saint Germain, I popped the question directly. I asked why Bonnie sometimes vanished and where she went.

"Not knowing bothers you, doesn't it, Paul?" Abdul's dark, piercing eyes made me squirm.

"Of course it does." Being the youngest of three children, I'd grown up trying to learn what my older sisters were talking about, what they were up to. They labeled me as nosy. I preferred the word inquisitive. So, yes, not knowing about Bonnie's disappearances bothered me. Frankly, it bothered the *hell* out of me.

He sipped his espresso, looked around. "Why?"

"I'm shocked you'd ask such a question. You know Bonnie as well as I do. Maybe better. She's a remarkable person, one who is as good-natured as she is selfless."

"You're not telling me anything I don't already know."

"Then you shouldn't have trouble understanding why I'm concerned about her."

He let out a long sigh. "I do understand."

Good, maybe now I was getting somewhere. "So why won't you tell me where she goes and why?"

"Listen, telling you what I know, what good would it do for anyone—you, Bonnie, or me?"

"It'd help lessen my anxieties about her." Anxieties didn't begin to describe all the thoughts and various scenarios that continually played through my mind. My writing was starting to suffer. I couldn't keep my mind off of Bonnie.

Abdul leaned toward me, a solemn look on his dark face. "Will it? Or will knowing merely *add* to your anxieties?"

I sighed and ran a hand through my hair. "I don't follow you." My frustration showed in my voice.

"My friend, because I don't tell you what you want to know, you're disappointed in me. And I can understand that. It saddens me that you feel that way, but knowing what I do, it is better that I live with your disappointment than tell of Bonnie's whereabouts." He paused. "If only there were some way that I could tell you and then have the knowledge instantly erased from your thoughts. If I could do that, I would not hesitate one moment to tell you. But if I told you, instead of being disappointed in me, you'd fall to your knees and *thank* me for sealing my lips so long. And for the little time you possessed the knowledge, you'd hate yourself for knowing and me for telling."

"All of what you say may be true, but I'll never know of its truth unless, of course, you answer my questions."

"As I said, I have good reasons for not answering." I had a sinking feeling I was getting nowhere with Abdul.

"I'm sure you do," I said, "but the point is, are those reasons as valid today as they were the last time we discussed the matter, in view of the fact that now Bonnie has been missing for such a long time?"

"And because of that fact, Paul, my reasons for not telling you are even more valid."

A couple kissing at the table next to ours momentarily caught my attention. I focused my eyes back to Abdul. "Why do you say that?"

"Why? Look, if I answer that question you'd be able to figure out the answers to the questions you originally asked, so I can't tell you. I gave my word to Bonnie that I wouldn't share what I know. And to me, my word is worth everything to me."

"I can respect that, Abdul. However, you make this whole thing sound so *mysterious*, as if it's some kind of cloak and dagger operation."

"I don't mean to. It's just that if I told you what you want to know, I'd betray Bonnie and myself by dishonoring my word. And I can't do either." Abdul glanced at his watch, popped to his feet, and, after snapping his fingers, said, "Paul, I just remembered an engagement I have with a friend."

"By all means, don't let me hold you up. I take it that this meeting is with one of your new Algerian friends?"

"Yes. We're supposed to meet at my place. There's some unfinished business to discuss, important business, and I don't want to be late."

"Of course and I understand."

"So, though I hate having to do this, *mon ami,* I really must rush. You see, this friend of mine doesn't like anyone being late. It annoys him."

"You don't have to explain. Take care, Abdul." I watched him hurry off.

"Well, that was a wasted conversation," I mumbled to myself. I'd learned nothing and all I'd succeeded in doing was frustrating both of us. I stood, threw a coin on the table as a tip and headed for Twenty-One Rue Galande. There was a decided chill in the air. I felt it clear to my bones—both the chill and the loneliness of being alone at Christmastime.

Two days before Christmas, I sat on the enclosed terrace of Café Le Fleur, which was directly across the street and diagonal to Notre-Dame Cathedral. It was one of Bonnie's favorite cafés. The view from the terrace was excellent. When you looked straight ahead, you saw the cathedral towering over nearby slated roofs. On either side, attached to the huge church, were flying buttresses that angled out like giant supportive fingers. The architecture was exquisite: reliefs, carvings, bell towers and gargoyles.

Though the view was exceptional, Bonnie frequented the café not because of the scenery, but because of a waiter friend of hers who worked there, Marcus Seldan. He was a part-time college student, who, as Bonnie said in her letter to me, was in love with a prostitute who worked the streets of Place Pigalle, an infamous red light district.

Marcus came to my table, and after I placed an order for a Coke, he fetched it, returned, and said, "So tell me, where's Bonnie hiding these days? I haven't seen her in a while."

"You're not the only one, Marcus. It seems nobody knows where she is. At least no one I've talked to."

"Maybe she returned to the States."

"Could be, although I doubt she'd leave without saying goodbye." Would she? Bonnie and I were close, too close for her to just walk away from our friendship. Still, the power of suggestion could be a strong force. "Did she tell you she was going back home?"

He wiped off the table next to mine, shaking his head as he did so. "No. When I said maybe she'd returned to America, that was just a wild guess, nothing more. I thought perhaps she might have gone home for Christmas."

"Oh." I looked away, surprised by the enormity of my relief.

"At any rate, I miss her," the waiter said.

"So do a lot of other people, including me. But then, she's done it before."

"Done what?"

"Disappeared, then reappeared without explanation."

"There's a chance she just wanted to get away for a while. You know how that goes—occasionally we all need to escape, to find space and time for ourselves. When the world closes in on us, and at one time or other it closes in on all of us, it's then we search for a quiet sanctuary where we can be alone and hear our thoughts."

"I know the feeling."

"Perhaps she needed such a place. Anyway, as I said, I miss her—a lot. Whenever Bonnie Silver walked into this café, she brought her own rainbow."

"She does that wherever she goes." She did that to my life, I thought, slumping lower in my chair. My "pouting posture" my mother had always called it.

"By the way, if you see her, be sure to tell her I asked about her and that this café could certainly use a few of her rainbows."

"You have my word. I'll do that."

Marcus entered the café and fetched his order pad. When he returned, he seemed pensive. "Paul, while I was inside I remembered an incident that happened early last week. When it took place, I didn't give it much thought, but now that I've had time to think about it, maybe it's worth mentioning. I'll tell you what happened, and you can let me know what you think."

"I'll be happy to."

"As I said, it happened a week ago. I was up in Neuilly, not far from the American Hospital of Paris."

"Were you sick?"

"No, I didn't actually go to the hospital. I merely strolled near it. I often go to that neighborhood. It's restful there, a place where a man can escape the hustle and bustle of central Paris and think in peace. Recently I've gone there often. You see, this…this girlfriend of mine, she…" After pausing, he sighed, "But that's another story."

"Marcus, I've heard about your girlfriend. Bonnie mentioned her in a letter to me."

"So, I don't have to tell you how much I love her."

"Not at all." I was finally beginning to understand the depths to which a man could care for a woman.

"Anyway, I was in Neuilly strolling and rummaging through my thoughts. Soon I found myself within a few blocks of the American Hospital of Paris, on one of those quaint Neuilly streets where moss-covered walls border sidewalks. A block or so straight ahead, I saw a woman approaching. I didn't think anything of it. I figured she was just another person, who, like me, was out for a stroll. But the closer she came, the more familiar she seemed."

"Was it your girlfriend? Ah, what's her name?"

"Marie…Marie DeClare." He shook his head, a sad expression on his face. "No. If I had wanted to find Marie I knew *exactly* where to go, Place Pigalle, where the 'working girls' are. But no, it wasn't her."

I sipped my drink. "Who then?"

"The way the woman walked caught my eye. Her steps were springy, bubbly. Seeing her gait, I instantly knew who she was— Bonnie Silver."

I sat up straighter in my chair. "You're kidding. What would she be doing in that neighborhood? She's never mentioned that she had friends there. And I've heard her talk about all her friends." Perhaps not, perhaps she'd only told me about the ones she wanted me to know about. Who was she staying with over in that neighborhood? A man? A fiery emotion snaked its hot fingers around my lungs and squeezed. I fought for air as Marcus continued recanting his story.

"At the time I couldn't be sure it was Bonnie, though the woman certainly looked like her. 'Bonnie, Bonnie!' I yelled, waving."

"Did she stop?"

"Yes, and then stared in my direction."

"Any indication she recognized you?"

He quickly glanced around at his customers, probably to make sure none needed his attention. Then he continued with his story. "None, except for her stopping. Then she did something odd."

"What?"

"She did nothing. Absolutely nothing. Just stood, frozen, gazing at me. I say 'gazing at me.' Maybe I should have said her eyes seemed aimed in my direction."

"I see your point and, yes, there is a difference."

"I shouted again, louder this time. 'Bonnie! Bonnie Silver!'"

"What'd she do?"

"Same as before, continued standing as if riveted to the spot, standing and staring. 'It's me,' I called, 'Marcus...Marcus Seldan. Remember? The waiter at your favorite café, Marcus.'"

"Did she recognize you?"

He shrugged. "I can't say."

"What do you mean, you can't say?"

"I mean, what she did next stunned me." Marcus placed a hand on my table and leaned toward me. "She spun and hurried in the opposite direction."

"You're kidding! That doesn't sound like Bonnie at all." Why would she snub her friend? I'd never known her to ignore someone she knew.

"I called her again. 'Bonnie, Bonnie!' Instead of stopping or even slowing, she walked faster, almost jogging, occasionally glancing back." Marcus paused. "I wonder why she'd do a thing like that?"

"Beats me, but there could be lots of explanations. Maybe the woman, whoever she was—she didn't *have* to be Bonnie, but someone who looked like her—maybe she was frightened, afraid you were a molester and she'd be attacked." I was making excuses, I knew.

"Attacked? Me attack her? In broad daylight? With me shouting, drawing attention to myself and calling out my name so that anybody who happened by could identify me and give a full description to the cops? Attack her? And in that neighborhood, where women are unafraid to walk the streets at ten and eleven at night? And you say she thought I might attack her? Doesn't make sense.

"In fact, I'm willing to bet a week of tips that the woman I saw was Bonnie. Our Bonnie Silver, the same person we both know and love. As many times as I've seen her sparkle into this café, I know that walk as well as I know my own. A face I sometimes forget, names too, but a walk, especially one like hers, I don't forget. I say again, the woman I saw was Bonnie."

"Look, if everything you say is true, why would she act as if she didn't know you and try to avoid you? After all, you're her friend, and you did identify yourself. So, why would she flee? What was she up to?"

"I wish I knew. I really do."

I rubbed the back of my neck where muscles twisted and tightened, creating a colossal headache. "Strange, Marcus, really strange."

"Very. I wonder what's going on with her? Ah, women, they're such riddles." Shaking his head, Marcus reentered the café. Seconds later, he returned and, while waiting for the next customer, stood beside my table. We chatted. However, I didn't mention his "girlfriend" Marie again. I was afraid if I did, I might add to the pain he was already suffering because of her.

We talked instead about the mysterious woman he saw near the hospital and the way she acted. Marcus was still convinced she was Bonnie. If it were, we agreed that something had changed her.

Without a doubt, something had. But what? Or whom?

Chapter 24

Finally, three days after Christmas, Bonnie came home again. She returned the same way she left—without warning and when least expected.

On the morning she returned I, as usual, stopped in the foyer to pick up my newspaper. After removing it from the mailbox and leaning against the wall, I poured over the lead article. Behind me, the door opened, a blast of cold air swept over me, and someone stepped inside, but, engrossed in the article, I didn't turn to see who it was.

"Well," the voice behind me chirped, "aren't you glad I'm back?"

I pivoted and, to my surprise, there she stood, the Phantom Lady herself, Bonnie Silver. I hugged her and babbled, "I'll be damned! Is this really you, Bonnie?" I pushed her away, yet held her by her arms. "I can't believe my eyes! And what do you mean, am I glad you're back? Of course I am." I continued holding her at arm's length, scanning The Prodigal from head to toe. "You're looking great, absolutely great, even *better* than before you left."

"That's bull, Paul, and you know it. What're you trying to do," she smiled, reaching up to caress my cheek with her hand, "flatter me so you can work some sort of scam?"

"Of course not. I meant every word; you are looking great. Me, scam you? Suggesting I would, hurts my feelings."

"I was only kidding," she tittered.

I hugged her again. "I know. So tell me, how've you been? How was your Christmas." Mine had been lonely without her, and I hated that I'd become so attached to someone who would only be in my life for a short while. I wouldn't be in Paris forever.

Like the first wink of daybreak, she beamed one of her certain-to-make-you-feel-good smiles. "It's a glorious day out there, how could I be anything but fantastic."

Claude and Marie Rose, the couple who moved into Betty Jean's studio after her death, entered the building, laughing, kissing, and oblivious to our existence. Bonnie and I moved over to the mailbox so the couple could romance their way up the stairs. Seeing Parisians kiss was a common sight. Kissing and intimate whispering could go on for several minutes—and often did.

"Have you seen Roger or Abdul lately?" Bonnie asked.

I tore my attentions from the kissing, groping, giggling couple. "Yes, I've seen them both. However, the person I haven't seen, the person I've *longed* to see the most was you. Where've you been?"

"Same place I was the last time, only this time I stayed longer."

"Why do you disappear so often and where do you go?" I could have shaken her for her cavalier attitude. I'd been lost without her, damnit!

"Like I said, to the same place."

"Now you're repeating yourself." My stomach was starting to churn.

"I know." She smiled again, lighting up my world and reminding me how much I'd missed her. As if I needed a reminder, I told myself, running a hand through my hair in frustration.

"Why do you do that?" I asked, trying my best not to spoil the moment by getting upset with her. "Why do you avoid answering my questions? Why do you give riddles and enigmas for answers?"

"You wanna run that by me again?" She had the cutest quizzical look on her face.

I sighed and ran the backs of my fingers down her face. "I've forgotten how I phrased it."

"Paul, this conversation is turning into a verbal treadmill," she smiled. "So why don't we hop off it? Did you by chance pick up my mail?"

"Of course. It's up in my studio. You want to go up with me and get it?"

"If you don't mind."

"No problem." I headed for the stairs. When I reached the first step, a streak whizzed by me. The streak was Bonnie Silver.

"Hey, slow down, will you?" She didn't. Bubbling laughter, she scaled the stairs like a gazelle.

"Bet you can't catch me," she laughed.

"Catch you? That's child's play, Bonnie."

It might have been child's play, but the truth was I couldn't catch her. She waited for me at the top of the first landing. "Momma's boy," she teased. I assured her I could have caught her if I'd *really* wanted to. Her response to that lie? "Bullshit. Grade A. Bullshit, buddy. And you know it."

Seconds later, we, laughing like children on Christmas morning, entered my studio. She sat as I fetched her mail and placed it on the table in front of her. "So tell me, did anything interesting happen while I was away?" she asked, thumbing through the letters. I told her about the anti-America demonstration on Rue Galande. She listened and then shook her head. "What a shame. I'll lay you odds that before that war ends there'll be other such protests, many more."

"I'll pass on that bet. Did you have a good Christmas?"

She shrugged. "Passable. How about you? Did you look at all the window displays in the stores, especially at Galleries Lafayette?"

I told her I had and that they'd been works of art. I told her about attending the Christmas Eve service at Notre-Dame Cathedral with its uplifting majesty. I told her about the packages from home and growled about my oldest sister sending me a fruit cake—something she knew I hated. What I didn't tell her was how much I'd missed her. I'd never thought of myself as someone who'd depend on another person to feel complete or to be happy. Yet the truth was sitting right in front of me, smiling and brightening my world. For some reason I couldn't let her know how dependant on her I'd become. Frankly, it was a bit of a blow to my male ego. "Anything else happen while I was gone?"

"Well, I found two strange men in your studio. Have you been to your studio yet? Because when I was there it was in a shambles. Everything was turned upside down. Your clothes and books were scattered everywhere."

She stilled. "They were in my place? Strangers?" I nodded, waiting for her to explode. Instead she said, "I have to commend them, they did a good job."

"Of going through your stuff, you mean?"

"No, of putting everything back in order. I got home over an hour ago, so yes I've been in my studio. I would never have guessed anybody had touched a thing."

"Doesn't surprise me. They were a thorough couple. As far as I could determine, they were in your studio for quite a while, six or seven hours. Wonder what they were looking for?"

She walked over to my window, looked out at Rue Galande, and shrugged. "Why ask me?"

"Why not? It's *your* studio. You, if anybody, should know what's in it. Maybe they were searching for things like...stolen property or illegal drugs." Having baited the verbal trap, I waited for her response.

It came quickly: "Of course I know what's in my studio! That's why it beats the hell outta me what they were looking for. But whatever it was they didn't find it, the creeps." She shuddered before turning away from the window. "Knowing someone has gone through your things, touching them, looking at them, assessing them gives me the number-one-grade-A creeps. I'm trying not to let it spoil my good mood, but it makes me feel violated in some way. Like I've lost all sense of privacy, ya dig me, Paul?" She glanced across the room at me, and I nodded.

"Well, that's all the time I'm giving those brainless creeps." She snorted. "All that time wasted going through my pad, when they could have been hunting down *real* criminals. Wasted time 'cause they didn't find a thing."

"How do you know that?"

She pressed her wrists together in front of her. "You don't see me in handcuffs, do you?"

"No, not…yet." Please let her be telling me the truth, I thought.

As if she could read my pleading thoughts, she said, "Look, there's one thing I know to be the indisputable truth: they couldn't find anything illegal in my studio because there was *nothing* illegal in it. I could have told them that and saved them lots of time and effort." She snapped her fingers and said, "The hell with them. The hell with 'em all."

She seemingly dismissed the search of her studio as something so trivial it wasn't worthy of discussion, so she changed the subject. "By the way, I haven't checked all of my mail. I was expecting an important letter." She picked up the sizable stack of mail and started sorting through it again. "Ah, here it is," she smiled, tearing open an envelope and hurriedly removing the letter. As she read, the smile lighting her eyes dimmed.

"Something wrong, Bonnie?"

She sat at my tiny dining table and sighed. "Well, the news isn't the best." She refolded the letter and returned it to its envelope.

"Your expression says the news was distressing."

"Do I look that bad?" She put both hands in her hair and pushed it away from her face.

"Not bad, just…*saddened*."

Folding her arms on the table, she laid her head on them, and sighed. "Well, to be honest, the news was a terrible let down."

"About what?"

"About something that at first seemed so encouraging, something many believed showed *great* promise, but the letter says the thing doesn't work and," she sighed again, "it won't now or *ever*."

"Work, you say? Work on what? Work how? What are you talking about?"

She ignored my queries. "Well, for me, it's back to square one, but in spite of the setback, I'll go on. Somehow. Some way. I have to."

"My lady, I feel stupid."

"Why?"

"Because we're having an interesting conversation, but I don't have the *faintest* idea what the hell we're talking about."

"That you don't understand my friend, really doesn't matter. In fact, you're better off not knowing. Besides, I was talking more to myself than to you. I'm sorry I dragged you along for the ride." Half smiling, she changed the subject. "You didn't have much to say about Abdul. How's he doing?"

"He's OK, as far as I can tell, except I suspect that when you see him again, you won't recognize him."

"Has he changed his way of dressing or his hairstyle, something like that?"

"No, it's more than a cosmetic change," I hedged. At her questioning look, I said, "You'll understand when you get to talk to him."

"Well that gives me something to look forward to—seeing Abdul and taking note of the change in him. Oh, it's good to be home. Really it is."

It was wonderful seeing Bonnie again. And though she doubted what I said about how good she looked, I was telling the truth. She looked fantastic, in fact, even better than before she disappeared. Her cheeks rouged more glowingly, her eyes twinkled with greater sparkle.

But, the question remained, where from time to time, did she go? I took comfort in the fact that in her letter she assured me that one day I'd know the answer to that question. On the other hand, what Abdul once told me also resonated in my thoughts. He said that I'd scorn the day I learned Bonnie's secret.

Chapter 25

On the last day of 1968, the *Herald Tribune* featured four in-depth articles about the conflict in Vietnam and America's escalating involvement in it. In one, the Pentagon announced that it recently deployed ten thousand additional combat troops to the war zone. Coming on the heels of the previous week's high casualty figures, this initiative outraged the peace-seeking Doves. Hawks, led by the feisty senior senator from Texas, applauded the war's increase.

Following the Pentagon's announcement, hundreds of demonstrations, some violent, erupted throughout America—thirty protesters arrested in Cleveland, sixty-six in New Orleans, and twenty in Washington DC. In addition, there was widespread anti-war rioting in Chicago—policemen stoned, five trampled. None of the downed officers were expected to live. Opposition to proliferating American military commitment resulted in "anti-Yankee" rallies in Amsterdam, London, Rome, and Moscow.

The previous day, an alternative press in Chicago, *Independent Voice,* published photos of four wounded American GIs, their arms shredded, legs, bloody stumps. Waving enlargements of the photographs, members of The American Mothers for Peace Coalition blocked the main entrances to the Pentagon. Policemen arrested and slammed the middle-aged protesters into paddy wagons. Photos of cops bludgeoning the activists covered the *Herald Tribune's* front page, while pictures of the four wounded soldiers filled the second.

Bonnie, Abdul, and I chatted over a bottle of wine in my studio New Year's Eve. We'd decided on having a little get-together before going out into the streets to celebrate the beginning of 1969 with thousands of other Parisians. Music would fill neighborhoods, as would fireworks, sounds of popping champagne corks, laughter, and the frequent exchange of *bisses,* that delightful French custom of kissing a person on both cheeks, all amid cheers of *Bonne Annee!*

We'd drunk about half the wine when Bonnie mentioned the photos in the morning's Herald Tribune and said she thought the Vietnam War had degenerated into a national calamity that feasted on the blood of young Americans.

"You know what's wrong with North Vietnam?" Abdul said.

"No," I answered, "not that we were talking about North

Vietnam, but since you raised the subject, what's wrong with it?"

"It doesn't know how to fight a country like America."

"Judging from published GI casualty figures," I chuckled, "they're doing a pretty damn good job. But tell me, how do you think they should fight America?"

"Their mistake is they're restricting the war to Vietnam, and I say that's stupid."

"I'm confused. If not in Vietnam, Abdul, where are they going to fight America...in Iceland?" Bonnie chuckled, slicing off some cheese and placing it on crackers.

"Listen, if the Cong was smart," Abdul said, voice straining as he reached for the bottle, "they'd expand the conflict."

"To where?" I wanted to know.

"Simple," he stated, topping off everyone's glass. "Transform the whole world into a theater of operation."

"Just how do they do that?" I asked.

"Easy. Dispatch undercover agents to Amsterdam, Rome, Chicago, in fact, everywhere."

"OK, let's say the Cong does that. Once in place, what would the agents do?" Bonnie tucked her hair behind an ear and peered at Abdul, obviously disturbed by his remarks.

"Arm them with plastic explosives, and they'll wreak holy havoc. In practically no time, America would be *begging* for peace."

"What would they bomb?" I wanted to know.

"Any place where people gather—schools, churches, hospitals, airports, you name it."

"Don't you really mean any place *Americans* gather?" I could feel anger battle with suspicion.

"No, you heard right. Any place people gather, *any* people, not just Americans."

"But the terrorists would end up butchering innocent folks, Abdul—mothers, newborns, the old, the lame, those who have nothing to do with the war, who might, in fact, be as opposed to America's involvement in it as Mother Theresa or Martin Luther King," I countered. "So how can you justify doing such carnage?"

Abdul shrugged. "So a few hundred are killed here, a few hundred there; that's a minor price to pay. It's called collateral damage."

"Wait, Abdul. Think about what you're saying. We're talking about human beings. We're talking about mangled bodies strewn in streets, bloody corpses buried under debris, men, women, and children indiscriminately slaughtered like cattle." I couldn't believe

172

what my friend was suggesting. Where had the Abdul I'd met months earlier gone? And what happened to put this seemingly heartless man in Abdul's place?

"Look," Abdul growled, leaning toward me and pounding his finger on the table to punctuate his words. "Some find my idea hard to accept, and I realize that, but the truth is, *war is war*; it always has been, always will be. In wars, people get killed—it's inevitable. It's the nature of the business. During battle, no one is innocent; all are participants. Neutrality is a myth. You're either on one side or the other. And that's how it is. So everyone becomes fair game, from the President of The United States to some nun or school kid in Switzerland or in the remotest hamlets of Africa."

Bonnie sat there staring open mouthed at Abdul, twin tears blazing a trail down her cheeks.

"Abdul," I said, "let me see if I understand you correctly. You want North Vietnamese terrorists to blow up young kids and little old women in, say, Lisbon or Madrid, people with no connection to the Vietnam War or with America whatsoever? Is that what I'm hearing?"

"Exactly." Abdul's expression was grim, his eyes hate-filled.

My heart nearly tore in two with the realization that my friend had morphed into someone I didn't know, and didn't *care* to know. "All right, for the sake of discussion, let's say terrorists do as you suggest. The question is: What's the point of it all?"

"Simple, kill enough, what you call, 'innocent people,' and the deaths will get the world's attention, at which time you let it be known that the killings will continue until America withdraws its forces from Vietnam. The international community will then pressure the States to end the war by condemning and ostracizing Yanks and boycotting their products. That'll hit them where it hurts the most—in commerce and prestige. If America still doesn't comply, slaughter more people, and on and on." Spittle shot from his mouth as he exploded with his opinions.

"Abdul," Bonnie said, "you make it sound so simple—so coldheartedly simple."

He turned his attention on her. "It is. Tighten the screw enough and eventually America, boycotted and condemned by the world, will end the war."

"Abdul, to be honest, your idea is merciless, callous...cruel." There was incredulity in her voice.

"You don't understand, Bonnie. In war, one has to be unfeeling, without pity."

173

"OK, Abdul," I said, "let's suppose that one of the innocent little old women blown to bits by Cong terrorists just happened to be your mother. How would you feel about your idea then?"

He pierced me with his dark eyes for a few long seconds. "The same...the very same. Like I told you, in war everyone is a combatant, my mother included. Does that answer your question?"

Bonnie's hand flew to her throat. "You...you are joking, aren't you?"

He looked her straight in the eye and didn't answer.

Minutes later, Abdul told us he had to leave. Bonnie and I tried to persuade him to stay, but he explained that he was committed to an "important" meeting with "some friends," even though it was New Year's Eve and he hadn't mentioned it earlier. I walked him to the door. After he left, Bonnie sighed and, like a deflating balloon, plopped onto the sofa.

"Paul." She looked up at me with tear-filled eyes. "What was that all about?"

"I told you you'd see a change in him."

"I had no idea. No idea at all that the change would be in his heart. You heard Abdul, heard all that talk about The Cong winning the war by killing innocent folks."

"And?" I scooped up our wineglasses and took them to the tiny sink in my kitchenette.

"Have you ever heard anything so absurd?"

I stepped from the kitchen area to the sofa and looked down at her. "No. Remember I told you that you probably wouldn't recognize Abdul when you saw him again?" I sat down beside her. "Sad isn't it?"

"Beyond sad. What in the world changed him? Granted he has always had his biases, his dislike for the French, but it's escalated, hasn't it?"

"Judging by how he talked tonight, I'm afraid so."

She shook her head slowly and wiped away a tear. "What on earth has happened to our friend? What has hardened his heart toward other human beings?"

I wasn't sure there was an answer, at least, one that made sense to anyone but Abdul, so I said nothing. I enveloped her into my arms and held her as she cried for her friend, Abdul—a man who no longer existed.

Chapter 26

After I told Bonnie, I thought she was going to either faint or cry. Or both.

"Are you OK?" I reached out to rub her arm.

"Yeah," she choked out a sob, "it's just that I need a second or two to settle." She lowered to the edge of her sofa and, after catching her breath, said, "Paul, I want you to tell me again what I thought I heard you say the first time, but pray that I didn't."

"You heard right,." Her voice hitched, "You mean they—"

"Right, they arrested Abdul."

"That's what I thought you said. And you say you saw it all?"

"Everything." I rubbed hands over my eyes and turned to stare out Bonnie's window, looking yet seeing nothing, except for the memory of Abdul being taken away by the police. I was still struggling with my friend's arrest—and why. I turned to look at her.

Her hands were clasping and unclasping as she obviously tried to grasp the news I was giving her. "So tell me about it. I want to hear every detail. Don't hold anything back."

I walked over to a chair, removed a stack of books and, placing them on the table, sat down. "Well, earlier today I was sitting on the glass enclosed terrace of a little café near Montparnasse. Ordinarily I don't go up there, it's too far. But I was tired of writing at my usual spot. I needed a change. You know the café I'm talking about, the one on the corner just up from where Abdul recently moved."

"No, I'm afraid it doesn't register."

"It's next to that big handbag boutique."

"Oh, right." She nodded. "Now I remember."

"Anyway, I went there and wrote. After three hours, my fingers cramped so I stopped to rest and flex them. Glancing down the street, I noticed a man standing in front of the building where Abdul lives. He was reading a newspaper, or appeared to be reading it. I thought it odd that he'd be doing so when it was so cold outside. Why not find a warm café? Occasionally the man glanced up and down the street, as if expecting someone, and then he'd look at his watch."

"Did you know the guy?"

"I'd never seen him before. Soon, Abdul and the friend of his who usually wears a blue suit headed down the sidewalk and entered a building. Seeing the pair, the man with the newspaper, folded it, and stuffed it into his pocket, then hurried to a car parked a couple of doors away. He leaned over and said something to its occupant, who immediately picked up a microphone and spoke into it.

"Seconds later, several men raced into view, two from around the corner and three from the terrace of a nearby café. The doors of two Renaults parked just up the street popped open, and men in jumpsuits exited, all but one carrying automatic weapons. The unarmed man shouldered a battering ram. Within seconds, they swarmed into the building that Abdul and his friend had entered.

"My goodness. Wonder what they were looking for?" Bonnie asked.

"A couple of customers, on the café terrace, where I sat wondered the same thing. 'What's up?' the guy beside me asked. 'Cops must be after a real big fish,' another commented. I left and hurried down the street, hoping to enter the building to see if Abdul was OK, but I couldn't get in."

"Why not?" She looked at me, her eyes wide with worry.

"A cop posted beside the entrance stopped me. 'Sorry, only those on official police business can enter.'"

I waited on the sidewalk near the door. Minutes later, several men with drawn pistols escorted two prisoners out."

"And I take it one was—"

I closed my eyes and nodded. "Right. Abdul. The other was his partner. Both were in handcuffs and leg irons." Bonnie gasped, her hand to her mouth. "Their guards looked jittery, as if expecting an assassination or escape attempt...or worse, a suicide bomber. Encircling the prisoners, lawmen scanned the crowd now gathered. Both policemen and prisoners inched towards a paddy wagon double-parked in front of the building. 'Abdul!' I called."

"Did he hear you?"

"I think so. At any rate, he turned, gazed at me, his face expressionless, eyes, two voids, and though we were only a couple of feet apart, I couldn't be sure he actually saw me. In fact, I wasn't sure he saw *anything*. He looked like a man lost in a nightmare groping for an exit."

She covered her eyes with her hands and shook her head. "Poor Abdul. Oh, I just can't bear it."

"Once the prisoners were in the paddy wagon, an officer slammed its doors, and the vehicle, tires squealing, sped down the street. Abdul stared out the rear window. He seemed dazed, as if in another dimension. And that was the last I saw of him."

"Do you have any idea what he's been charged with?"

"The cop at the door said both were suspects in the recent café bombings." She gasped again. "I guess you've heard about those?"

"Who hasn't? They're horrible. Innocent lives ended in the blinking of an eye. Sickening. But...but Abdul couldn't have been involved in those! Why this is awful! These charges, they can't be true. They just can't be! Tell me more about him. Oh, my poor, dear Abdul." She shook her head as if refusing to accept the reality of things.

"What do you want to know? I think I've told you everything."

She stood and started pacing back and forth in her small studio like a caged tiger. Stopping, she rapid-fired questions at me. "How did he look? Had he been roughed up by the cops?" I shook my head. "What was his expression, his demeanor? What'd you see in his face, his eyes?"

"Blankness in both. He seemed disengaged."

"From what?"

"Everything. Himself included."

"So, there were no clues about what was going on in his thoughts?"

"Bonnie, I didn't need any clues because I was sure I knew what was in his thoughts."

"Oh?" She sat, hugged a throw pillow to her chest, and started a slow rocking motion as if to consul herself. "How? How could you possibly know what Abdul was thinking?"

"You remember the last time we talked to him, don't you?"

She closed her eyes. "Of course. That was just last week."

"Remember those...heartless things he said?"

She opened her eyes and aimed them at me, sadness filled them. "How could I forget?"

"Recalling what he said New Years Eve, I figured I knew what he was thinking."

"Like you, I remember what he said all right." She stood and started pacing the room again. "I remember that I couldn't get over the change in him. I wanted to chalk it up to some mood he was in— some *dark* mood. Maybe he'd argued with someone earlier or had too much to drink. I tried to rationalize his behavior, his sinister thoughts. Told myself he really didn't mean any of those evil things he said. Well, I guess I was wrong. And all the while, I thought I knew him."

"Did you?"

"Sure. After all, he was one of my closest and dearest friends."

"Bonnie, when you get down to the nitty-gritty, who can say he truly knows *anyone*, including himself?"

News of the "grande" arrest spread through The Latin Quarter like pollen in a cyclone. The following morning in the dairy across from Twenty-One Rue Galande, it was the subject *du jour*.
"What those bastards did was disgusting!"
"Makes you want to puke."
"Both are barbarians!"
"No, worse…brutes with no conscience."
"How could they justify murdering strangers? How could *anybody* justify doing that?"
At Café Le Balkan, customers debated what punishment would be appropriate for the "guilty thugs." There, of course, had been no trial to determine the suspects' guilt or innocence, but the disputants weren't concerned about "such a minor technicality." Some recommended the use of the iron maidens and/or thumbscrews on them. Others insisted that a year on the rack would be too lenient for "the bastards."
More charitable customers, though outnumbered and outshouted, said life behind bars was "the only humane sentence." Tempers flared. Several debaters almost came to blows. Two did, and the café owner, aided by a big stick, ejected them.
One tabloid printed a three-column article profiling the "cold-blooded terrorists." Similar write-ups, though less incendiary, appeared in *Le Monde*. "Algerian Hitler" screamed the headline of one journal. "Bloodthirsty Killers," declared another.
Bonnie and I sat at a table in the café, trying to ignore the murmured and shouted conversations swirling around us. We'd been sharing the morning papers, both English and French versions. She laid one paper aside after reading part of an article to me. "Paul, do you suppose Abdul is reading all this stuff the newspapers are printing about him?"
"Who knows?" I gulped my coffee, grimacing as it scalded my mouth.
She waved a hand at the *Le Monde* she'd just laid aside. "The press is having a field day, an attack frenzy, making Abdul look like Attila the Hun."
"Yes, on the Hun's worst day."
"Poor Abdul. I hate to think of what's going through his mind."
"Same here."
"One thing is for sure; it's not good. So, what do you think,

Paul?" She leaned towards me, her eyes wide in questioning.

"Think about what?"

She let out a sigh. "About going to visit him. I don't abandon my friends."

"That's a good idea. That'd be an effective way of letting him know that in spite of everything, there are still those who give a damn about him."

"So, it's decided, we go."

I stood, grabbed my coat and scarf, and held out my hand. "Right, we go."

I'd heard a thousand horror tales about French bureaucracy. Most were, I thought, exaggerations based on half-truths. Bonnie and I soon discovered there was more to these stories than hyperbole.

To visit Abdul, we had to have six forms signed and stamped by five different bureaucrats, the final one a cantankerous old hag who specialized in hating Americans, or anyone else who threatened her claim to the title of Grand Potentate of Red Tape, Government Double-Talk and Bureaucratic Bullshit.

After convincing Lady Macbeth to affix her John Hancock to the admission passes, Bonnie and I entered a cavernous reception hall, through the center of which stretched a glass partition with rows of chairs on either side. Fronting the chairs ran a long counter, on which telephones sat. Bonnie and I took seats and waited.

Minutes later, two armed guards escorted Abdul through the far door to a chair directly in front of Bonnie and me. He sat and, after glancing at his handcuffs, he looked up. The three of us then picked up telephones.

"Abdul?" Bonnie spoke first, unbuttoning her jacket as she did.

"Yeah, Bonnie."

"How've you been?"

He smiled, but the smile was anemic. "For someone on this side of the partition, I'm as well as can be expected."

"Are they feeding you OK?" Bonnie wanted to know.

"Well, the food isn't exactly the kind they sell in Algerian restaurants on Rue Huchettes, but I shouldn't complain about that."

"At least it's food and it's edible, right?" She choked out, tears pooling in her eyes.

"Sometimes."

"I see. So tell me," Bonnie said, "have you been able to get your hands on a newspaper?"

"Yes."

179

"I hope what you're reading about yourself in the press doesn't upset you."

"Bonnie, I've never lost a moment's sleep over what the press says. I take the long view of newspapers because news is a short-lived thing. Newspapers are merely yesterday's history and tomorrow's landfill—gone and forgotten. Anyway, I do appreciate you guys coming. But there is something you should know. One, I did what I did because it was the *only* thing I could do. And two, if you're wondering if I'd do anything different, I wouldn't."

Tears started racing down Bonnie's pale cheeks. I took her hand and squeezed it gently for comfort. "Why not?"

"My dear friend, like everyone, I was born into a mass of circumstances woven by chance and history, one fabricated long before I was born. The decision to do what I did was not mine alone. History and circumstance made the choice for me, made it the day Frenchmen with greed in their hearts set foot on Algerian soil. When they did, fate cast me to play a prescribed role. And for playing that role I must now pay with the only currency French law accepts: the remaining years of my life. And after I pay, I will do what we all must do, move…to another plane. Hopefully, a happier place, where colonialism and its cruelties are unknown."

The guard tapped Abdul's shoulder with a baton and barked that his visiting time was up. Abdul stood and the chains coupling his ankles clanked. Bonnie and I glanced at each other, and, after saying goodbye to Abdul, we left.

That was the last time we saw Abdul. A month later, a tabloid printed the following: "At 6:50 Tuesday morning, Abdul Bushaeve, the notorious 'Café Bomber of Paris,' died in his jail cell. The body of the convicted Algerian murderer dangled from a leather belt he had converted into a hangman's noose. How the belt came to be in the prisoner's possession is under investigation."

The length of the article was striking. Prior to Abdul's death, stories about "The Mad Paris Bomber" filled three or four front-page columns daily in nearly every Parisian journal. The piece announcing his suicide was the last article on the last page, written in fewer than thirty-two words.

Chapter 27

A week passed and once again, Bonnie Silver disappeared. The preamble of her vanishing came the evening she and I walked to The American Cultural Center, a popular meeting place for Americans, as well as Frenchmen and Germans. In fact, it was a place for anyone who wanted to learn more about America and American life. Occasionally musical groups performed there and in addition to being a venue for concerts, the Center housed a small library of books by Americans that visitors could borrow.

Bonnie and I were about to leave The Center when I glanced at the bulletin board and saw a flyer announcing that the Sunset Singers would perform there the following night.

"How'd you like to go to the concert with me, Bonnie?"

"Love to."

"How about I pick you up, say, 'round six? How does that sound?"

"I'll be waiting, with rings on my fingers and bells on my toes." We laughed, hooking arms, as we strolled up the street.

At six the following evening I knocked on her door. She wasn't in, nor would she be home the next five days. On the sixth day she, as if by magic, reappeared. She knocked on my studio door, and when I opened it, she looked at me strangely with those aqua blue eyes of hers.

"Why, hello stranger, or should I call you the *Prodigal Daughter?*" She didn't answer. "Did you enjoy your sabbatical?" She looked away. It was obvious she didn't want to discuss her absence.

She cleared her throat, glancing up at me briefly before she spoke. "The Sunset Singers, Paul, how was their show?"

"I don't know."

"What do you mean?" She fiddled with her red knitted scarf.

I leaned against the doorjamb and stuck my pencil behind my ear. "I didn't go to the concert."

"You should have."

I crossed my arms over my chest. "I'd planned to go with you, remember?"

"I know, and I'm flattered you invited me, but you should have

181

gone without me. I'm sure you would've enjoyed yourself."

"Could be, but it wouldn't have been the same without you there to share it with. So tell me, why weren't you home when I stopped by for you?"

She shrugged a shoulder. "Something came up; something requiring my immediate attention."

"Couldn't somebody else have handled it? Whatever it was?"

"I wish someone could have. I really do. What a blessing that would have been. But it wasn't to be, nor will it *ever* be. I'm the only person who could have taken care of it."

I peered down at her, wondering if now she'd tell me the truth or would she give me another stellar performance of *The Evasion Dance.* "Only you?"

She shrugged a shoulder. "Yes. And, like I said, that's the way it was and always will be."

"Don't you think by now I deserve a better explanation than that? You come in and out of my life like the coming and going of the tides. Frankly I'm getting sick of it. Getting!" I exhaled a harsh bark of laughter. "Hell, I've been sick of it now for months. Are we friends, or not, Bonnie?"

She locked wounded aqua eyes on mine. "Please understand that I can't tell you." She reached out with a gloved hand, laying it on my arm.

I jerked my arm back. "Can't or won't, Bonnie? Do you have any idea the thoughts that go through my mind when you're gone? You're driving me crazy with these disappearance acts." I ran both hands through my hair, trying to regain a measure of calm. I was yelling at her, and God help me, I wanted to shake the truth out of her. "Slowly and surely crazy."

Tears were pooling in her eyes, and I was feeling like a first class heel. "I need your understanding, Paul. Please don't be angry." I was weakening and hated it.

I opened my arms and she stepped into them. We stood there for several minutes, both trying to comfort the other with promises neither could make. She couldn't or wouldn't give me the truth. I couldn't look the other way any longer.

In the end, I told her I understood, but I didn't. And a whispering voice told me I might never understand.

Two days later as I was leaving the apartment building, I happened upon Bonnie in the foyer. Arms circling a large box stuffed with groceries, she strained to mount the stairs.

"Let me give you a hand, OK? Hand it over." I reached out. "Come on, my momma raised me to be a gentleman."

She backed away. "Thanks, but I can handle it. If you want to help, get the others."

I looked around. "What others? I don't see any more." "They're outside in the taxi. Mind bringing them up?" Her breath strained with exertion as she continued to climb the steps.

"No problem." I scratched my head in wonder and turned toward the door. How did the woman stay so thin if she ate large quantities of food like this? I fetched the two boxes and carried them to her studio. While helping unpack the boxes, I asked, "What do you plan to do with so much food? Have a picnic for the Sorbonne freshman class?"

"Paul, what do people do with food?"

"Eat it, of course," I said, a can of tomato soup in each hand.

"Brilliant," she smiled, "so, there's your answer."

"But this much food, Bonnie? Come on, give me a break. I'd say you got enough grub to last—"

"Long enough," she interrupted, voice softening. "Long enough."

"And how long will that be? Two weeks? Three? A month?"

"Like I said, long enough. So why don't we let it go at that? Now will you pass me those three cans of baked beans?"

"Before or after I bow, Slave Master Silver?"

She switched on a smile, lighting my world as always. "Either way, peon, either way."

A couple of days later I bumped into Bonnie on the stairway. Again, she was carrying more groceries.

"Bonnie."

She stopped. "Yeah?"

"Let me ask you something."

"Sure." She shifted the bags in her arms.

"And you promise you'll give me straight answers."

"You have my word."

"Are...are you pregnant?"

"Me pregnant? Do I look pregnant to you?" Her voice squeaked in an annoyed, insulted kind of way.

I smiled trying to unruffle her feathers. "No. I only asked because of all the food you're buying. I figure you have to be pregnant, supplying food for either twins or triplets. My sister, Carol Ann, ate like that when she was pregnant with my nephew."

"Trust me, I'm not pregnant. I've never even...well, I'm not, that's all."

"Then why all the food?"

She rolled her eyes. "I thought I answered that earlier. To eat. What else? Paul, you *do* have a college degree, don't you?"

"Yes."

"So why can't someone with a sheepskin understand what 'eat' means? E-A-T. What part of the word don't you comprehend? The first letter? Second? Third? Or the concept the word represents?"

"None of the above."

"So, you got any more questions?"

"Nope, I've exhausted my quota for today."

"Good," she smiled and continued mounting the stairs.

Because of that encounter with Bonnie, I learned that she wasn't pregnant. At any rate, she said she wasn't. And if she said she wasn't, she wasn't. The Phantom Lady was a walking shopping list of adjectives—irreverent, whimsical, and unpredictable, among others—but dishonest was not one of the adjectives. Still, the nagging question remained: why was she buying so much food?

The next day I went to her studio and knocked. I heard movement inside, but no one answered.

"Bonnie, it's me."

"Paul?"

I rolled my eyes. "Yes, Paul, as in Paul Lasser! You sound like you've never heard the name before. I'm your neighbor, the guy who lives downstairs---your friend, remember? So come on, open up. I've got a bottle of wine to share."

"I'm not opening the door."

"What? Sounded like you said you're not opening the door."

"You heard right. I'm not opening the door."

I leaned against the wall next to her door. "Bonnie, are you OK? I mean, are you playing with a full deck today?"

"Yes, all fifty-two."

"So why won't you open the door?"

"Are you deaf? Like I told you, because I'm not. That's why."

"Did I say something to hurt your feelings?" "No," she replied on a sigh.

"Look, I apologize for that crack I made about your being pregnant. I wasn't implying you're overweight. You really don't look overweight." The fact was she was too thin. She was losing weight of late.

"That's not it."

"Then what the *hell* is?" I slapped my hand on her door. "Why won't you open the door?"

"Because I'm not."

"Is that answer supposed to make sense?"

"Must *everything* make sense, Paul?"

"No, not really, but making sense would certainly help me follow this conversation, which, at the moment, I'm not following at all. Bonnie..."

"What, Paul?"

"I give up. I'll talk to you later, OK?" I headed for the stairs. Women can be so damned moody. Who can figure them out?

"Paul, you...you *do* understand, don't you?"

I stopped on the top step and looked back, talking once more to a closed door. "I'm trying to, but you're not making understanding easy."

"I realize that. And I'm sorry. I wish I could tell you everything, but I can't. At least, not now." For several seconds, she was silent. Then. "Paul."

"Yes?"

"Don't...don't go away mad because I need your help."

I returned to her closed door. "Me? Help you? Sure! How?"

"Paul, just remember that—regardless of what happens, regardless of what I say or do, and I'm sure to do and say things that'll seem odd to you, but in spite of all of that, don't desert me. Understand?" I didn't answer. I was trying to make sense of what she was saying. "Paul?"

"Yes."

"Did you hear me?"

"Every word."

"And?"

"Baby, you and I are inseparably close—almost like two halves of a whole. We both know that. So, if you tell me you need me, you can count on me. *Always.* For anything. On that, you've got my promise. So, you don't have to ask me to stand by you. I will, and for as long as the need exists. That I thought you understood."

"I did, Paul, but I had to hear you *say* the words. And, Paul?"

"Yes?"

"When I said I needed you, I meant it."

"And, I meant I'll be here for you."

I heard muffled sobs coming from her studio. I put my hand on her doorknob, jiggled the knob. "Bonnie, are you crying?" I wanted to break down the door to get to her, to hold her, to help her through this mood, this funk, this depression she seemed to be in.

"No," she shot back. "Of course, I'm not."

I walked to the stairs.

"Paul? Wait."

I stopped and turned. "I am."

"Ah…"

"Go on."

"I…I want to say…" Her sobs were louder, more frequent, without inhibition, flowing like streams cascading a mountainside. "Ah, I want to say…'night, Paul."

"'Night, Bonnie."

Seconds later, I stood in front of my studio door. From there I could hear Bonnie doing what she swore she was not doing…crying.

Chapter 28

The following morning I walked across the street to a little café, Café Ami, and, after ordering an espresso, sat on the terrace, bundled in my coat and hat. My grey knitted scarf was tightly wrapped around my neck and my feet were encased in three pair of socks. From there I had an unobstructed view of Twenty-One Rue Galande. If Bonnie left the building, I'd be able to see her. For most of the day, I sat, wrote, and watched. No Bonnie. At around four, I went to her studio and knocked.

"Yeah?" Bonnie's voice drifted from her side of the door, aka *the blockade.*

"It's me...Paul."

"Oh?" I could hear shuffling inside as if she were approaching the door.

I put my shoulder against the wood trim around the door, getting comfortable for the long exchange I figured we'd have through the solid wood access to her studio. I smiled slightly at the poster of the multi-colored peace sign she'd hung on her door the day after our surviving the students' riot. "Do you plan to come out today, Miss Phantom Lady?"

"How do you know I haven't been out already?"

"I have ways of finding out such things, and I know you haven't. So, are you coming out?"

"What do you think?"

"It doesn't matter what I think; it's what you *do* that counts. So, are you coming out? I take you to out for onion soup." No answer. "Bonnie?"

"Yeah?"

"Tell me something. Are you in there stoned out of your mind on grass or LSD? Or—"

"*Hell* no!"

"Are you sure?"

"Paul, why would you even think something like that? The only thing I've ever gotten high on was life and the beauty of it. Gimme a break, will you? How'd you come up with such a question? Me? Stoned? That's a stupid question."

"It may be, but I've tried asking all the non-stupid questions and they don't fit. Nor do they get answered."

"Well, what you just asked is the wrong size too." She sounded indignant.

"So, if you're not smoking pot or dropping acid, why have you locked yourself in your studio and refused to come out?"

"Why don't you leave me alone?"

"If that's what you want me to do, Bonnie, I will."

"When?"

"*After* I find out what's going on in there." I could feel my frustration building, and I knew she could hear it straining my voice. "And I'll find out. Take my word, I will."

"So, you think you will, huh?" Her voice was equally as determined. Great, I thought, the battle of two hardheads.

"Not think, Bonnie. I *know* I will."

"Bullshit!"

"I wouldn't say that if I were you."

"Why not?"

"Because, as you'll see, I'll find out what's going on, and when I do, you may have to eat your words. And I don't think you want to eat what you just said."

"You won't find out, Paul."

"Wrong, I will."

"Ha!"

"Miss Know-It-All. Just wait. You'll see." I turned and stomped down the steps, stalked in my studio, and slammed the door behind me. That woman could be the most infuriating, the most frustrating, the most…

Again, the following morning I sat on the terrace of the café across from Twenty-One Rue Galande. And again, I didn't see Bonnie leave. What was going on? Maybe she was right after all…maybe I wouldn't find out why she locked herself in her studio—and by doing so, locked out not only me, but also the rest of the world.

Later that afternoon I headed for my studio. I stopped in the foyer to see if I had any mail. I didn't, but Bonnie did—a single letter enclosed in a fancy, pale gray envelope that was made from top-of-the line paper—first class stuff. The return address? "The American Ambassador, the American Embassy of Paris."

What the hell was going on? Correspondence for Bonnie Silver from, of all places, the Ambassador's Office of the American Embassy? Why would Bonnie Silver be getting a letter from the AEP? The only explanation I could come up with was that the US ambassador, aware of her unpredictable irreverence, was officially warning her to stay away from the embassy because he already had more headaches than he could handle: anti-war protesters blocking his limousine, demonstrators burning draft cards in front of the embassy, etc.

I carried the letter to Bonnie's studio and knocked.

"Yeah, who is it?"

"Me."

"Oh. Hi, Paul." She almost sounded glad to hear my voice. Maybe I could persuade her to open the door, especially once she heard about the letter.

"Hi, Bonnie."

"How are you?"

"Fine," I replied to the locked door.

"You sure?"

"Positive. Although I'd be better than fine if I could see your beautiful face." I waited for her typical response, but got nothing. Silence. I exhaled a frustrated breath. "What about yourself?"

"I'm still kicking, and that's something a lot of folks can't say."

"That's for sure. Bonnie, there was a letter in the box for you. I brought it up."

"Thanks. That's very kind of you."

"So, I know you'll open the door so I can hand it to you." I smiled, tapping my hand with the edge of the grey envelope.

"You *know* that, right?"

"Yeah."

"Then you know wrong."

My smile disappeared. "You don't understand, Bonnie. This is an important letter."

"How do you know it's important?"

"Because of who sent it; it's from the American Embassy of Paris, no less."

"You're putting me on." I could hear shuffling inside as if she were walking to the door. Maybe she'd open it after all.

Thinking I'd soon see her sweet face, my mood brightened. "I kid you not. It's from the American Embassy."

"OK, so I'll tell you what to do, open it and read it to me."

"Read your mail? That wouldn't be right, and you know it."

"You have my permission, Paul, so read it to me."

I was discovering that Bonnie was smarter than I thought, a lot smarter. Frankly, I wasn't sure if I liked it. "OK, OK, I'll read it to you, if you insist."

"I do." A pause. "So, what're you waiting for, Paul?"

"Give me a sec, will ya? First, I have to get the letter out of the envelope. 'Dear Miss Silver,' I read, and stopped. "Bonnie?"

"Yes."

"I guess you know that what I'm doing is probably illegal. It would be so much simpler if you opened the door and—"

"Don't start that again, please. Don't. And since I've given you my permission to read the letter, it's not illegal. You're just making excuses, and we both know it."

"OK! OK!" I grumbled. "So what if I look like an idiot standing out here in the hall reading a letter to a closed door.

"*'Dear Miss Silver,'*" I continued, "*'Acting on reliable information provided this office from an impeccable source, a full-scale investigation was recently conducted. As a result, I wish to inform you that a ranking official of the French government will contact you within days, offering sincere apologies for what has transpired. Rest assured that this office will see to it that those responsible for the infringement on your rights will be dealt with to the fullest extent of French law.'*

"*'Sadly, I must report that due to the unspeakable actions of a zealous and misguided French law official, who harbored anti-American biases and who hoped to embellish his resume in a scheme to secure a higher paying position, for months you have been the target of an illegal undercover investigation. This official, whose sole aim, evidence indicates, was to indict you, a person chosen at random, on false charges of distributing illegal substances and conspiring to overthrow the French government.'*

"*'The inquiry revealed that the lawman in question possessed no probable cause for conducting such a probe and did so without authorization from either his superiors or the courts. Because of his twisted zealousness, he is an embarrassment to the French government and will be dealt with accordingly and harshly.'*

"*'On behalf of that government, and until you receive official correspondence from it, allow me to offer apologies that this regrettable incident ever occurred, and my hope that you will enjoy the remainder of your stay in France, free from police misconduct.'*

"*Respectfully yours, Ambassador William Sebastian Clark.'*"

"Is that...is that all the letter says, Paul?"

"That's it."

"Oh," she sighed.

"A bored 'Oh,' is that your only reaction? You don't sound at all enthusiastic about the good news I just brought you."

"Should I?" she said, matter of factly, as if we were discussing baseball scores. Her question was ridiculous. It didn't deserve an immediate response, so I didn't give one. "Well, Paul, should I sound enthusiastic?"

"Of course you should. Can't you see how lucky you are? You could have ended up warehoused in some French penitentiary, doing maybe twenty to life on trumped up charges. And when you hear that authorities nabbed the guy trying to railroad you, what do you do? Become Miss Nonchalant of the Year." I folded the letter and reinserted it into its matching envelope.

"Look, I *hadn't* done anything wrong, and I knew that."

"What difference does your innocence make? In a court of law, being innocent is often a liability. If you don't believe that, ask a few of the innocent prisoners sitting on death row."

"That the innocent are sometimes punished is something life has already taught me, Paul, and continues to teach me...all the time. Not only do the innocent suffer before the bar of justice, but also in the court of life."

"That's for sure. Anyway, the letter explains a lot, doesn't it? It tells why those cops questioned me about you, and why the men rummaged through your studio. It's all becoming clearer now. Anyway, what do you want me to do with your letter? If you'd just open the door I'll be more than happy to hand it to—"

"I'm not opening the door, Paul!"

"So what'll I to do with the letter?"

"Keep it."

"What?"

"You heard right, keep it. Either that, or toss it."

"Bonnie, you're impossible!" I waited for a rebuttal. None came. I was tired of beating my head against a brick wall, or in this case, a locked door. "I'm going to my studio."

"Paul, wait. I want you to understand something before you go. I realize that the way I've acted recently and the things I've said may be...well...confusing."

"Confusing?" I ran a hand through my hair. "That's the understatement of the year. Damned frustrating would be more like it."

191

"But I want you to understand that I didn't lock myself in here because I wanted to. And that's all I can tell you now, except that I really want to tell you more, but I can't."

"This is really getting old. Why are you hiding?"

"One day you'll know the truth, Paul."

"Sooner or later?"

"I can't answer that. I realize that what I've said and what I'm about to say you'll find hard to believe, but I'm grateful and happy that you stop by from time to time to check on me. And I hope you'll continue to do that."

"I will." As if I *could* stay away from her; the woman was like a magnet, and I was but a jumbled, confused mass of steel.

"Paul." She cleared her throat. "I'll…I'll…be seeing you."

"I certainly hope so."

"Me too."

Several days passed and Bonnie continued her self-incarceration. I, of course, knew she couldn't stay locked inside forever. Eventually she'd exhaust her food supply and would have to come out. But when?

That Thursday morning I resumed my vigil at the café across from Twenty-One Rue Galande. As usual, I sat on the terrace and wrote, occasionally glancing at the apartment building's entrance. By noon, I'd filled the only composition book I brought. I needed another, so I headed to my studio. After crossing the street, I stepped onto the sidewalk and looked up. I was directly under Bonnie's studio. Gradually her studio window opened, and, to my amazement, she appeared.

Once the bloom and blush of morning, her face was now the graying haze of sundown. Her hair, always undulations of softness, was disheveled. Crests of gray underscored her cheek, replacing the rouge that ordinarily glowed there. Silent, she stared straight ahead, eyes, empty orbs. Though I was only yards away, she appeared to be unaware of my presence, in fact, unaware of anything or anybody. Her expression was as blank as a sheet of paper.

"Bonnie," I called. She looked in my direction but gave no indication she either saw or heard me. "Bonnie!" Her face was the personification of emptiness. "Bonnie?"

Where was the *authentic* Bonnie Silver? The impersonator in the window, who was she? Certainly not the woman I knew. What being now inhabited Bonnie's body and looked in my direction, looked but seemed not to see, hear, or feel? What had the counterfeit Bonnie

Silver done to the real one, who was the distillation of freshness and light?

"Bonnie, you can't stay locked in your studio forever!" I yelled. You've have to come out." No reply. "You're being *unfair*, unfair to Roger, to me, to all who love you." It was as if she hadn't heard me. "More important, you're being unfair to *you,* Bonnie Silver." More silence. "Can't you see the truth in what I'm saying? Can't you..." Slowly, she raised a hand.

I saw her lips mouth my name, "Paul."

"Yes." I was thrilled that she actually reacted to me.

"Don't go."

"I...I won't."

"I'll be back. Don't...don't go, Paul."

She disappeared from the window. Seconds later, she reappeared, holding a scrap of paper, and with a flick of the wrist, she wafted it to the sidewalk. I hurried to where it landed, then looked at her. Rallying my last molecules of strength, I somehow managed to tear my eyes from the impostor in the window and focused on the note.

"'Call an ambulance. I'm dying.'"

Chapter 29

Moving as fast as my legs could carry me, I bolted around the corner to Café Le Balkan and, after buying a phone token at its checkout counter, I charged into a telephone booth, dialed 15, then instructed the dispatcher to send an ambulance immediately.

When it arrived—within minutes, though each seemed an hour—I, pacing back and forth in front of my apartment building, flagged it down.

"What's the problem?" the driver asked.

"There's a sick woman upstairs, fourth floor," I shouted, pointing. "She needs immediate help! Hurry! She's dying! Follow me!"

Seconds later, the driver, his partner and I bounded the stairs to Bonnie's studio. The door was unlocked, and we rushed inside where we found her sprawled across the bed, eyes closed, and perspiration glazing her brow. The natural blush that once lived in her cheeks no longer held residence there. Her skin was like bleached leather, grainy and pale. "Bonnie!" She creaked open her eyes. "Bonnie!" Slowly she closed them. "Bon…Bonnie, baby, do you…do you hear me?"

If she heard me, she showed no signs that she did.

Seconds later, Bonnie lay on a gurney in the back of the ambulance. I knelt beside her, and though only inches from her, I wasn't sure she recognized me or, for that matter, even saw me. Her eyes, though open, seemed comatose, totally lacking vitality. I looked into them. She wasn't home.

"Bonnie. You're going to be fine…just fine." I didn't know if I was saying the words to reassure her, or me.

Abruptly, the driver swerved the vehicle around a corner, then, tires screaming, it catapulted forward, as if shot from a Howitzer. Glancing out the rear window, I recognized several landmarks and realized we were on our way to the American Hospital of Paris.

Bonnie's hand was now warm, almost searing, and though her lips quivered, she uttered not a sound except to whisper, "Paul…Paul."

"I'm here, baby…I'm here. Don't leave me. Stay with me. You hear? Stay…"

The ambulance siren wailed its "wee-whaa" sound, the cry of a wounded jungle beast alerting all to "make way...make way!"

Soon, the vehicle screeched to a stop. "Bonnie, we're here...we're..." Her face was as expressionless as it was ashen. Perspiration glistened her cheeks, but her lips seemed parched, a duo of deserts circled by a moist expanse.

The rear doors of the ambulance swung open, revealing two men in white smocks standing inches from the bumper. Behind them hung a sign over the hospital entrance: "Emergency Room." The paramedics slid the gurney forward as I hopped from the vehicle and joined them on the asphalt; the three of us then rushed inside. "Hold on, Bonnie, hold on," I ordered, or prayed, or both.

A nurse cradling a clipboard stood at the entrance, and as we approached, she stared at Bonnie and immediately her expression changed from professional detachment to surprise, and finally, to a mixture of shock and dismay. "Oh my God!" she gasped. Bonnie remained motionless and unresponsive. "It's *Mademoiselle* Silver!" the nurse heaved. "Hurry! Please hurry!"

How did the nurse know Bonnie's name? That was the question, but for the moment, finding its answer was the least of my concerns. Of greater immediacy was seeing that Bonnie received the medical attention she desperately needed, and as quickly as possible. Now her hand was even warmer, her lips and cheeks, more ashen.

Inside the hospital where two hallways intersected, one of the paramedics turned to me. "I think we have everything under control now," he said. "We'll handle her from here on." They raced the gurney down a long corridor. Meanwhile, I walked to the admission desk, knowing I'd have to provide information about the new patient: her name, address, etc.

The clerk looked up. "Can I be of service, *Monsieur*?"

"Yes, ah, I'm here for the patient just brought in."

"I know. I saw you enter. Is *Monsieur* in need of medical attention for himself?"

"No." Although my heart rate was highly elevated and I felt a thousand pound weight on my chest after finding Bonnie in near comatose condition.

"What then?" the clerk asked.

"Well, I'm aware you can't admit a patient without first getting certain pertinent information. So I'm here to supply that information for—"

"Kind of you, *Monsieur*, but that won't be necessary."

"Are you saying you don't need the information?"

"I'm saying that the admission information won't be necessary for this particular patient."

"Why?"

"Because we already have the data on *Mademoiselle* Silver. You are Paul Lasser, are you not?" I nodded, surprised that she would know my name and equally surprised that the hospital already had Bonnie's information. I supposed my mental questions showed on my face. The clerk smiled slightly. "*Mademoiselle* Silver has you on her list of contacts, you and her father."

"What? List of...why?" I leaned against the reception desk, grasping it so hard that my knuckles had turned white. What in the world was going on?

"As I'm sure you know, from time to time *Mademoiselle* Silver has been receiving special treatment at this facility, in fact, for at least two years that I'm aware of, perhaps even longer. The staff has come to know her quite well, not only know her as a patient, but know and *love* her as a person, for she is a most remarkable individual."

"I'm well aware of that, *Madame*."

"When she added you to her list of emergency contacts, she said you were her closest friend."

"No, *Madame*, I'm really more than a friend. I'm closer, in fact, than a blood relative, if you get my meaning."

"Knowing the woman, I think I do understand."

"You mentioned that *Mademoiselle* Silver has been receiving treatment here for a long while. Treatment for what?"

She suffers from..." The clerk probed my eyes. "If she hasn't told you, then perhaps I shouldn't either."

"Suffers from *what*?" A shockwave entered my skull and quickly traversed to every pore, every molecule of my body, its jolt so powerful that I shuddered from the force of it. Bonnie suffered from an illness? That can't be! And she's been coming here for a couple of years for treatments? For what? I felt as if my warm blood had suddenly been replaced with ice water. I was chilled to the bone and my heart was beating a loud, staccato beat that echoed in my head—not the heart's usual lub-dub beat, but *for what...for what?* "What? What has she received treatment for? Tell me what's wrong with her!" I knew I was sounding like a frantic lunatic, but at this particular moment, I was both.

"You didn't hear?"

"No!" *Hell no!*

"Sir, the nature of *Mademoiselle's* ailment, I cannot give you."

"Do you mean you don't have that information?"

"*Monsieur*, you are asking me to divulge what I cannot."

"Why is that?" Why was getting information like pulling hen's teeth? I tried to trim down my frustration, to keep calm. I resisted the urge to reach out and choke the truth from the thin-lipped woman.

"It's a matter of medical ethics, *Monsieur*, not to mention the law, neither of which I wish to violate. I trust you understand."

I rubbed my hands over my eyes, resigned myself to that fact, and sighed. "I do."

"However, there are some facts I can share with you without breaching either my oath or the law."

"Please, *Madame*, I would appreciate it if you did."

"Well, as I said, *Mademoiselle* Silver has been receiving treatment here for a considerable time. She, of course, was aware of the nature of her ailment, as well as its prognosis. However, not once have I seen her yield to despair or depression. The hospital has treated countless others suffering the identical condition. Sadly, some drowned in despondency, dying prematurely, long before their hearts stopped beating, if you understand what I'm so clumsily saying."

"Oh, I understand perfectly."

"*Mademoiselle* Silver has always been upbeat, a beacon of sunlight. I've often wondered if the staff treating her has not received more therapeutic benefits from her smile and disposition, than she from the hospital's high-tech instruments and therapy."

"Knowing Bonnie as I do, it was a one-sided contest, slanted in *Mademoiselle* Silver's favor."

From a box of tissues on the counter, the admissions clerk removed one and nervously fingered it. "*Monsieur*, you have my sympathy."

Sympathy? Why...why *that* word? Why that awful, final word? Perhaps she meant sympathy for what she could not tell me. Surely that was it. "I appreciate that. And believe me, what you told me has been most helpful." Still holding the tissue, she looked away and then wiped her eyes. "Again, *Madame*, I thank you."

I walked into the waiting room, sat, and picked up a copy of the latest issue of *Time* that lay in the chair beside me. It featured reports of increased B-52 bombings in Vietnam, plus four articles detailing outbreaks of antiwar and civil rights demonstrations in the States. Several of the protests, said one story, turned violent, resulting in numerous arrests, cracked skulls, and deaths. I flipped to a story about an anti-draft riot in Baltimore and began reading it. Or, I should say my eyes stared at it; my mind, however, was fixated on Bonnie.

Thinking of her lying in a nearby room impaled in pain, I couldn't focus on what was taking place in faraway Vietnam or America. Compared to what was happening to Bonnie, events chronicled in the news magazine seemed trivial. Nothing, *nothing* mattered, except for Bonnie. I closed the periodical and tossed it into the chair beside me.

Four hours later, I was still in the waiting room, which was now packed with people, people chatting, snacking, reading, or snoozing. A hospital waiting room, I discovered, even one crammed with visitors, can be a lonely place, and especially if a person dear to you lies a few doors away, and you have no idea if she will live or die.

I was in agony, probably not as much as Bonnie, but in pain, nevertheless. Hers was physical, mine emotional. I rubbed my hand over my heart; it physically hurt, so great was my concern and worry for the woman I cherished more than my own life. The hurt multiplied when I realized there was nothing I could do, except sit, stare at a clock with frozen hands, and wait. Wait...wait as seconds slowly dripped past.

Finally, a nurse entered the waiting room

"Is there anyone here for *Mademoiselle* Bonnie Silver?"

I jumped to my feet. "Yes, me."

"Would you mind coming this way?"

"Certainly." The nurse and I walked a few paces down the hall and stopped. "How is the patient?" I needed to know.

"Resting comfortably."

I breathed a long sigh of relief. Maybe things weren't as bad as I'd feared. Maybe they put her on some miracle drug and she was improving every second. "I'm happy to hear that."

"When I say 'resting comfortably,' *Monsieur*, I mean she is as comfortable as can be expected... under the circumstances."

My heart sank. "Of course, *Madame*."

"*Monsieur*, I came to tell you *Mademoiselle* Silver will not be allowed visitors for the remainder of the day. Perhaps you'll be able to see her tomorrow."

"Perhaps, you say?" Was this all the information I was going to get? I had so many questions about my dear friend, the woman who'd come to mean more to me than anyone else in Paris—quite possibly in the entire world.

"Yes, perhaps," the nurse hedged.

"I see. Please, tell me something of her condition, *Madame*. You see, I care for this woman with every cell of my body."

"Of course, *Monsieur*."

"What is the prognosis? How long do you think she'll be in the hospital?"

After sighing and locking her eyes on mine, she paused, then whispered, "This time, *Monsieur*, she won't be going home. More than that I must not reveal. I am sorry, but you are not a family member. This is all I can say." She turned and walked down the hall.

Chapter 30

That evening, after leaving the hospital, I walked. I walked and thought about all the questions I had regarding Bonnie's frequent disappearances—and the indisputable, cutting pain that came with knowing the answers. I walked and weighed the significance of remarks she'd made in the past. I walked and worried; walked and ranted to the heavens in fear and frustration. I couldn't bear knowing that I was going to lose my heart-mate. Yes, I walked and cried. For hours I walked. Before I knew where I was headed, I was at the little café that Roger frequented, and there he sat on the terrace at his usual table—alone.

I told him that Bonnie was in the hospital and how serious her condition was. I, of course, expected some kind of reaction from him, but, face as blank as a cloudless sky, he stared straight ahead and said nothing. In fact, I wasn't even sure he was breathing.

"Roger, did you hear what I just told you about Bonnie?"

"I heard." His words were barely audible. One lone tear forged a trail down his black cheek.

"So, aren't you going to...I mean, after all, one of your closest friends is in the hospital, so naturally I expected you, after hearing the news, to do or say *something*. Scream. Curse fate's unfairness— and heaven knows it can be unfair or appears to be. I expected some reaction from you. Something. Anything. So why did you suddenly turn into a mute?"

"You really wanna know?"

"Of course."

"I didn't say anything because I...well, I couldn't. News about Bonnie froze my vocal cords." He stood. "I'm gonna have to split, man."

"Where're you headed?"

"I think I'll stroll along the Seine for a while. It's always relaxing there. The sound of water lapping the banks calms me. Maybe I'll smoke a joint. I need to try and erase Bonnie's illness from my thoughts for a while."

"I'll see you later, Roger." I was sure he heard me, but he didn't answer. Hands stuffed in his pockets, he walked on, and, eyes fixed on the sidewalk, said nothing.

Hospital visiting hours began at ten in the morning. At five of ten, I stood in the hall in front of Bonnie's room. I was more than eager to see her, beyond impatient, beyond anything I could describe. The stems of the bouquet of daisies and yellow roses I'd brought her from a street vendor were getting crushed in my steely grip.

I took several deep breaths to calm myself. "Get a grip, man." What happened to the cool, calm, and collected man who took everything in stride? Be cool!" I ordered myself. "Be cool!" I knocked on the door of Bonnie's room.

"*Monsieur*," her nurse said, "you will only be allowed to visit the patient for a short while."

"How short?"

"Five minutes. Doctor's orders."

"I'll remember that."

"Five and *only* five!" She eyed me up and down, and deeming me the obedient sort, she opened the door further.

"I understand," I promised. When I walked into Bonnie's room, what I saw shocked me, but, looking back, I now realize I shouldn't have been shocked. She looked dehydrated, feeble. Her face was pale. A jumble of tubes leading from a machine by her bed coiled near her shoulder; several extended to her arms and one to her nose.

I tried to lift her spirits by telling her how "good" she looked and by showing her the flowers I'd brought her. She weakly motioned to her nose, indicating that she wanted to smell them. I held the pathetic floral offering, symbolizing my friendship, my devotion, my love to her nose. The nurse quickly snatched them from my hand, saying she'd put them in a vase. She quietly left the room, and Bonnie and I were alone.

I placed my hand over hers and said that I was certain that in "no time" she'd be out of bed doing everything she normally did. After listening to me say these things, she turned and faced the wall. "Paul?" Her voice was weak and scratchy.

"Yeah?" What had I done now? She seemed upset.

"Are you through?"

"Yes."

"Do me a favor, will you?"

"Anything." A truer word had never escaped my lips, for at that moment I'd have done anything for her, anything to make her feel better, anything to bring back the Bonnie I loved.

"Please don't try that again."

"Try what? I don't understand what you're talking about." I

201

paused, thought of the empty lies I'd just uttered, and said, "OK, Bonnie, I won't."

She nodded once. "Time for secrecy is over. So is the time for false hope. We have to face what the future holds, don't we?" She shrugged and fiddled with a tube going into her hand. "I'd like to snap my fingers at the world right about now and tell it what I think of this nonsense. But what is…is." She sighed. "So, tell me, how is Roger doing these days?"

"He's fine, except he's not taking the news about you very well, but that's to be expected. In time, I'm sure he'll adjust. He needs a while to regain his balance and shake hands with reality."

"It's a shame I can't be there to comfort him."

"Knowing how compassionate you are, Bonnie, I'm sure not being with him saddens you tremendously."

"More than you'll ever know."

"As usual, you're more concerned about the welfare of others than you are about your own." She shrugged, then asked if I'd pass her the glass of water sitting on the little table by the bed. I held it to her parched lips. After a few sips, she nodded, and I placed it on the nightstand. "Now, maybe you can help me."

"How?"

"By explaining a few things, things that have been bugging the hell out of me."

"Like what?"

"Well, some time ago the concierge told me she saw you leave Twenty-One Rue Galande one morning at around three, and that you carried a leather bag she'd never seen you with before. She said that you, though within inches of her, spoke not a word—no smile, no greeting, nothing, acting as if she was invisible. What was that all about?"

"Paul, that morning I suffered a severe attack and was in excruciating pain, so I was on my way to the hospital. And about that bag? I carried my toiletries in it."

"Oh. And there's something else. Do you recall that letter you received from some guy in Chicago?"

"Yes. It was from William Jones, a medical researcher at National Health. He wrote to tell me that the new medication heralded in the press as a miracle cure for the condition I have, turned out to be ineffective, a total bust. In spite of the bad news though, I realized that I somehow had to suck it all up and move on."

I took her hand, rubbing my thumb over it. "Did you?"

"Did I what?"

"Were you able, as you say, to suck it all up and move on?"

"What choice did I have, Paul? Proof that I was able to suck it up lies in bed before you now…and speaks."

"And Bonnie, there's something else." I leaned over her and looked into her aqua blue eyes. "Baby, why didn't you…for the love of God, *why* didn't you tell me about your sickness and the treatments you've been receiving here? If you had told me, I wouldn't have been so worried when you disappeared from time to time."

"Why should I have told you, Paul?"

"*Why?*" No woman on the face of this earth had the ability to make me as happy or as frustrated as this woman lying before me. Had she no clue how much she meant to me?

"Yes, why? Let me ask you something. Wasn't it true that you already had more than enough crosses to bear without being saddled with mine? The whole world is in turmoil right now. A war in Vietnam which seems to have no end. Not to mention the racial time bomb about to explode in America. Add to that the personal problems you, I, and the rest of us Americans in Paris have to confront daily just to survive in this beautiful city. Weren't these burdens enough? Why would you want me to stack yet another one on top of those? Why? Isn't everyday life screwy enough?"

"But, Bonnie, compared to you those problems are miniscule, inconsequential."

"I could think of no reason to saddle you or, for that matter, anyone with my problems."

"Still, I think it would have been much better if you'd told me. I could have helped you, been with you so you wouldn't have been going through all those treatments alone. We could have faced everything together."

"Hush, Paul," she said, raising an index finger to her lips, "just hush…enough…enough."

We held hands, and with our faces nearly touching, we whispered things that needed saying, shared feelings and hopes that would never be realized.

Then the nurse appeared at the door. "*Monsieur.*" The nurse pointed to her watch.

"Of course, *Madame*, of course."

I stood. "I have to go. I wish I could stay, but I'll be back tomorrow. I promise."

Bonnie mustered a smile. I breathed a kiss across her cheek and two on her forehead. As I walked to the door, I wanted to look back at her. It pained me not to, but I didn't, I couldn't. I knew that if I looked at Bonnie I would have seen a mere shadow of the indomitable woman I once knew.

The following day when I returned to see Bonnie, I brought her pink tulips and yellow daffodils. She spent most of the allotted five minutes inquiring about the tenants at Twenty-One Rue Galande and the "neighborhood regulars." She wanted to know in detail how each was. She was genuinely interested in them. Later, as I stood near the door, ready to leave, it occurred to me that not once had she mentioned herself or her sickness.

"Bonnie, do you know what's going to happen the next time I come? We'll talk, not about your friends and the tenants at Twenty-One Rue Galande, but about *you*, Bonnie Silver."

The tube attached to her arm shifted slightly as she shrugged. "So, you want me to talk about myself, huh? What a damn *boring* conversation that'll be, Paul, the most boring imaginable. Look, if I'm gonna be the sole topic during your next visit, maybe you shouldn't come." She smiled, but her smile was missing its usual radiance, the radiance of early sunlight winking through Parisian skies. Where had that radiance gone? And when would it return? When?

I walked back to her bed. "Don't be upset, love." I kissed her on the lips and gently laid my forehead against hers.

"Our first kiss," she whispered, a tear trickling from her eye.

"Baby, I'll...I'll see you tomorrow."

"God willing, Paul."

"Yeah...God willing."

Chapter 31

Every day, sometimes twice a day, I went to see Bonnie. By order of her doctor, my visits were limited to five minutes. Her nurse, a Lady Macbeth clone, made certain I didn't overstay. "Five minutes, *Monsieur*, five, and *only* five!" She meant every syllable. There was only one exception to her "five minutes" decree, during which she allowed me to stay ten minutes. Why? I never found out. Maybe someone diluted her regimen of snake venom that day.

One morning, holding a fragile bouquet of forget-me-nots, I walked into Bonnie's room to find a graying man I'd never seen before, sitting beside her bed, caressing her hand. He nodded a greeting, then popped to his feet, and smiled as if he and I were old friends finally reunited. He reached for my hand and shook it vigorously. His grip was firm. His smile glowed with sincerity and warmth.

"A pleasure meeting you!" he said.

"Same here," I responded, shooting a questioning look at Bonnie.

"Paul, this is my father, Henry Silver," her love obvious, as she looked at her father's face. She beamed me a smile and reached out a hand. "Are those beautiful flowers for me?"

I handed them to her and breezed a kiss on her forehead. "They're not half as beautiful as you. Nor could they ever brighten the world the way you do."

Henry's smile grew wider. "So, at last I get to meet Paul Lasser. My daughter speaks fondly and often of you."

"But now that you've seen me," I smiled, "you of course realize that none of the good she said about me is true."

"Quite the contrary," he chuckled, "quite the contrary. Young man, pull up a chair and join us."

"Thanks."

For the next several minutes, the three of us chatted about various mundane things. Did Henry have a pleasant trip? (He did.) Where was he staying? (Hotel Victor Hugo on Rue Copernic.) Was this his first visit to Paris? (It was.) What was his impression of the City of Light? ("The splendor of Paris leaves one breathless.") And on and on we chatted.

However, no one mentioned the matter that brought us together—Bonnie's illness. I think we wanted to, and several times tried to, but each attempt ended in a stillbirth. So Henry and I went on asking prosaic questions, about prosaic matters, followed by equally prosaic answers, all of which, considering the circumstances, had little importance and even less relevance.

Soon, the nurse appeared at the door and pointed to her watch. Henry and I left. As we walked down the hall, he said, "Paul, allow me to thank you for the kindnesses you've shown my daughter. She tells me you visit every day, in good weather and bad. She calls you her 'pyramid of support.' Hearing her say that means more to me than you can imagine. So I want to thank you for your kindness."

"You owe me no thanks. In fact, you owe me nothing. I visit Bonnie because I want to and because I *need* to. She is like no one I've ever known."

"Still, I feel obligated to express my gratitude. Trust me, if I had known of the seriousness of her health, I would have come much sooner, but I had no idea of the condition she was in until a few days ago. Of course I knew why she'd come to Paris. They're doing a new and radical treatment here for her illness." He ran a hand over his face, fatigue evident in his features. "She assured me things were going well. That the treatments held promise."

"I'm not surprised that she kept you in the dark, Henry. She told me she didn't want to burden others with, what she called, 'her problem.' 'The others,' she referred to, I now see she wanted to protect you, too, her own father."

"I'm afraid so. You can't imagine my reaction when her doctor phoned and told me she was not doing well." He glanced over his shoulder in the direction of her room, a haunting expression marring his face.

"I'm sure the news jolted you."

"No, it decimated me, rolling over me like a Russian tank."

"You have my sympathies."

"You're most kind."

"Believe me, my words come from the heart. Henry, would you please tell me what Bonnie has? What is this evil, soulless enemy that's taking her from us?"

Henry turned mournful eyes on me. "Acute Lymphocytic Leukemia."

The following morning I arrived at the hospital earlier than usual, at around nine. I went to the cafeteria, which was on the ground floor. It was quiet there, an ideal place to write. The coffee served was tar black and Herculean strong, just the way I liked it.

The view I had, as I sat at a table by a window, overlooked a grassy court in which several old men sat in wheelchairs, some slobbering, all with heads tilted forward. Looking bored, their attendants stood beside the aged and wrinkled patients. The old men sat quietly, patiently, waiting like those anticipating the arrival of some invisible visitor---a visitor whose coming was inevitable. Oblivious of when, how, or where the visitor would come, they, having no alternative, waited for the supreme visitor who would escort them on an infinite journey.

I removed my composition book from its leather holder and began writing. Time passed quickly, and before I realized it, it was five of ten, time to go upstairs and visit Bonnie. I started gathering my things—pencils, erasers, little sharpener—and was about to place the composition book into my leather portfolio when a nurse approached.

"*Monsieur.*"

I looked up. "Yes, *Madame.*"

"Are you *Monsieur* Paul Lasser, the one who comes to visit *Mademoiselle* Bonnie Silver?"

"Yes, you're speaking to him. And you are?"

"*Madame* Simone Deburn, the nurse for *Mademoiselle* Silver."

"But you're not her regular nurse, are you?"

"No. Today is her day off. My supervisor told me I might find you here. So I came to—" Abruptly, she stopped speaking. When she resumed, her voice quivered, then strained. I didn't know why the hesitation. Peering into her eyes, I tried to glean the reason. Finally, I did. My stomach dropped. My heart twisted in pain. "*Madame, please don't,*" I beseeched.

"Don't?"

"Yes, don't. You can tell me anything, but please don't tell me that—"

She reached out to touch my arm. "I must, *Monsieur.*"

"No," my heart cried. "*No! Madame*—"

"I must say it, *Monsieur.*" A kindness, a pitying kindness was in her eyes.

"In the name of God, don't say it!"

"*Monsieur, Mademoiselle Bonnie Silver is dead.*"

Though I anticipated what she'd say, her words still jolted me. The leather binder I held dropped to the floor. I blindly staggered a few steps away from her, then turned, "*Madame,* I foolishly hoped the news you brought would be about something else. Anything else. That the Mona Lisa is a forgery. That Charles DeGaulle, a Nazi. That morticians buried Adolph Hitler in Napoleon's tomb. Or that the Arc de Triomphe is a giant toy made from a Lego set. Any of these calamities I could have suffered, or even greater ones. But not...*not* that my Bonnie is—"

"*Monsieur*, I can imagine your grief."

"If only you could, *Madame*. If only you could." Her image blurred before my eyes as tears blinded my vision. "Please forgive me," I choked out. "I'm afraid I'm losing my composure. I'm not usually so emotional."

She gave me a tissue to wipe my tears. "You don't have to apologize." Her voice was gentle.

"Tell me, when did she...when did she...Dear God, I can't even *say* the word."

Her eyes held great compassion and understanding. "Pass, *Monsieur*...pass."

"Yes, thank you. Pass. When did she..." I ran a hand through my hair, closed my eyes as if to block out the pain coursing through my system, racing toward my heart. I took a ragged breath and whispered, "Pass."

"Early this morning, as dawn was breaking."

"Do you know the...exact time?"

"Shortly after five. I happened to be in her room at the time. Before departing, she mumbled something about a 'daredevil walk' across some bridge or other. To me, her words made no sense. Do you understand what she meant?"

I nodded. "Perfectly...perfectly."

"She also said, 'Free like an eagle.' She spoke gibberish."

"*Madame*, I'm sure her words to you were just that, gibberish, but to me they're abundantly clear. Socrates himself couldn't have uttered wiser thoughts."

She looked at me strangely. "I see. Anyway, *Monsieur*, it might comfort you to know that she seemed at peace when she departed, her face bright as dawn's light."

"Thank you for sharing that."

"She also said, 'High above the Seine and soaring like an eagle...' her final utterance."

"*Madame*, if the end must come, and it must for all of us, I can think of no better way for *Mademoiselle* Silver to exit. I do appreciate your sharing this information. It comforts me more than words can say." I turned my back to her, trying to come to grips with my all-consuming emptiness. My Phantom Lady—gone.

She reached out to touch my shoulder. "I thought you'd want to know."

I nodded, too much in pain to turn my tear-drenched face toward her. "I did. Thank you."

"*Au revoir, Monsieur.*"

"*Au revoir, Madame.*"

Some time later when I walked past the waiting room, I saw Bonnie's father inside. I entered and sat beside him. As if in a trance, he stared at the far wall.

"You've heard?" I whispered.

His voice was flat, devoid of emotion. "Yes, I've heard. I came all this way to be with my little girl and yet I was not with her when…when she needed me."

"You came. That meant the world to her, I'm sure. She loved you very much and spoke highly of you. Henry, I'm sorry beyond what my words can say."

"I appreciate your commiseration, Paul."

"If there has ever lived anyone who deserved a longer life, it was Bonnie Silver. She had only begun to share her goodness with the rest of the world."

"Yes, only begun. If I could have died in her place, the day of my death would have been the happiest of my life, a festive day of rejoicing."

"Henry, life for us all would be blessed if we could die for loved ones who passed prematurely. And doing so would spare us grief, which is often worse than death."

"Well, as I see it, Paul, the only thing left for me to do now is arrange to transport Bonnie's body home."

"Home?"

"Yes, to Goode, Virginia."

"I don't think she would want you to do that, Henry."

He finally looked at me, his face pale, his eyes red-rimmed. "From a father's perspective it's the only proper thing to do. To return his daughter to the place she was born."

"But you don't understand. Granted, Bonnie was physically born in Goode, no question about that, but she discovered life and *herself*, in this city, coming alive here, not in Goode, Virginia. So, Paris is her true home, her *real* place of birth, and I'm sure it's here she wants to spend eternity."

He shook his head, looking at me as though I had indeed suggested something bizarre. "I—"

"Don't misunderstand. I don't mean bury her body here. What I mean is sprinkle her ashes into the Seine, sprinkle them from her favorite bridge, *Pont Michel*. She had an almost mystical attachment to that bridge and to this city."

"Well, I appreciate your suggestion, and I'll keep it in mind." His words were a polite dismissal. Still, I could not let the matter rest. I felt I had to do this for Bonnie.

"I wish you would because the Phantom Lady definitely found her soul home in Paris."

"Excuse me, but did you just refer to my daughter as the 'Phantom Lady'?"

"Yes, that was my pet name for her. A nickname she gave herself, actually." I recalled that first zany note she'd penned and tacked on the bulletin board above the mailbox the day she'd stolen my newspaper—the day my life suddenly brightened.

"The Phantom Lady?"

"You know Bonnie's sense of humor, Henry."

A brief smile flitted at his lips and he nodded. "Yes, bubbly and effervescent. Infectious." He shook his head once. "Irreverent, at times, too. Yes, I understand." He exhaled a mournful sigh. "My little girl. Gone."

We talked briefly and I left him. I squinted when I stepped out of the hospital into the bright sunlight. My mind was absorbed in the final words Henry and I spoke; he said he understood.

Understand? Henry didn't understand. How could he? How could anyone understand who hadn't shared those enchanted moments "daredevil-walking" the bridge at the foot of Boulevard Saint Michel as dawn blushed and freshness perfumed the Latin Quarter air like a Chanel fragrance. When two Americans, pulsing with youth and energy, knew the joy of flying like eagles above mountain tops...flying and free, and coming as close to heaven as two mortals can without the aid of angel wings. How could he understand all of that, understand what Bonnie and I, having shared, knew so well?

The only people on Planet Earth who could truly understand?

The Phantom Lady of Paris—now gone—and me.

Chapter 32

Ten forlorn days after Bonnie's death, spring arrived in Paris. Crystal skies sparkled like diamonds, and the fragrance of blossoms was everywhere. Trees on Boulevard Saint Michel transformed into impressionists' canvasses and in the Luxembourg Garden, flowers dazzled with violet and gold. When you sat on the terrace of a café in Saint Michel Plaza, breezes whispered past, cooling and refreshing. Spring had come. It came early, mere days after Bonnie left.

Latin Quarter inhabitants who hibernated through much of winter reappeared and once again strolled boulevards. All the cafés on Boulevard Saint Germain were now open (many closed during winter months). Their terraces bubbled with laughter and conversation. If one paid attention, there were sounds carried on the breeze—the gurgle of wine filling goblets, the pop of champagne corks, and the hiss of espresso machines spewing the aroma of fresh coffee. It was an aroma that called back memories of Sunday mornings and good times at home. Spring had come. It came early, only days after Bonnie left.

On Sunday afternoons, couples, their toddlers in hand, strolled Boulevard Saint Michel. Cradling toy sailboats, youngsters frolicked into Luxembourg Garden and as parents looked on, the young dynamos of energy splashed through wading pools, squealing and laughing—orchestrating the melodic sound of youth and immortality. Spring had come.

Gypsies once again panhandled on street corners, their favorite, the intersection at Saint Germain and Saint Michel, where they stopped passersby, glibly spinning tales of "hard times," and "starving babies," and the imperative need for a few francs to buy milk and/or medicine for their emaciated, "near-death" children. Translation? "We need money to buy wine." When Gypsies returned, there could be no doubt, spring had come.

Neighborhood bums reappeared and bought bottle after bottle of *vin ordinaire*, drank themselves into stupors, then snoozed away the afternoon. Spring had arrived. It came soon after Bonnie left. Yet springtime in Paris did not delight me, for Bonnie—the woman I loved—was gone.

Its arrival came much too soon, for its coming meant I would soon return to America. My time in the City of Light was coming to a close. My feelings, raw though they were from the loss of Bonnie, were mixed; Paris was not the same without her. Yet leaving the city we'd shared was like leaving her memory, her spirit, the essence of her that had forever changed my life and my way of thinking. Simply put, I was struggling.

I chose June sixth as the departure date. Before leaving, I decided I'd talk to Roger a final time, which I did as he sat in his favorite café, a bleak place. The only café in Paris that sold coffee and gave away gloom with each cup.

I sat across from him. "I thought I'd let you know I'll soon be heading stateside, Roger."

"Oh? When?"

"June sixth."

His expression was bleak. "That early, huh?"

"Yeah. I need to allow myself extra time because I have to write a few teaching units for the coming school year. Plus I want to go visit my folks for a couple weeks. Have some of Mom's good cooking."

"I'll hate to see you go."

"Kind of you to say that," I commented, scribbling my American address and telephone number on a scrap of paper, then handing it to him. "When you return to America, how about giving me a call? We'll get together and talk about the good times we had in The City of Light. I'd love doing that."

"Same here, man."

I handed him the little scrap of paper. "So tell me, when will you be going back home?"

He gazed at the paper but said nothing. Finally, he sighed, "Well, ah… "

"Look, Roger, do me a favor, will you?"

"Sure."

"And I want you to be honest with me and, more important, I want you to be honest with yourself."

"Honest about what?"

"About…well, let me put it this way. Do you think you'll *ever* go home again? Or do you think you'll be forever marooned here in the City of Light?"

"Why of course I'll go home," he chuckled.

I folded my arms across the table. "When?"

"Soon," he replied defensively.

"Soon?"

"Yeah." He twisted his coffee cup around on its saucer. "Like I said...soon." He folded the little piece of paper and slipped it into his wallet. Seconds later as we stood and shook hands, our eyes connected. When they did, he looked away.

"I'll be seeing you...in the States, I mean."

"Of course, man...in the States. Where else?"

"Right, Roger. Where else?"

After I'd been in America a couple of months, I received a letter from Bonnie's father, Henry.

> *Dear Paul,*
>
> *Again let me express my gratitude for the kindnesses you showed my daughter. Because of you, her passing was as free of pain as dying can be. It comforts me to know that during her final days she, though a stranger in a distant land, was never alone, thanks to you.*
>
> *I don't have to tell you I treasured Bonnie. She was iridescence in my otherwise colorless life. When depressed, I needed only see her smile and its glow exhumed my spirits. With the wizardry of a wonder worker, she brought joy to my grief, harmony to the discord of my life, and to its darkness, light. I'm blessed to have had such a daughter, though, as heaven decreed, I would have her for only a brief time. As she did for mine, I'm sure she enriched the lives of all who knew her, no doubt yours included.*
>
> *Like any parent, I've always tried to do what was best for my child. With that in mind, I recalled your saying Bonnie's final wish would be that someone sprinkle her ashes into the Seine. At the time you made the recommendation, I didn't think much of it—too old-fashioned, I suppose. And so, I had her body flown to America. But when it arrived, I reconsidered, finally realizing that you were right after all. So I ordered a cremation. Later, I returned to Paris with her ashes, stood on Pont Michel—the bridge you suggested—and from there shared Bonnie with the city she loved so dearly—and with eternity. Now she rests in peace, rests where she wanted to be. Not where she was born, but to paraphrase your words, in the place of her spiritual birth—Paris, France.*
>
> *Again, thanks for all you've done. I'm sure if Bonnie*

were here she would thank you also, far more eloquently than my clumsy words ever can.
Eternally grateful,

Henry A. Silver.

P.S. Enclosed is a small envelope. In it, you'll find a pinch of Bonnie's ashes. She would want to share a part of herself with you, as you shared your love with her.

I removed the little envelope, opened it, and looked inside and there I saw the Phantom Lady, once a comet blazing over Paris, now a pinch of powder and an eternal presence in the City of Light.

The following day I went to a jewelry designer. I ordered a special necklace made with a treasure chest in which the jeweler enclosed Bonnie's ashes. The silver chain I wear around my neck at all times. My life's treasure—Bonnie Silver—is always with me.

A year later, in a kind of sentimental journey, I returned to Paris. From De Gaulle Airport, I boarded a commuter bus to the Latin Quarter. As antsy as a three year old on Christmas Eve, I pressed my face to the window and gazed out. It was delightful seeing the princess again. Adorned, as she always was, in her most dazzling gowns, Paris was as elegant and youthful as ever, and even more regal than when I last saw her.

After checking into my hotel in The Left Bank, I headed for Café Le Balkan for an espresso. How good to be back in my writing café, where I'd spent so many glorious hours writing and observing French customers.

From there I walked down a side street until I came to the dim little café that was Roger's favorite and, no surprise to me—in spite of what he told me the last time we spoke—there he sat at his usual table, mulling over a demitasse of espresso. I say he was at his customary table. More accurately, I should say he was either there or in his hometown, Flatwater, Mississippi, or maybe in both places at the same time. It was hard to tell where Roger really was, even when his body was in Paris.

Upon seeing him, my first reaction was to coil my arms around my old friend and then exchange hellos and high fives. I did neither, for I realized that after our greeting, I wouldn't know what to say or how to say it. My words would have come out clumsily and, no doubt, wrong. But of one thing, I was certain; if Roger and I talked, I'd feel uncomfortable, and he would too.

Better to say nothing, allowing him time and space to deal with his demons—trapped, as he was, between heaven, Paris, and his hell, Flatwater, Mississippi, and certain to suffer regardless of which "home" he chose, or if he selected neither. I realized that even if I wanted to help Roger (and I did), I couldn't. Only Roger could help Roger.

I headed for Rue Galande, anxious to see if the street I'd walked so often, came to know so well, and loved so dearly had changed. It had. But not much. Traffic on the thoroughfare was as congested as ever. Cars moved slowly, almost bumper-to-bumper.

The little bakery across from Twenty-One Rue Galande was still in business (tantalizing tarts brightening its windows like neon signs), as was the dairy (packed with chattering housewives), the pharmacy (still drab by Walgreen standards), and the clothing boutiques (mannequins sporting the latest styles). The usual assortment of neighborhood bums loitered in the alley near the dairy; others, no doubt stoned, slept nearby on a vendor's cart or in a doorway or a gutter. Not surprisingly, several Gypsies panhandled at the corner. And oh yes, I saw Rue Galande's living legend and unofficial mayor, "Old Man Henri."

As usual, the gray-headed retiree walked his poodle. Seeing the pair of inseparable companions reminded me that there were some things on Rue Galande that would probably never change, not as long as Paris was Paris; the Latin Quarter, the Latin Quarter; people, people; and French dog owners loved their pets with incomparable passion.

There was one thing on Rue Galande, however, that had changed. The café near the corner where neighborhood "regulars" relaxed and chatted away the afternoon over wine or coffee, was now out of business. In its place, a McDonald's: customers in and out in three minutes or less—little time to chat and unwind. I agreed with the pithy wording a British columnist recently called the proliferation of fast food restaurants in Paris—"progress." I shook my head in disgust. Progress it was not.

Twenty-One Rue Galande looked as it did when I lived in it. A nick was still on the foyer's doorframe, put there by the handlebars of Jean Paul's bicycle. Jean Paul and his blind wife, Marie Claire lived on the fourth landing, across the hall from Bonnie's studio. Marie Claire, an angel on lease from heaven, could "see" more of a person's character with her cataract-curtained eyes than the sighted could with twenty-twenty vision. There was a new floor mat in the foyer, smaller than the old one, and a different color--gray. And to my dismay, someone painted the foyer walls fuchsia. Disgusting.

The first thing I did after entering the building was dash to the third floor, the landing on which I once lived. "Curtis Logan" read the nameplate on my former studio door. So, Curtis Logan now lived in "my" studio. The moniker sounded American.

I wondered who he was, if he, as I surmised, was from the States, and, parenthetically, what chance toss of destiny's dice brought him to Paris. I also wondered if, while in The City of Light, he would be as lucky as I'd been. Would he, too, meet his Phantom Lady? Impossible. There could *never* be another Bonnie Silver. Not even The Almighty, with His infinite power, could clone Bonnie. Surely with His great wisdom, The Omnipotent, was wise enough not to try.

I returned to the foyer and noticed that the bulletin board over the mailbox was still in place. Seeing it reminded me of the many notes the Phantom Lady and I exchanged on it. Smiling, I ran my fingers over the corking and tingled elation. Then, I recalled my last visit to the hospital to see Bonnie that fateful morning and when I did, my elation quickly disappeared.

I returned to my hotel at around seven that evening. From my room I had a good view of The Left Bank, including the apartment building where I once lived. Seeing it unleashed a deluge of memories, memories of the day Bonnie pilfered my newspaper, of the morning she pounded on my door, and later when we walked to the little café for onion soup. I remembered when she and I daredevil-walked the railings of *Pont Michel* and the many times we chatted in the foyer of Twenty-One Rue Galande. I recalled the day I held her hands in the ambulance as it sped to the emergency room of the American Hospital of Paris. Vividly I remembered the last time I visited her and the news the nurse brought as I waited in the cafeteria…the most devastating news I had ever heard or will ever hear again. I remembered. God, how I remembered.

Later, I lay in bed and within minutes, I dozed off. For nearly four hours, I slept soundly. Then, I sensed a presence in the room. Startled, I awoke and peered towards the door, where the presence seemed to be, and there in the semi-darkness I saw what was or what appeared to be the Phantom Lady, saw her as clearly as I did the bed before getting into it or the light switch before flipping it off.

My breath caught in my throat. "Bonnie…is that…is that *really* you?"

"Sure it is. Why do you look so surprised, Paul? Who were you expecting? The Mona Lisa? Or Venus De Milo maybe? Yes, it's me. And, Paul, before I forget, I want you to tell me something."

"What?" I raised up on an elbow.

"Why?"

"Why, you say?"

"Yes, *why* have you been so sad...for so long?"

"Isn't that obvious? It's...it's because you...because you—"

"Because I died? Is that what you're fumbling to say, Paul?"

"Exactly. Because you died."

"Paul, you shouldn't grieve over that."

"Why not?" I sat up, resting my back against the headboard.

"When you grieve over a death, Paul, you capitulate to death, and that you must never do. Never. Instead, you must *triumph* over death. Do you understand, Paul?"

"Triumph over death? How do I do that?"

"With hope, Paul. Hope. Hope is death's antithesis, its natural rival, and death, with all its horror, will never prevail over hope. Besides, Paul, there's something I think you've forgotten and forgotten so soon, too."

"What's that?"

"Do you remember the morning you and I daredevil-walked the railings of *Pont Michel*?"

I smiled. "How could I forget?"

"Good, so you remember I told you that I dreamed of one day feeling the freedom an eagle feels when flying mountain-high."

"I remember as if it happened yesterday, Bonnie."

"Well, I now know how eagles feel when soaring in the stratosphere."

"What's it like?"

"Like being transformed into something as ethereal as dreams. Like riding a beam of light into another dimension where death is banished and grief doesn't exist. It's exquisite, like nothing I've known." She paused. "So, Paul, tell me."

"What?"

"Why aren't you rejoicing?"

"Why should I?"

"For two reasons. The first is because at last I'm where I want to be, doing what I longed to—flying on wings of light...free."

"Bonnie, I am happy for you. In fact, ecstatic. But you forget one thing: You're gone, and I'll never see you again. I can't begin to tell you how much I miss you. How empty I've felt."

"I understand. Trust me, I understand, but remember this: though you won't see me, Paul, you'll *feel* my presence and know I'm there. In the café where you wrote each day, I'll be there. On the sidewalk

217

fronting the Cluny Museum, among the street performers...there also. Your senses will tell you I am. I'll be in the foyer of Twenty-One Rue Galande where we rendezvoused. In the plaza near Saint Michel fountain. Look for me, Paul. In Shakespeare and Company bookstore. There too. In Notre-Dame Cathedral. Luxembourg Garden. I'll be in *all* these places.

"And in spring, Paul, when you stroll Latin Quarter boulevards and a breeze whispers past. That's me; I'll be in the breeze, caressing your cheek with a kiss. Your heart will tell you it's me. Heed your heart, for it sees better than the eyes. Heed your heart and you'll see me. And there's something else I want to tell--" She stopped. "Paul?"

"Yes?"

"I have to leave now."

"Why? You've only been here for a few moments."

"Trust me, I want to stay, Paul. I do, but—"

"Bonnie—"

"I can't stay, Paul."

"Don't go...don't go." I panicked. I couldn't bear losing her again.

"Remember what I said; you won't see me, Paul, but I'll be in all the places we know so well. *Look* with your heart."

"Bonnie?" No answer. "Do you hear me? Where are..." The room was soundless, as soundlessness as a vacuum. "Bonnie, where..." Like a pricked bubble, she had vanished.

Five days later at De Gaulle Airport, I boarded a Trans Atlantic jetliner. Upon arriving in America I, to assuage grief, immersed myself in work. Rising at six each morning, driving forty minutes to the high school where I taught, teaching five classes, returning home, correcting papers, writing lesson plans, working on my novel, going to bed, and the following day getting up at the same hour to repeat the identical routine. I became a work android, leaving no time in my busy schedule to even *think* about Bonnie Silver, let alone brood over her.

At the end of August each year, I began my annual work marathon, plowing through the daily look-alike schedule until the middle of June, at which time I switched off the work machine, for the school year was over, and I felt drained.

Near the end of June for the past four years, I've returned to Paris and remained there for six or seven days. Revisiting the city, especially the Latin Quarter—the neighborhood my soul calls home. My trips have become a delicious diversion. Seeing my old haunts were a delightful way to refresh for another year of work.

During the trips, I've learned many valuable lessons, the greatest being that the person who spoke to me that night in my hotel room was right when she assured me that the Bonnie I knew and loved would *always* be in the City of Light. Now I have evidence that she is, and I'm certain not only me, but anyone who visits Paris, strolls her boulevards, lounges in her cafés and bistros, and most important—to use Bonnie's words—anyone who heeds his heart will "see" her. For as long as the City of Light is a metropolis of splendor, romance, and magic—and it has been for countless years— the *Phantom Lady of Paris* will reside there.

If you doubt, visit the city on the Seine, and with your heart, you too will "see."

THE END

www.ingramcontent.com/pod-product-compliance
Lightning Source LLC
Chambersburg PA
CBHW070731280626
47159CB00023B/3083